Kathleen E. Woodiwiss, Johanna Lindsey, Laurie McBain, Shirlee Busbee...these are just a few of the romance superstars that Avon Books has been proud to present in the past.

Since 1982, Avon has been continuing a different sort of romance tradition—a program that has been launching new writers of exceptional promise. Called "The Avon Romance," these books are distinguished by a ribbon motif on the front cover—in fact, you readers quickly discovered them and dubbed them "the ribbon books"!

Month after month, "The Avon Romance" has continued to deliver the best in historical romance, offering sensual, exciting stories by new writers (and some favorite repeats!) *without* the predictable characters and plots of formula romances.

"The Avon Romance." Our promise of superior, unforgettable historical romance...month after dazzling month!

SANDRA LANGFORD

MIDNIGHT'S LADY

AVON
PUBLISHERS OF BARD, CAMELOT, DISCUS AND FLARE BOOKS

AVON BOOKS
A division of
The Hearst Corporation
1790 Broadway
New York, New York 10019

First Avon Printing, February 1986

AVON TRADEMARK REG. U. S. PAT. OFF. AND IN
OTHER COUNTRIES, MARCA REGISTRADA, HECHO EN
U. S. A.

Printed in the U. S. A.

WFH   10 9 8 7 6 5 4 3 2 1

To Leona

There is no armour against fate.
—James Shirley

Chapter One

London, March 1770

The fog rolled along the strand like some great gray beast, obscuring the buildings from the eyes of the weary traveler. The faint glow of candles inside the frosted warehouse windows warmly beckoned the girl to enter, but a light mist had begun to fall and she knew she could not take the time to stop and enjoy the warmth.

Lauren de Fanchon had arrived that night by packet from France, where only a week ago she had buried her mother in her native soil. It had been more than ten years since Lauren had walked on British land, but she still had bitter memories of how England had declared her father a traitor.

Now, as she gingerly made her way through the night, across ropes and barrels that littered the area, she was determined to find the grandfather who had turned his back on her family when they had needed him. She did not know London very well, but she knew the address where he lived. She had sold the last of her mother's jewelry to make this trip, and the small

1

bag she carried contained nothing of value, only her few meager garments.

As Lauren walked, she was unaware of being watched, intent on her own thoughts. Turning down a narrow street, she pulled the hood of her cloak closer about her face, but stopped short when she realized she had reached a dead end. She turned to retrace her steps and saw her path blocked by two large boys wearing clothes too small for their frames, their shirt-sleeves ending at their elbows, their breeches not meeting their bare, grimy knees. The boys' stance was menacing and she could see a feral gleam in their eyes even in the darkness.

She straightened her shoulders and took a step toward them, thinking they might back up and let her pass, but she was mistaken. They, too, took a step forward. She stopped and eyed them warily, mentally sizing up their strength.

"Let me pass!" she ordered in trembling tones.

They laughed, as if she had just told a merry tale.

"The lady wants ter pass, Leo," the tallest of the boys said, giving his companion a wink.

"Ain't that a coincidence. We wants yer to pass, too. Pass yer money, that is!" They both laughed loudly, pleased with their wit.

"I have very little money, but I'll give you a coin or two if you'll go away."

"We don't wants yer charity, lady," Leo sneered.

She lifted one eyebrow. "Oh!?" she asked in disbelief. "You would rather steal than take what is offered?"

"At least we works fer our money. It ain't easy

smelling out a plump pigeon and then getting it alone."

Lauren gave a shaky laugh. "Then you are not very proficient in your endeavors, because you have definitely not found a plump pigeon. I have only a few shillings to my name."

They looked skeptically at each other. Her voice and manner were of the moneyed class, but what was she doing alone in this neighborhood? Why wasn't she whimpering like any other upper-class woman would be doing by now?

Leo pulled a knife from his pocket and took an angry step forward. "Hands it over so we don't have ter get rough wid ye."

Lauren's heart was pounding so loudly she was sure they could hear it. She glanced behind her and saw no avenue of escape.

"Take what I offer and go away. I told you I have very little."

"It be more'n we gots," the other boy piped.

She clutched her possessions closer and made a dash past them, but they caught her arms, jerking her back against the wall, where she hit her head. Everything spun crazily for a moment and then her head began to throb sickly, but she recovered her senses as she felt the tug on her bag. She struggled against them, holding on for dear life, but they gave her a vicious push and she fell to her knees, moaning as her fingers lost their hold on her precious bag. She heard a wild whoop of glee and then the clatter of running feet before she slumped wearily to the ground.

She began to cry, great sobs shaking her slender frame. Lauren had cried so little in the past, but now, once released, the flood of emotion would not stop. She remained seated long after the tears had dried, the dirty streaks down her face the only evidence of her grief.

Lauren slowly stood up, grimacing as she noticed the dirty stains on her clothing. She pushed a stray lock of dark hair from her forehead and straightened her shoulders. Her sad eyes looked down the deserted alley and she wondered what she was going to do now. She had no money to spend the night at an inn. The thought of sleeping in the street, exposed to all kinds of danger, was certainly no comfort, either.

A sudden wave of self-pity overcame her as Lauren remembered how, eight years ago, she had mourned her loss of freedom when her father had died and she and her mother had sought the safety of the convent. Now she was free, but realized that never in that small, enclosed world had she feared harm or known hunger as she did at this moment.

"Well," she said aloud. "I can't stay here all night."

She walked to the entrance of the alley and peered down the dark, gloomy street. Singing and laughter came from several of the buildings, proving that not everyone was miserable tonight.

Lauren stopped when she saw a group of men arguing about something; one man gestured angrily and then another man punched him in the mouth. In the blink of an eye, fists, cudgels and oaths came from everywhere. Then bottles started flying and Lauren quickly slipped behind some crates to hide and wait for the fight to end. England was a savage, ill-mannered country, she thought, and she began to wish she had never left France.

The noise finally died away and she looked over the crates, watching as the men limped away, holding their heads. Cautiously, Lauren came out from her hiding place and began to make her way down the street. Her head was pounding and she felt sick; the rumbling of her stomach made her realize she had not eaten anything all day.

The smell of food was tantalizing as she passed a window, and stopped to stare greedily at the warm, crowded room. Men in seamen's garb and women dressed in bright, gaudy gowns laughed and sang while tankards of ale flowed freely. Two men sitting near the window saw her standing outside and exchanged knowing looks. She unconsciously licked her lips as she saw a joint of mutton crammed into the wide slobbering mouth of a man with a painted woman on his lap.

The two men winked at each other and rose to make their way across the crowded room to the door.

"Would ye care to join me and my friend, missy?"

Lauren jumped with surprise and looked at the two men standing beside her.

"Er, no, thank you," she said, shaking her head. She cast one more wistful glance through the window.

The tall, bearded man noted her reaction and smiled. "Are ye sure ye wouldn't like a nice hot bowl o' stew?" he asked.

Her eyes lit up, but were quickly dimmed. "I have no money," she sighed.

"Ain't that a pity," the man smirked. He sent his companion a quick look. "Ain't it a pity the little lady hasn't a bob, Ewan?" he asked in mock sorrow.

Ewan was a short man with shaggy red hair and blunt features. "Aye, it's a pity, it is," Ewan returned, viewing Lauren through slitted, smoldering eyes. "We can't let the lady go hungry, Graham."

Graham bowed awkwardly, unused to pleasant gallantries. "Allow us to offer ye dinner."

Lauren could hardly believe her luck. She gave them a warm smile, mentally changing her opinion of England and her people. These two men were certainly being kind to someone in need.

"I am rather hungry," she murmured.

"Then say no more," Ewan swaggered, holding out his arm.

Lauren tentatively placed her small hand on his dark sleeve and allowed him to lead her to a table in the corner. Once they were seated, she pushed back the hood of her cloak, blushing as their eyes openly studied her. She glanced down self-consciously and saw a stain on her bodice as well as a small tear that gave a glimpse of her smooth, white skin. She placed her hand nervously over the rent.

"I know I look a mess." She gave a choked laugh. "I really do thank you for your kindness. All my money and possessions were taken from me a short while ago."

Ewan and Graham exchanged skeptical glances as she looked casually around the room.

"Is there someplace I could tidy myself?" She asked.

"Maisie!" Ewan called, and a thin, sickly woman came to the table. "We'd like three bowls o' stew, and could ye take the lady someplace so she can wash herself?"

"Ain't we gettin' fancy!" Maisie cast a sour eye at Lauren. "Follow me," she lisped, walking away and leaving Lauren to scramble hurriedly out of her chair in order to keep up with her.

Maisie led her up a flight of stairs and down a dark hallway. She pushed open a door and motioned Lauren inside with a jerk of her head.

"There's water and towels," she pointed out. "Ye kin find yer own way down." She turned with a flounce of skirts, leaving Lauren alone.

Lauren idly noticed that a bed was the only other furniture in the room and that the place was not very clean. She looked in the cracked mirror and a gasp escaped her for she looked nothing like a well-brought-up young lady with her hair straggling down her back in tangled waves and smudges of dirt on her face as well as her gown. Her bodice and her sleeve were ripped, she guessed, when the young boys had grabbed for her bag.

She scooped up a handful of cold water, splashed her face, and repeated the motion, scrubbing her cheeks. She pushed her hair away from her forehead and an expression of pain crossed her features. Looking closer, Lauren saw a large bruise on her temple, and when she lightly touched it, she winced. She had no comb

or brush so she ran her fingers through her hair.
She replaced two pins, which were all that remained, but she still looked rather wanton with
her riot of thick, black curls flowing so freely.
She thought she looked like a gypsy, not the
demure girl from the convent at St. Cyr.

Lauren made her way down the stairs and
placed a hand on her stomach as she heard it
rumble in a most unladylike way. Sister Mar-
tine would be shocked if she could see me now,
she thought, and a giggle escaped her. For the
first time since reaching England she was not
quite so sad or worried, and the thought of a hot
bowl of stew made her smile widen.

As she approached the table, Ewan nudged
Graham and they quickly broke off their whispered conversation. Ewan stood and held out a
chair, which she gratefully accepted.

Maisie appeared with three bowls, a loaf of
bread, a bottle of ale and three glasses. The
glasses looked foggy and Lauren wondered how
clean they were, but she shrugged philosophi-
cally, thinking that beggars could not be choos-
ers.

Ewan and Graham attacked their food like
hungry wolves, while Lauren looked weakly at
the watery stew with a big glob of fat floating
on top. She felt a little sick and decided to try
the ale. It was too strong and she ended up choking and gasping at the sour taste.

"Have ye gots any relations hereabouts?"
Ewan questioned, wiping ineffectually at some
stew that had dribbled down his chin.

"My grandfather," she returned absently. She

was concentrating on her food, wondering if she dared eat it, so she missed their sly look.

"Grandfather, is it?" he asked, thinking a poor old man was no threat to them. "Does he know ye're comin'?" The two men watched her closely.

"No. It's to be a surprise." She was becoming aware of the bold stares she was receiving from the men in the room. She shifted uneasily and, suddenly, when she looked at Ewan and Graham, they no longer looked like kind men; Lauren noticed, for the first time, their rough garb and the lustful gleam in their eyes. She swallowed with difficulty and her mind flashed over several ways she could get out of this predicament. She pushed the bowl of stew away with shaking fingers and stood up to leave.

"Thank you for your kindness, but I must be going now." She smiled weakly and rubbed her hands down the side of her gown to remove the nervous perspiration.

"But ye told us no one was waiting for ye. Why do ye have to hurry off?" Ewan had a sober expression on his face and Graham's eyes were narrowed and intent.

"I—I was wrong. My grandfather knows I'm coming. He's waiting for me right now!" she hurriedly improvised, but they clearly did not believe her.

"'Ere now," Graham snarled, coming to his feet and grasping her wrist. "Ye're lyin'! Ye're not thinking of runnin' out on us, are ye? And after we were so nice to buy this food!" There was an ugly look on his face.

"N-no—no," she stammered. "Certainly not." She sat down.

"'Ere, Maisie!" Graham bellowed as Maisie made her way across the smoky room. "We be wantin' ter pay."

He threw a few coins on the table and as she bent over to scoop them into her hand, he dropped one down her loose blouse. She threw him a glare of dislike and then flounced away as he grinned after her.

"Let's go," he announced, and Lauren wearily let him pull her to her feet.

Once outside, Ewan took her wrist. She jerked away from him, but he took hold of her arm again and gave it a vicious twist.

He felt her shudder and laughed. He was one who enjoyed preying on those weaker than himself. "Ye got to treat women rough," he told Graham, "They really like it."

"Just remember," Graham warned. "I gets her first."

Lauren paled at his words and her lips began to tremble. She had feared something like this and his words confirmed it. How foolish she had been to trust them, she thought. No one in this place cared if she lived or died.

The fog was still thick and the heavy mist was beginning to dampen Lauren's face and clothing. She shivered both from cold and fear, and she thought that tonight was the most miserable night of her life.

As they went down the narrow street, women lingered in the doorways and called out bawdy comments to the passing men. Lauren knew she would have to do something soon or be beyond help.

"Oh!" she cried, stopping with a pained expression.

"What's the matter with ye?" Graham demanded in a curt voice.

"I've hurt my foot," she said, her brow wrinkling with distress. When she bent to rub her leg, Ewan loosened his hold on her arm. She straightened and took a small, limping step. "I don't think I can walk."

"Ah, hell!" Graham burst out, casting an angry glance at Ewan. "We can't go carrying her through the streets."

With their attention diverted for the moment, Lauren saw her chance and broke into a run. She startled the two men and they stood with dumfounded expressions as they saw she was perfectly capable of running on a bad foot. They came to their senses as their prey disappeared around the corner.

"Blast that damned strumpet!" Ewan exclaimed furiously. "I'll teach her to play wily tricks on me."

As they started after her, they both silently pledged to repay her for the wound to their egos.

Lauren knew they were behind her and that spurred her on to greater speed. She had really angered them and if they had any leanings toward kindness, those feelings were now buried beneath the bitterness they felt at her scheming. They would know she had found them distasteful, so her humiliation would be twice as bad.

Down the narrow winding streets she ran, straining for breath through lips parched with fear and lungs bursting with anguish. Faster and faster she ran until everything was spinning dizzily around her and she became lost and confused. She stopped and pressed trembling hands to her chest, but the sound of running feet from behind quickly made her sob desperately and hurry on through the dimly lit streets.

She saw a group of coarse, gaudily dressed women standing in front of a door through which a haze of light came, and she ran to them, panting as she sought her breath.

"P-please!" she implored, casting an anxious glance behind her. "Please! You must help me."

The women gave her haughty looks and turned their backs. When she reached up and grabbed the sleeve of one, the woman angrily shook her off.

"A pox on ye! Get away!" she ordered. "We wants no trouble."

Lauren stared in dismay at their lack of concern and a whimper escaped her. She wished fervently that she was somewhere safe and sound, and if the convent had appeared before her in that moment, she would gladly have entered its portals and never again raged against its confining walls.

The footsteps were getting closer and she heard a hard laugh. "There she is! Let's get her."

Turning away from the unsympathetic women, Lauren slipped on the wet cobbles and fell to her knees. Her eyes were wild as she saw the two men approaching; she knew they offered her hell on earth. With renewed vigor she scrambled to her feet and took off, showing amazing agility for one so tired and desperate.

She careened around a corner and met solid

resistance to her flight. The breath left her body and she fell back to stare in horror at the dark cloaked figure that loomed up before her. Finding no help from other quarters, she doubted she would find succor here, so she turned to run in the other direction. However, her escape was halted as she found her arm caught firmly between the stranger's fingers. She struggled like a wild animal, hit, kicked, and tried to bite the hand that held her captive, but he was definitely the stronger, and he jerked her angrily until she went limp in his arms.

The two figures of Ewan and Graham came around the corner and stopped short at the sight of their quarry in the net of another.

"That girl be ours, guv'nor. I know ye wants to be a sporting gent. Just give her to us and we'll be on our way," Graham said in a wheedling voice while Ewan stood beside him, rubbing his knuckles as if eager to punch a jaw.

"You may certainly have the girl," the man returned in even, cultured tones, very different from the other men's speech.

At his words Lauren felt the blood turn to ice in her veins, but when he continued she relaxed against him in relief.

"But only if she wishes to go with you."

She looked up, mesmerized by the golden depths of his eyes which were so warm and welcome after the evil lusting stares she had seen of late that she felt like crying in her gladness.

"Do you want to go with these,"—he gave Ewan and Graham a look of distaste—"these men?"

She was too stunned to speak; Lauren only

answered with an emphatic shake of her head. He smiled at the other men and lifted a mocking eyebrow.

"It appears the lady has no wish to accompany you."

"'Ere now!" Ewan grunted. "This has naught to do with ye. Give the lass over and we'll not bash in yer fancy head," he scorned, looking with disdain at the well-dressed figure of the other man.

Graham laughed as if his friend had made a fine joke. "Aye," he chortled. "We'll takes pity on ye, seeing as how ye don't know the way of things. We found 'er and she's ours."

The man lifted the light cane he carried and gave a mocking salute to the two facing him so menacingly. "But my dear fellows, she does not wish to go with you," he said laconically.

The two aggressors looked at each other in amazement. The damned booby did not seem worried at all.

"Ye're a simple-minded one, ain't ye?" Ewan glowered, standing with his feet firmly planted, braced for battle.

"No, I don't think so," the man replied, unperturbed. "I thought I was very lucid. I have no intention of giving the girl to you."

"I guess we'll have to teach ye a lesson, guv'nor," Ewan snarled, advancing on his enemy. But before he reached his target, he found the tip of the cane had sprung open and a nasty looking blade was against his throat.

Ewan's eyes opened in dismay and he swallowed convulsively as Graham took a hasty step backward.

"I wouldn't make any sudden movements if I were you," the gentleman said calmly. "My hand is none too steady, shaking with fright as I am." And as if to emphasize his point, the blade scratched Ewan's throat and brought a thin line of blood to the surface. The gentleman gave a mocking laugh as Ewan's eyes dilated with terror. "If you value your worthless skin, viper, then I suggest you and your friend take yourselves off before I change my mind and decide you're not worth gracing the earth."

Ewan backed away cautiously, eying the blade with misgiving. Once out of range, he turned and ran, taking his companion with him.

Lauren sagged against the man in relief and noticed that he smelled warm and sweet, unlike those foul-smelling ruffians.

"Th-thank you, sir," she said weakly.

Her voice was soft and educated where he had expected coarse tones to match those of her attackers. He placed a finger under her chin, lifted her face and studied it closely, catching his breath as he comprehended the full beauty of the girl.

Her hair was a dark curly cloud about her small, piquant face, her lips were soft, full, slightly open as she returned his look, her cheeks were flushed, and he noticed her high cheekbones and the straight narrow nose. Beneath her clothes, her figure was slim but he could make out enough curves to make it interesting. When his gaze returned to her face, he found himself lost in wide, beautiful violet eyes that filled her face with heart-stopping poignancy.

His hand was unsteady as he reached out to

brush a tear from her cheek, and when she smiled tremulously, his heart raced. He had a sudden desire to pull her closer and claim her trembling lips.

He shook his head, wondering why he was being so fanciful about a woman. He must have had too much to drink in his already tired condition.

"Come!" His voice was curt to cover his thoughts and Lauren shivered at his tone. He saw her reaction and softened his voice. "I think you need a drink and a warm place to rest. This ordeal has shaken you."

She was too bemused to speak, so she allowed him to take her elbow and escort her down the dark street. It was strange how safe she felt with him. She had none of the fear she had experienced with Ewan and Graham, but felt her heart leap within her breast when she looked at him. He was such a handsome man, moving with controlled grace as if straining at a leash, eager to be off to more pleasurable pursuits but tempering himself for her benefit.

Lauren wanted to thank him for his help, to offer some words of gratitude, but she found her tongue was tied in knots and her brain was strangely dull.

They turned several corners before they came to an inn with a sign creaking in the night as it waved back and forth in welcome. Inside, they found the landlord snoring loudly as he rested his head in his hand. At the rapping of the cane on the table he came wide awake, sitting up with a snort.

"We'd like a private room," the stranger ordered, "and some food and wine." He looked at the young girl huddled in her cloak. "Also bring us some brandy."

The landlord hurried around the desk and up the stairs, leading the couple behind him. He was stout with a red-mottled face, his eyes appeared small since his cheeks were so round and plump, and he was panting slightly from the exertion of climbing the stairs so swiftly. When he reached a door on the second landing he pushed it open, revealing a room with the bare essentials for comfort. A bed, table, two chairs, and a washstand were the only adornments to an otherwise nondescript place, but Lauren noticed that it was immensely cleaner than the place where she had met Ewan and Graham.

"I'll have all you want in two whistles, m'lord," he fawned, recognizing nobility when he saw it. He backed out, bowing low.

Lauren looked around the room and blushed. She wondered why they were in a private room instead of the common room below, and as if reading her thoughts, the man said: "I thought you would be more comfortable here after your adventure. I'm sure you don't want to be ogled any more than necessary."

She was surprised at his understanding and gave him a fleeting smile. "Thank you," she murmured.

His dark cloak as well as his hair were beaded with moisture. The gentleman removed the garment and threw it across a nearby chair, then raked his hands through his hair. He sat in a chair and stretched his long legs as he watched her through hooded eyes. He grinned when he noticed that she was studying him as well, and Lauren lowered her lashes until they concealed the violet light of her eyes.

Never had she seen anyone so handsome. His features were finely chiseled: high forehead, narrow nose, his chin strong and slightly square with a small cleft in the center. His hair was as dark as her own and brushed neatly from his face. She wondered if he had just come from a ball since his clothes were evening attire. Dark breeches molded his legs and thighs so that she found a strange fascination in just looking at him. His shirt was frilled and his jacket fit snugly over strong arms and a muscled chest.

When her eyes met his, she found him smiling at her in a way that made her both hot and cold, and she wondered what this stranger thought of her as she stood before him like a bedraggled cat.

She looked lovely and desirable to him. There was no artifice in her smile or coquetry in her glance. The silence was heavy in the room, but neither noticed; they were caught up in their own thoughts.

To Lauren he was like something out of a dream, and his warm eyes and dark charm mesmerized her. His gaze made her think of the times at the convent when she had listened to other girls whisper about making love. Lauren's eyes dropped to below the man's waist as she remembered one girl's particular detail in describing her lover. She shivered suddenly and her teeth began to chatter. Her dress was soaked, but that was not what caused the chill that shook her. She pulled her cloak closer but she could not stop shaking.

"You must take off those wet clothes," he said, his voice deep and rich, grating along her nerve endings like a fine-tooth comb.

Lauren turned away, disturbed by her thoughts. "I-I—" she gulped and tried again. "I have n-nothing to wear other than the clothes on my back."

The corner of his mouth lifted in a smile. "Do not fear. I shall turn my back while you remove your dress. You can wrap yourself in the blanket on the bed."

He promptly turned, but she still remained unsure as she stared at his back.

"We don't have all night, you know," came his faintly mocking tones, and she wondered if he had eyes in the back of his head. "The landlord will soon return with our food, and by then you will have caught a chill."

She dropped her cloak and hesitantly reached for the laces on her gown. She began slowly untying them as she sent swift glances at his immobile back. Gingerly, she stepped out of her sodden garment and grimaced ruefully: her chemise was just as damp and torn as her dress. Lauren looked again at him and then resolutely removed the rest of her things before she pulled the covering from the bed and wrapped it around her shivering body. She found an odd comfort in the rough scratchy material.

"I'm finished," she said weakly.

He turned to face her and his golden eyes made the heat creep into her body, warming her as effectively as if his gaze were that of the sun lending its warmth for her use.

Suddenly Lauren feared her feelings more than she had feared those two men who had chased her. Although they would have abused her, it would have been physical abuse; she sensed that this man could hurt her in a more profound way. He held a strange fascination for her, and her emotions spiraled out of control at a mere glance from those strange golden eyes.

There was a tap at the door, breaking her thoughts, and he sent a glance at her to make sure she was covered, then moved forward to open the door. The innkeeper entered carrying a bottle and two glasses on a tray.

"The food will be up in two winks," he panted, setting the tray on the table. "I'll just go and see that all is right and ready." He smiled and departed, leaving them alone again.

"I don't believe we have introduced ourselves," the man smiled. "And since there is no one here to give the introductions then allow me to present myself. I am Julian Grey."

To prevent anyone from linking her to the Warwick family, Lauren had decided not to use her father's name; she felt no guilt in using her mother's name.

"My name is Lauren de Fanchon," she announced calmly.

"French?" Julian mused, thinking how well she spoke English.

"Partly," she said, but did not elaborate. "I just arrived in London tonight."

"Did you come to meet family?" he asked,

coming to his feet and walking to the table, where he poured brandy into the two glasses.

"Perhaps." She nervously twisted her hands together. He was asking questions she did not want to answer.

He crossed the wood floor and offered a glass to her. She shook her head to refuse.

"I insist," he pressed. "It will do you good."

She took it and watched as he easily threw his drink to the back of his throat. With a Gallic shrug she repeated the action and felt a trail of fire course down her throat. She doubled over, coughing and gasping, while Julian watched in amusement.

"Are you all right?" he asked humorously.

"I see nothing amusing," she choked. She could not see him, for her vision was blurred by tears. "Why didn't you tell me it burned like that?"

"That's one purpose of the drink. It warms the blood."

She did not comment as she tried to regain her composure. There was a warm feeling in the pit of her stomach but the rumble of hunger reminded her that she needed food. She pulled the blanket closer, keeping her head lowered so she would not have to look upon his raw masculinity, which so disturbed her senses.

The innkeeper knocked before he entered with two trenchers of food. Behind him came a small lad with a bottle of wine. The large man set the food on the table and placed two eating utensils beside them. The boy handed the bottle to the man as he sent a shy smile to Lauren.

"That'll be all, Jack," the innkeeper told the

boy, seeing how he was watching the lady. He scuttled away and the man tried unsuccessfully to open the bottle of wine.

Julian raised a hand in dismissal. "Leave it," he ordered.

The innkeeper hastily bowed and departed, sure that the gentleman and lady wanted to be alone in their dalliance.

Julian opened the bottle with none of the difficulty of the innkeeper. He poured two glasses and placed them beside the trenchers.

Lauren felt her mouth water at the sight of juicy pork pie and slices of warm bread.

"Please be seated," Julian offered, and she realized she had been staring dumbly at the food.

She slipped into her chair and immediately began to eat. She was dainty in her motions, but the food quickly began to disappear from her plate.

Refilling her wineglass, Julian watched in amusement as she ate. He felt an amazing tenderness for this half-starved waif of the night, a desire to protect and care for her. Her life had not been easy if what he had witnessed tonight was anything to go by. She was half child, half woman, and her unexpected advent into his life seemed predestined.

"Won't you eat?" she asked, noticing his lack of interest in the food.

"No. I am not hungry at the moment. You may have my food if you wish."

She reached for his bread and placed it on her dish. "This is excellent food. It's nothing like what I was offered earlier."

A frown touched his brow as he remembered the two men. "Were those men friends of yours?" he asked, surprised at how angry he felt when he remembered them chasing her.

She was startled. "Oh, no! I thought they wanted to help me, but—" She blushed bright red and reached for her wineglass. "They did not have friendship in mind."

"No." Julian grinned. "I don't think they had friendship on their minds."

She drank a little of the red wine. "This is quite palatable," she said, smiling.

Julian nodded his head in acknowledgment of the compliment. "I'm glad you enjoy it. And"—he cast a sardonic look at the empty trencher—"the food."

She looked embarrassed. "I'm sorry. I should have restrained my appetite, but it is so long since I ate."

"Don't apologize." He shrugged carelessly. "Food was meant to be eaten."

Julian refilled her glass a third time and she sipped the rich red liquid and felt it go to her head as well as her stomach. She liked the warm, drowsy effect it had on her; there was a delicious kind of lethargy in her bones from being full and replete.

"How did you come to cross the path of those two specimens of humanity?" Julian asked.

"They just appeared." She told him of her experiences since her arrival, and finished by saying: "I'm indebted to you for helping me."

He waved away her gratitude. "I am happy to be of service."

He watched her for a moment longer. "You

are very lovely, Lauren." He liked the sound of her name on his tongue. "I'm surprised some young man in France didn't make you his wife."

"There was someone who wanted to marry me, but I couldn't bear the thought." She shivered, thinking of the gouty old Comte whose land had bordered that of the nunnery.

"Perhaps you share my views on the married state." His voice was dry. "I have seen few happy marriages, and I'm surprised how quickly the marriage vows seem to dampen a man's ardor and loosen a woman's true character. My sister has a very good marriage, but then she is one of a kind, and her husband knew what he was getting into before he offered for her hand."

"My mother and father had a very good marriage," Lauren said pensively. "But my mother never got over losing my father; she was never the same after he died. I don't think I like that part of love—it opens one up to all kinds of pain."

"There is more to you than a beautiful face and figure."

She blushed and turned away. She was unused to compliments. The nuns who raised her had taught her it was wrong to be vain.

"I'm really very ordinary."

He took her fingers in his and felt them tremble. "Don't underestimate the power of your beauty, for in this world it is the strongest weapon a woman can have."

Her eyes widened as she met his golden gaze. "What makes you think I need a weapon?"

He lightly stroked his chin and she noticed how lean and brown his fingers were. "You are

alone in a city that can be unpredictably cruel
or kind. You have already tasted its cruelty. But
remember, it will be kind to you more often if
you have money or beauty and the ability to use
them to your advantage."

"I don't underst—oh! You mean become a *fille
de joie?*"

One or two of the girls at the convent had
dared to say they would become rich men's mistresses; it was the only thing open to them that
would guarantee money and excitement. Was
that what he was suggesting for her?

Lauren looked at Julian through her lashes.
The devil was surely tempting her tonight—the
devil or a stranger called Julian Grey.

"You have the face of an angel, do you know
that? But I have often found that an innocent
look can hide the blackest heart. I don't know
if I should trust you or not."

Lauren reacted instinctively to the harsh note
in his voice and attempted to rise to her feet,
but she swayed precariously and reached out to
steady herself. The blanket slipped from her
shoulder, baring one pink-tipped alabaster
breast to his view.

"Lauren!" his voice was deep and husky.

She glanced down at her dishabille and tried
to pull the blanket into place. She looked ques-
tioningly at Julian.

He closed his eyes to shut out the picture of
her beauty, but it remained scorched on the inside of his lids. When he opened his eyes again
she moved over to the bed and fell down upon
its soft covers. "I'm tired," she murmured.

Julian rose slowly to his feet. "I'll leave you now."

"No!" she cried, holding out her hand in an unconscious appeal. "Don't leave me." She did not want to be alone again.

She was only half aware of what she was offering, but Julian took her words as acquiescence. He was unused to innocent girls. He enjoyed instead the practiced courtesans and married women who knew the rules of the game. Those innocent creatures of the *beau monde* were always chaperoned and too prim in their conversations to interest him. But Lauren was a strange mixture of innocence and worldliness, a born temptress.

Julian moved across the room and was surprised to find he was as eager as any callow youth about to bed his first woman. Still, he felt uncertain and was wary of frightening her with his bold desires.

Lauren lay back and closed her eyes. The wine and brandy had created a lethargy in her that was rather pleasant. It was like she was watching herself from a distance.

He removed his jacket, waistcoat and linen shirt, and carelessly threw them to the floor. When he sat on the edge of the bed, Lauren stretched and rolled over, dislodging the blanket until he could see the satiny sheen of her skin and the tiny waist that gracefully sloped to smooth, softly rounded hips. Hastily, Julian removed his other garments. He felt as light-headed as Lauren, but it was not due to the wine. The blood rushed furiously through his body with a primitive beat and the ache in his groin grew steadily stronger.

He bent and placed his lips on the curve of her waist and slowly began to move upward, nibbling, tasting, delighting in the warm, womanly scent of her body. She was smooth and pale, like some rare jewel from the Orient that all desired but few possessed.

Lauren felt something tickling her like the warm lick of a flame and she turned toward it like an unwary moth tempted by light. Her eyes fluttered open and when she found herself gazing into warm golden eyes, she smiled sleepily. There was the light! It was so bright and golden.

She slowly let her lids fall because she found it an effort to hold them open. She felt his lips touch hers and found them warm and intoxicating. She thought they were rather like the brandy that had slipped down her throat in a heated rush to reach her stomach, only to somehow turn around and go to her head.

He lifted her body and pulled her closer. Lauren rubbed against the crisp dark hairs on his chest like a cat rubs against its master's leg. She gave a small, secret smile. So this was what was meant by losing one's head, she thought. Julian saw the smile and caught his breath. "I was right about you, little vixen," he growled deeply. "You were born to make love to a man."

She heard his words but they had no meaning. His voice was a warm, fuzzy blur and she found comfort in the tone. It skimmed across her like a breeze, lifting her spirit as it caressed her skin.

"Lauren! Oh, Lauren!" he groaned, taking in

the scented ebony darkness of her hair. He was holding her so close that the shiver that shook him also shook her, as if they were already one. "To look upon you is sheer agony, but to hold you in my arms and taste your honeyed lips is like a sip of ambrosia that bewitches the senses and makes mere mortals think they are gods."

"Julian," she murmured. "I've never felt like this before."

"Then you, too, have tasted of desire."

Her eyes drifted open, revealing soft, violet depths, and he thought that even the most exquisite jewels could not match their glow. A spark started between them as her gaze met his, becoming a beckoning flame that hypnotized them, drawing them into its heat.

His lips descended with a dreamy slowness, and her mouth lifted instinctively to his like an innocent flower gladly yielding itself to the bee. When their lips touched, hers melted beneath his scorching firmness, and he groaned deep in his throat as he gathered her closer.

Lauren could feel the heat coming off Julian's body in waves and she tentatively lifted her hands lightly to touch the back of his neck. With a sigh, she leaned into him until she could feel every sinew and muscle in his thighs and legs. Her hands slid down his back and she felt the tensing and rolling of his flesh as it reacted to her soft strokes. A heat began in her stomach, spreading quickly down her legs until she ached with a raw hunger for something that was totally alien to her. She tried to pull back as a slight tremor of fear touched her, but then his mouth claimed her in hard possession and she eagerly met his touch. She forgot why she should resist.

Julian's tongue lightly traced the outline of her mouth and she trembled as an exquisite ripple of pleasure coursed through her body, shaking her to her very depths. Never, never had she felt like this, so warm and tingly. The little girl was being immersed in the woman in Lauren, and the woman was somehow being controlled by this man.

"Open your mouth." Julian breathed against her lips, and she passively obeyed, too far removed from reality to question the wisdom of his commands. His tongue penetrated deep within her and she gasped before her tongue joined his in provocative play.

A teasing hand at her breast set off a panic in the numbed recesses of her brain, but his other hand, at the small of her back, urged her closer until she forgot everything in the swirling mists of desire that swept around her like a whirlpool, dragging her deeper and deeper into a world of sensuality where her mind had no power and her body was eager and pliant in his hands. And what marvelous hands they were!

Julian's dark head dropped to the quivering mound of a breast and he gently tasted the pink bud until it was pert and swollen. Lauren's breath caught with a gasp as he raised his head to meet her lips, and suddenly she knew a hunger she had never thought existed. Instinctively, she knew how to rub her thighs against Julian to bring a moan from him, and the sensuous longing that coursed down her spine had her shaking like a leaf clinging to a branch in a storm, afraid to let go lest it be blown into nothingness.

"Lauren! Wild, sweet Lauren," he murmured beneath his breath, and her name had never sounded more beautiful to her ears. She felt a headiness that carried her to euphoria. She was unsure whether the wine had loosened her inhibitions or if it was Julian alone who was lifting her high on this bold cloud of desire. It didn't seem to matter; if this was passion, then it fulfilled all her wildest imaginings.

She ran her fingers through the crisp darkness of his hair, and as their eyes locked the hunger of the moment intensified until she could almost hear the crackle of emotion between them. Slowly, Lauren lifted her lips in supplication and the invitation was eagerly accepted as his touch seared her like a flame. Julian's lips slid down her arching throat, and she moaned with savage satisfaction as he found pleasure in the taste and touch of her body, before he again settled hungrily on the perfect peak of her breast.

Julian was on fire for this slip of a girl; he had never felt such overwhelming desire. Even sultry, practiced Monica had not been able to ignite such a burning need in him. But this slim nymph he now held in his arms was everything a man could ever want or ever need; he was starving for Lauren as if he had been without a woman for years.

Julian used all his considerable skill to bring her to a pitch of wanting that would equal his. He worked his art on her until she was a mindless, writhing hellion, straining eagerly against him.

He moved slowly over Lauren, sliding skin against skin. He placed his lips in the hollow of her throat and felt the frantic beating of her pulse, and then he lifted a dark tendril of her hair and kissed it. It smelled as fragrant as her skin. He wound the strand around his wrist and tugged gently until she lifted up to meet his lips. Those beautiful sensations again filled her until she was clutching his broad shoulders. She wanted to be taught more.

Tiny nerves sprung to life beneath his fingers as his hand moved sensuously across the silky smoothness of her belly. When his hand was between her legs, Lauren gasped and tried to pull away, but his leg was across her, firmly holding her in place. He made soft, soothing noises to quieten her and slowly, surely, with leisurely even strokes, he brought her achingly to life until she was dragging her nails down his back as wave after recurring wave of ecstasy swept over her. She felt caught in some mystical web of feeling where everything ceased to exist except this moment of pleasure. She was floating in a place where only Julian and his touch could reach her, and the world had faded into insignificance.

Again he parted her thighs, but this time Lauren did not protest. She felt on the verge of some great discovery and wanted to find it in Julian's arms.

When he entered her, her eyes flew open and a scream formed in her throat, only to be stifled by his mouth on hers. He remained unmoving while she moaned and restlessly twisted beneath his weight.

"Shh! love," he whispered.

There was surprise in his eyes, but once she had quieted, he slowly began to move. She remained motionless, but he went on gently caressing her, murmuring soft love words until she relaxed. As he moved, her body gained a will of its own. She arched closer and he moved faster. She could feel the sheen of perspiration on his body and sensed the tension growing within him.

Lauren felt a delicious tightening in her stomach as she wound her arms and legs around him. Her eyes were clenched shut as she strained for some invisible peak. She clung to him as her talisman in a swiftly dissolving reality and then the feeling came—that wonderful flowering and expanding that made her arch in abandon as a frenzy of sensations bounced around in her until she could find no starting point or ending place. She wanted to remain thus, but it was already fading like some nebulous dream as she floated back to reality.

Warm and satisfied and still a bit tipsy, Lauren stretched like a sinuous snake sunning itself on a rock. The room seemed to be tilted and she tried to focus on Julian. She did not believe this was really happening, and she half expected to wake up back in her room at the convent.

Julian breathed heavily as he rested his forehead on hers. His grip tightened as a burst of tenderness filled him.

"I had no idea you were a virgin," he said,

speaking aloud to himself. "You are indeed a rare woman."

She could not find her voice and her eyes closed as she snuggled against his furred chest. As she drifted off to sleep, her dreams were not of the passion she had just experienced, but rather of feeling warm and secure, floating on a cloud that cushioned her from all guilt and remorse.

Sweet nymph, 'tis true you worthy be,
Yet without love, nought worth to me.
—Fulke Greville, Lord Brooke

Chapter Two

Julian Grey, the Earl of Keaton, watched the young girl as she slept and thought he had never seen anyone more lovely in her innocence. A wry smile touched his lips at the word innocent, for that was no longer the case thanks to him. Heaven knew he would give anything to take back the hours that had just passed. But then he shook his head in a gesture of sardonic disbelief. Was that really true? he asked himself. Could he really wish away the heavenly moments just spent in this sweet girl's arms? Her response to him and the warm silken touch of her body against his had affected him like he was some awkward boy eagerly seeking to learn his first lesson in the joys of the flesh.

He placed his hands behind his head as he stared up into the darkness. Lauren moaned softly and turned on her side, seeking his warmth in her unconscious state. He smiled as she nestled against him. He didn't usually like to dally in bed once he was satiated, but tonight was different. He felt a strange kind of peace

34

come over him as he listened to the soft sounds of her breathing.

A frown gathered between his brows as he suddenly remembered his mistress, Monica Ridgely. Monica was anything but peaceful. He closed his eyes in an effort to let sleep ease the tension of his rather unpleasant day.

The letter from Monica had put Julian in a foul mood. He cursed violently as he pushed back his chair, its legs scraping noisily across the parquet floor. He threw the letter down in a gesture of distaste as he came to his feet. A seductive scent rose from the missive lying on the polished surface of the desk, but the sweet smell only increased his bitterness. He moved angrily away from the oak desk as if he found the nearness of the letter offensive.

He pulled back the heavy gray velvet drapes and watched as the rain made tiny rivers down the panes of glass. He blinked as lightning flashed, illuminating the water-drenched gardens of his estate. The click of a door disturbed his mood and he threw a brooding glance over his shoulder. He sighed wearily as he saw his sister enter the room.

Felice Taylor was small with dark hair and twinkling blue eyes. She had a pleasing vivacity much admired by others, but Julian was unable to appreciate it at the moment.

"I'm busy, Felice," he said impatiently, walking to his desk to shuffle through his papers.

She gave him a warm smile, unaffected by his tone. "So I see. The Earl of Keaton is so busy looking out the window that he has no time to talk."

"I'm in no mood for company," he said sharply.

She gracefully sat in the brocade chair that faced his desk. "I know why you are in a temper—" she began, only to be interrupted as he raised one eyebrow haughtily.

"Indeed? And how did you come by this information? No doubt the husband?" There was a sneer in his voice.

She sighed. "I understand why you are upset."

"Upset?!" He gave a hard laugh. "That is not the word I would have used, but yes, anyone with a thought in his head would understand why I'm upset."

She began again, as if he had not spoken. "I understand why you are upset, but I think it might be for the best."

His golden eyes were cold as he surveyed his sister, wondering if she had lost her senses. He raked back his dark hair off his brow before he turned and paced over to the window, again staring out over the vast gardens to the woods beyond.

"I have no intention of being blackmailed into marriage!"

"You are four and thirty, Julian, and although you are a handsome man, you must realize that you are not getting any younger." He remained still, as if he had not heard her.

She watched his proud back and knew instinctively how he loathed the position he was in and how he would chafe at any restriction put on his independence. Felice loved her brother, and knew he had a wild reputation with women. He treated his mistresses with a careless disregard for their feelings, often changing them as he would his jacket. His current mistress, Monica Ridgley, was a widow with a wild reputation of her own, although she tempered hers with a false show of respectability. Monica had lasted the longest of any of Julian's mistresses, and it seemed as if she had finally found a way to have him well and truly hooked.

Felice sighed softly as she watched her brother. Her friends and acquaintances thought him a rakehell, but she knew better. She had been a mere child when the family had lost everything through their father's gambling. Their mother had tried in vain to save face, but one night she took an overdose of laudanum. No one had known whether it had been an accident or if everything had suddenly become too much for her. The worst part was that Julian had been the one to find her because their father had failed to return during the night. The next day they learned that he had been killed in a duel after being accused of cheating. Loss of fortune, mother and father was a triple tragedy for a twelve-year-old boy used to security and the good life. Now all he had was his name, title and a younger sister.

A distant cousin claimed the children, taking them to live in his home. His wife doted on Felice, but Julian was a different matter. They disliked his proud, willful ways, and punished him often, usually taking a cane to him. They constantly told him how bad and wicked he was and how he would one day end up in hell. In-

stead of making Julian obedient, their repri-
mands only made him wilder and more
headstrong.

An old friend of Julian's father paid for his
education, but away at school, Julian fell in with
a rowdy, fun-loving set of young nobles who preferred wine, women and gaming over seeking
an education.

Julian soon grew tired of his aimless life. He
wanted his old estate back and enough money
to bring Felice to live with him; the one thing
he really missed was his little sister. If he was
going to gamble he might as well use his win-
nings to create the life he wanted. Julian discovered that he did not share his father's bad
luck with cards. As the stakes grew higher, so
did his fortune. He invested it wisely and soon
he was a very wealthy businessman. He bought
his childhood home and redecorated it at great
expense. He used his title to bring him in contact with the more polite aspects of society and
then he brought Felice to live with him. Felice
lacked for nothing and when she was presented
to society, she met and fell in love with Lord
Brendan Taylor. While Brendan did not have a
great fortune, he was Felice's choice above all
others, so Julian allowed her to marry him.

Frequent visits from his sister and brother-
in-law showed Julian that his sister's marriage
was a good one. Felice and Brendan still loved
each other after six years of marriage, a long
time to Julian, who tired of his relationships in
a matter of months. The only sadness in Felice's
marriage was that she had not been able to pro-

duce the child she and Brendan wanted so desperately.

"She's gone too far with her scheming." At Julian's words, Felice came back to the present with a start.

Felice slowly rose to her feet and crossed the carpet. She placed a comforting hand on his arm, feeling the muscles tighten beneath the cloth. "You have been with Monica almost a year now, Julian. Surely you have some feelings for her or you would have left her a long time ago."

His jaw tightened angrily as he acknowledged her words. "I admit that I found something more with Monica than with other women, but she knew from the beginning that I would never offer marriage. Any fleeting feelings I may have had for her died the moment I received that letter," he said, throwing out his hand at the paper resting so prominently on his desk. "She knew there was no question of love on my side."

"But you need someone, Julian."

"I have women, Felice. I can find all the women I need."

"Yes, I agree that it is not difficult to find a woman, but for one reason only! You satisfy the needs of the flesh, but what of the heart? The heart needs to be fed as well."

He gave a harsh laugh. "You have been married long enough to have lost that romantic streak that was always so strong in you."

"What about a family, Julian?" she persisted.

"I have all the family I need." His eyes softened. "You are my family, Felice."

"But what of children?" Julian made a dis-

missive sound, which she ignored. "It has always been a great sadness to Brendan and me
that I have not been able to conceive." Her eyes
filled with tears and her fingers trembled as she
clutched his arm. "I would like to see this house
filled with laughter and happiness. At least I
could be a doting aunt if motherhood is to be
denied me."

Julian started to make an angry retort, but
seeing the distress so clearly visible on her face,
he relented. "I would make a terrible husband,
ma petite," he said softly, his hand gently stroking her dark hair. "I would be even worse as a
father. Would you really wish me on some poor
unborn child?" he asked drily.

"Yes!" She emphatically shook her head. "You
would be a marvelous husband to the right
woman and a perfect father to the child she
would bear you."

"Sad to say they have not made the woman
that I would desire enough to give up my freedom," he grinned.

"You have so much kindness in you, Julian.
You can be gentle and loving. You just try so
hard to hide it from the world."

He raised his hand to gently wipe a tear away
from her face. "I love you, Felice, and that is
enough."

"But will it always be enough, Julian?" she
asked softly, her blue eyes filled with tenderness. "I cannot give you what Brendan and I
share, and it is my greatest wish that you should
have joy such as ours."

She gazed intently into his handsome face,
taking in the rakish contours that made him so

attractive. It was a sensual face with a straight nose, high cheekbones and a firm jaw. His countenance was rather serious and thin with abundant dark lashes framing his golden eyes. His body was slim and elegantly proportioned and he moved with an easy grace that drew women's eyes. He always caused a stir when he entered a room and Felice was aware that it was not only his large fortune that had every eligible young lady secretly thinking about him. His charm and slightly bored air had them forgetting his jaded reputation as they set out to catch his attention all the more.

"I find happiness in numbers, Felice. I could never settle for just one woman."

She laughed as she ruefully shook her head. "I can't wait until you fall in love, Julian, for I shall be quite delighted to throw your words in your face." A mischievous smile curved her lips. "She might even lead you a merry chase that will take the wind out of your sails."

"There's not a woman alive I can't handle, as Monica will soon discover. Brendan lets you get away with far too much, Felice. He hasn't mastered you yet."

She haughtily lifted her nose in the air. "It would do your ego a world of good to find someone you can't master. Your women think you far too perfect, even with your condescending ways. Brendan would never treat me so boorishly."

"And he's spoiled you because of it. He'll never bring you to heel now," he drawled lazily, smiling at the look of irritation that flashed in her eyes.

"Well! I shall have to begin looking for that

female. You are getting too high in the saddle and far too sure of your own charms."

"Search away, Felice, but Monica will not be the one to trap me. If she isn't careful, she might even find that the trap is on the other foot and she could meet with an accident."

Felice gasped. "Don't even speak of such things in jest lest they come to pass."

He laughed aloud. "I have no intention of murdering Monica, regardless of how pleasant the thought might be."

Felice lifted the ruffled skirt of her morning gown. "Brendan will be down in a moment, so I should go and see if breakfast is prepared."

Julian caught at her free hand. "I am glad you found the time to visit me. I have missed you."

She gave him a warm smile. "The estate can manage without us for a while, and Brendan knew I was longing to see my favorite brother."

"Stay for as long as you like. I always enjoy your company." He lightly touched her chin. "Now let's see no more sad faces."

Her glance went to the letter on the desk. "What will you do about Monica?"

"I'm not quite sure, but I intend to wipe the smug smile from her conniving face."

After Felice had gone, Julian picked up the scented letter and crushed it in his hand. How dare she try to blackmail him into marriage! He cursed violently, throwing the letter to the floor before he stormed from the room to search for his valet.

*   *   *

Julian was unaware that at the very moment he was talking to his sister, Monica Ridgely sat before her satin-draped dressing table and pouted. "I think a little Spanish wool here, Rachel." She pointed to her left cheek and the maid quickly added the necessary color.

"Are you sure you know what you're doing, Monica?" a feminine voice scorned from the doorway. Monica glanced over her shoulder to where her old friend Leah Bradwell stood.

"Ah! The voice of doom has come, Rachel," Monica laughed, waving a hand to dismiss the maid.

"You are foolish to try and manipulate a man like Julian," Leah persisted as she crossed the boudoir and sat on a small chair beside the bed.

"There are many ways to get a man, and I am not averse to trying them all if it will help me get Julian."

"He's been your lover longer than any other woman has been able to hold him, so let that satisfy you. He's never looked twice at me and I have given him enough opportunities to share my bed."

"I want more! I want to be the Countess of Keaton, and I shall be!" Monica stated with confidence.

Leah shook her head. "That letter was a mistake. I'd never have the audacity to insist that he marry me immediately or else I would go tattling to the King about the affair."

"Julian needs the King's good wishes if he is to expand his shipping firm. My late husband was a confidant to the King and so I dare to hope that I might make myself sympathetic in his eyes."

Leah laughed. "You? Sympathetic?!"

"You know how King George is about the moral uprightness of his subjects. He'd like us all to be as stuffy as he is."

"I still think you've gone too far," Leah interrupted. "Why don't you just breed a child and then he might marry you?"

Monica turned on her stool. "Are you mad?" She gave Leah a scornful look. "As much as I want Julian, I have no intention of ruining my figure having brats." She patted the stray curl into place. "This way is much easier."

Leah looked at Monica and noticed the velvet robe that slipped enticingly from one white shoulder and how the garment parted seductively to reveal half of a rounded breast.

"I see you are expecting him," Leah grinned.

Monica's painted lips parted in a smug smile. "If I know Julian, he'll be here as soon as it's dark. I know my message will bring him to me posthaste."

Leah shivered. "If I'd sent that note, I would have come to my senses by now and be on the first packet to France."

Monica laughed huskily. "Julian wants me, Leah. Once we have talked, I'm sure he will come to his senses and realize what a fine wife I will make him."

Leah stood, shaking her head ruefully. "Add a little more perfume, Monica. You're going to need all the help you can get."

"Go away, Leah," Monica smiled. "I know what I'm doing."

"That's what every fool says before his down-fall."

Once Leah was gone, Monica sat before the mirror with a frown on her face. What if Leah were right, she thought. Had she overestimated Julian's desire for her? A remembrance of the last time they were together lightened her features and gave a purely feline smile to her reflection. No, Julian might be angry, in fact she was sure he would be, but once in her arms he would accept his fate and she would be his wife.

The time seemed to pass slowly, but soon she heard his voice below and her heart began to race with anticipation. Monica positioned herself seductively on the bed as she waited for him to appear. The door opened and there Julian was, looking magnificent in his evening dress. He did not look angry, she realized with a start. In fact he looked like he was ready for a night in bed. Things were going better than she had expected. She moved, exposing one slim leg to his inspection. She felt a warmth invade her body as his heated glance lingered on her charms.

"I thought you would never come, Julian," she whispered, holding out her arms.

She was momentarily surprised when he turned away, walking instead to the table where she had a decanter of brandy and glasses ready for him. He poured a drink and turned to face her, lifting his glass in a mocking salute before he downed the liquid in one swift motion.

"I really must congratulate you on your mettle, Monica, but you really were just throwing idle threats around in that letter, weren't you?"

His tone was soft, but she sensed the hardness in his words.

"Several people know of our affair, Julian. It would be a simple thing to prove to the King."

"I have no intention of marrying you, Monica," he stated calmly. "You knew that before we entered into this relationship."

"I have made you happy, Julian," she insisted, sitting up in bed as she became aware that his earlier interest had been feigned and he was finding no arousal in her half-dressed state. "I would make you happier as your wife."

"Wife? You?" He gave a harsh laugh that made her flush with mortification. He moved to the side of the bed and gave her a scathing glance, viewing the charms so eagerly displayed before him and finding her lacking. "There was never any question of my choosing you for a wife. Why should I buy the cow when I can get the milk for free?"

A resounding slap echoed in the room and Monica warily sat back on her heels as she watched him rub his reddened cheek.

"You must admit that you are rather shop-worn for a wife."

"You despicable beast!" she screamed wildly.

"Women never do like hearing the truth, do they?" he asked coldly.

"And men like it even less!" she hissed, throwing her long blond hair angrily over her shoulder. "But you have to hear the truth now. If you don't marry me before the week is out, then I shall go to the King and tell him of the awful acts you forced me to perform. He was a very good friend to my late husband, so I think he will be very disappointed in you, Julian." At his cold, closed face, she softened. She did not want him like this. She had thought the mere threat would bring him to her where she could seduce him with her body, showing him all the pleasures they could share for many years. "You like lying in my arms," she said softly.

"Any woman would have sufficed," he announced with a twist of his lips.

"That's not true!" she remonstrated. "I pleased you longer than anyone else."

He bent closer to her face. "Any joy I found in your arms was killed the moment you thought you could manipulate me to your whims. You know so much about me, Monica, and yet so little if you thought I would give in to your demands."

Her eyes were a bright, glassy blue. She swallowed nervously, feeling the lump that came and went in her throat. "I can make you happy. Give me a chance."

"You have taken away any feelings I ever had for you." He gave a malicious laugh. "I'll admit that I enjoyed possessing your body. You're quite a little courtesan, Monica, and you know all the tricks of the trade, but I wouldn't touch you again if my life depended on it."

"You might think that now, Julian," she taunted. "But once we're married you will change your mind."

"Forget it, Monica," he said coldly.

"You will agree! Can you really want the scandal that will ensue? I heard the King hinting to you that it was time you settled down. He's such a family man himself, he thinks everyone else should be one as well." She leaned back on the pillows, a satisfied smile on her face. "I have trapped you, Julian, as successfully as any hunter would trap a rabbit."

His teeth snapped together angrily. "This is no meek rabbit in your trap, Monica. You should have thought of that before you set this plan in motion. I will admit that you have a full hand, but I have an ace. I can leave the country."

"But you won't," she said with certainty. "You are depending on the King's favor to help you seal this new shipping route. I know how much it means to you. You will marry me before the week is over or face the worst time of your life."

"My dear, nothing could be as bad as having to face you across the table every day. I'd rather marry a scouring maid than have you in my bed."

He strode from the room, slamming the door behind him. That small sign of his rage made Monica give a feline grin. She knew she had won.

Lauren moved in her sleep, jolting Julian from a fitful doze. He watched her for a moment, remembering how soft and yielding she'd felt beneath him. He suddenly wanted to drink again of her sweetness, and he wondered briefly if perhaps the alcohol he had consumed had addled his wits.

He vaguely remembered entering a dark pub and downing drink after drink as he sought to forget his problems. He smiled when he remembered thinking that the only way he could keep from marrying Monica was if he were already

cursed with a wife. It was a strange idea and
he laughed harshly at the thought. The sound
penetrated Lauren's sleep and she shifted restlessly, as if disturbed by Julian's anger.

He glanced again at the girl and gently removed a strand of black hair from her cheek.
Little did he know what he would find when he
had left the pub last night to wander down the
dark street—the street that had led him into
Lauren's arms.

Julian wanted nothing more than to forget
the unpleasantness of the day. He much preferred to dwell on the memorable moments just
spent with the beautiful Lauren, but his eyes
were growing heavy and he could not keep a
yawn at bay. As the dark waves of sleep began
to claim him, his last thought was that tomorrow he would know what to do.

A dream, a breath, a froth of fleeting joy.
—William Shakespeare
The Rape of Lucrece

Chapter Three

Lauren struggled up through the thick mists of sleep that pressed heavily on her closed eyelids. She tried to open her eyes, but the shaft of light coming through the window was painfully bright and she gave a small whimper as she raised her hand to shield her eyes. A dull ache throbbed in her head and she felt sick to her stomach. She grimaced at the heavy feeling in her arms and legs as she licked dry lips.

Her lashes flickered hesitantly and then she was staring up at wooden beams and cracked plaster. Her mind was so hazy that for a second Lauren could not place her surroundings. She moaned softly and tried to rise, but something held her long dark tresses securely to the rumpled bedcovers and she fell back, her head beginning to pound, causing the dull sickness in her stomach to worsen. Again she looked at the ceiling, noting vaguely that a spider was spinning its web about a poor fly as it struggled helplessly in the sticky threads.

Lauren was determined to sit up, but her scalp felt the painful tug on her hair—it was caught

50

somehow. She put her hand to her head as she turned to see what was hindering her movements.

There, stretched lazily beside her in brazen boldness was a totally nude man! He was still asleep, looking rather pagan with his sunburned skin so brown against the snowy white sheets. His hair was thick and black and curling against his forehead. His chin was obstinately square with a cleft in the middle, and a smile touched his mouth, as if he were dreaming of something very pleasurable. She noticed that his chest was covered with dark, crisp hairs that trailed down to his manhood.

Lauren looked away as embarrassment stained her cheeks. Her brow wrinkled in confusion as she searched the fuzzy chambers of her memory for some rhyme or reason for this man's presence. She shivered in the cold room, suddenly becoming aware of her own state of undress. She covered her breasts with crossed arms and her breath came in short frightened gasps. Her brain began to clear and the events of the night before returned with startling clarity.

She swallowed painfully and then slowly tried to remove her hair from beneath the man's body without awakening him. She pulled and he groaned and stretched, making her stiffen like a statue. When he settled back into sleep, Lauren again tried to pull her hair from under his shoulders, but this time the movement awakened him. One eye came open, causing her breath to catch and hold. He opened his other eye and gave her a reckless grin, showing even white teeth.

"Couldn't wait for me to wake up, eh, sweet?" he asked roguishly. There was a drowsy look in his golden eyes, but it was rapidly being replaced by a hungry look of anticipation. His hand grasped a handful of dark hair. "I thought I had dreamed you last night." His voice was low and husky, rippling along her nerve endings and making her shiver.

He mistook her reaction and pulled her closer. "But you are cold," he murmured, placing his lips on her shoulder. "Let me warm you!"

Lauren felt as if she had been turned into stone. She was unable to move or even breathe for fear he might become violent and leap on her.

He gave a self-satisfied laugh as his eyes traveled leisurely over her pale flesh. His hand moved up and cupped one luscious breast and she shivered in his arms, thinking he was like some dark savage hawk. She strained away from his touch. She opened her mouth to protest and moaned as his lips covered hers, plundering the depths of her sweet cavern before his tongue teased and played with hers. She twisted against him to break his hold, but she only succeeded in pressing her breasts closer to his dark, furry chest. Without knowing it, she was spurring him on, exciting him more than ever.

His fingertips found the base of her spine and moved slowly up and down, bringing soft little moans to her throat. "Put your arms around my neck," he ordered huskily, and his breath was a warm whisper that echoed in her mind. She felt as lost as a small mouse trapped in the claws of a hungry cat. To refuse him might make him all the more eager, and, besides, she could find no words to do so; her voice seemed lodged somewhere between her heart and mouth.

He gave Lauren no choice as he lifted her arms, and her fingers were tentative tentacles that slowly felt the crisp hair at his nape before they dropped limply down to the cool brown skin at his side. Julian's eyes glowed warm and golden as he scanned the alabaster smoothness of her shoulders before his gaze moved on to scorch her breasts with a heat that made the flat pink tips harden into tiny rosebuds. His lips were hot as he claimed one peak, and she gave a muffled cry, trying in vain to push him away.

Her head swam dizzily. "D-don't," she sighed into his mouth. "Oh, please d-don't!" and then she knew nothing as blackness closed over her like a warm blanket, blocking out everything that caused her distress.

When Lauren opened her eyes it was with a feeling of *déjà vu* as she saw the spider on the ceiling, the fly now encircled. She moaned softly and then a small noise made her swallow nervously, as she turned toward the corner of the room. Julian was sitting in a chair, leaning back on two legs, but he was now fully dressed.

"I've heard of women swooning with passion, but this is the first time I've experienced it," Julian said drily.

She blushed a dull red as she rolled onto her stomach. "Go away! Just go away!" she cried.

The chair scraped the floor and then she felt the bed give with his weight. She refused to look at him, embarrassed about what had happened between them.

"I had no idea you were a virgin before I took you." His voice was soft.

"Would it have made any difference?" she asked huskily, her head buried in the soft sheet.

His fingers lightly traced a track down her spine and she jerked angrily, making him remove his hand. "Probably not," he admitted slowly. "But I wish to make amends."

She lifted her head, staring at him with misty violet eyes. "There is naught you can do. I can never be my original undamaged self."

"In my opinion you are now better than before, Lauren. Virginity is a highly overrated commodity. I much prefer women with a little experience."

"I'm sorry I was such a disappointment," she snapped, covering her face with her hands.

"A disappointment? I wouldn't say that. I was very enlightened. I have never tasted such heady nectar."

"I don't wish to be reminded of it!" she snapped indignantly.

"Ah, but I do. Little did I know last night that I would come upon such a delightful sprite in need of rescuing." He chuckled attractively and Lauren shivered, as if the sound had touched a sensitive nerve. "A damsel in distress was more than my chivalry could ignore, for I have always had the urge to play the hero."

"A hero does not ravish the woman he was supposed to rescue," she said coldly.

He laughed. "I know. I fear that I was too tempted and much too mortal to be a true hero."

"Well, the deed is done so go away and leave me alone," she muttered into her pillow.

"I have a proposition to make to you that could solve both our problems." His calm, even tones made her lift her head, looking at him in surprise.

"What do you mean?"

"I know I was wrong to take you last night, but I thought you were willing and were just being coy." At her gasp of protest he held up his hand. "I know now that I was wrong. I want to marry you."

Her eyes widened in disbelief and she sat up, pulling the sheet around her body. "Are you mad?"

He laughed. "Yes I am, but at another woman, not in the crazed sense. I want to take care of you."

"I can take care of myself!"

"As you did last night?" he asked softly. She reddened and he continued, "I'm sorry, but you must admit that a woman alone in London with neither money nor work is bound to get into trouble. I offer you a house, servants and food on your table."

"B-but we don't love each other," she said shyly.

He laughed harshly and she flinched at the look in his eye. "Why must women always bring up that stupid emotion. Everything must be shaded in black and white, with none of the gray that makes up the majority of life."

She lifted her chin haughtily. "Then pray tell me what you mean. Surely you do not care for my lost virginity."

"You have the problem of being without funds or a place to live. I also have a problem."

She lifted one eyebrow. "Whatever can be your problem, sir, since it is surely not a guilty conscience?"

"So the sweet has a bit of spice to it? I like that. But no, it is not a guilty conscience. A woman of my acquaintance is pressing for marriage and she is in a position to force my hand. I have no intention of being blackmailed by her. While you were unconscious an idea came to me. If I were married, Monica would have no power. After all, it is rather hard to force a married man into marriage."

"This is ridiculous! You'll marry me to avoid marriage with another?" She laughed, forgetting her own sorry circumstances.

"It will be a secret marriage since Monica is the only one who needs to know of it. I will show her the papers and produce you if necessary. When a decent interval has passed we will go our separate ways. I will see that you have a sizable amount of money, enough to live comfortably the rest of your life."

"And what if you should decide to marry someone else in a few years?"

"I think it will be very easy to avoid that temptation."

"I don't know." She looked uncertain.

"Think, Lauren. Money, servants, a roof over your head. You can have lovely dresses and jewels."

"I need some time to think," she said, looking away from the strong appeal in his eyes.

He sighed heavily. "Very well. I will leave you

now since I have some things to attend to, but I'll be back this evening and shall expect your answer. Think, Lauren! It would solve both our problems with very little trouble."

"I will let you know this evening." Lauren caught his sleeve as he was leaving. "Julian, I want you to know that whatever I decide I do not hold you totally responsible for last night. I was frightened, alone, and had too much to drink. Your offer to take care of me was honorable."

"Do not think me gallant, Lauren," he muttered. "I need you as much or more than you need me."

After he was gone Lauren dressed quickly, throwing her cloak over her shoulder to conceal the torn bodice. She had something to do and she knew she would not accept Julian's offer. She did not need time to consider it; she had only appeared agreeable so she could get away without an ugly scene. She knew her grandfather would not refuse her appeal for shelter and understanding.

A memory of the lovemaking of last night lingered in her mind more than she cared to admit, but she shook it from her thoughts and quickly left the room in search of her past.

Rodney Warwick sat at his ornate desk, his features thin and gaunt, and stared coldly at the girl standing before him. His fists were clenched so tightly that the knuckles were white, and his eyes were coal black, hiding a soul equally as dark.

He had not believed his ears when the footman had announced that a young girl was requesting to see his father. Now he was glad he had had the foresight to view all his father's visitors and correspondence.

"What do you want?" he asked in an acid tone, finding no joy in her beauty.

"I think you know what I want, dear Uncle," she bit back.

He leaned back in his chair and studied his niece. He had never dreamed Stephen's wife and daughter would return to England. "You want money?" He gave a hard laugh. "Of course! Everyone wants money. How much do you need so that I never have to look at you again?"

Her lips thinned and her fingers tightened on the cloak. "I want no money. I wish to see my grandfather."

"I'm afraid that's impossible," he returned in a silky voice.

"Impossible?"

"He's very old and sick. I don't think it would be a good idea to upset him with your presence."

"Maybe we should ask him what he thinks."

A cold, cynical smile appeared on Rodney's thin lips. "I run the estate now. I may not have the title of Earl yet, but I do control the money, and I think it would be wise if you were to take what I offer and disappear."

"Would that ease your conscience?" she asked, holding onto her temper with great difficulty.

He looked startled and then he scowled dangerously. "What are you insinuating?"

"I am insinuating nothing! You may have fooled my father and grandfather, but you'll never fool me. I know that you had something to do with my father's disgrace and I intend to find out what it was."

He pulled at his lower lip as he looked at her, but she had seen the instant of shock that he quickly hid with a bored expression. "Strong words, Lauren, but can you prove them?"

She looked away from his taunting face, hating him as she had never hated anyone. "I shall find a way."

He laughed at that. "Do you really think anyone cares after all these years?"

"I care!" she threw the words at him.

He shook his head sadly. "You are a beautiful girl and should not be thinking about a past that is better forgotten. Your father was my brother. Why should I disgrace him?"

"You had everything to gain from my father's ruined reputation. You may think you are very clever, Uncle, but you're not. I was but a child and yet I saw the smirk of satisfaction on your face that my father and grandfather missed in the moment of their grief. You disgraced him so you could have all this," she announced, waving her hand at the elaborately decorated room. "Have your ill-gotten gains made you happy?"

"Get out of here! Go back to your mother and leave this country. There is nothing for you here but grief."

"My—my mother is dead," Lauren said slowly. "She died penniless, depending on the help of nuns to care for us. What makes me so angry is that she never did anything to suffer as she did. She always believed in my father's innocence, though that did not prevent her from feeling the shame of being ostracized by the very people who once claimed to be her friends. Father would have given you anything, Uncle, if you had but asked, but you were too greedy. You wanted it all to yourself!"

Rodney stood up and wavered slightly behind the desk. "Get out of here! Leave me alone if you know what's good for you. The shock of seeing you could kill Father, and you wouldn't want that, would you?"

With a muffled sob Lauren turned and ran out of the study, down the hall and out the front door without giving a second look at the magnificent furnishings along the walls. She ran and ran until her sides ached, finally coming to rest on a small park bench. Her vision was blurred by tears and she felt more wretched than ever as her heart seemed about to burst from her agony.

While she had not expected Rodney to welcome her with open arms, she had thought her grandfather would. He had cried at the loss of his son and his family. Lauren remembered him hugging her before they were hurried into the carriage and sent away like thieves in the night.

As she sat there feeling lost and alone, she was unaware of the people around her. She did not see the young mother scolding her child, or the two young men arguing over a friendly bet. She was remembering a time and place she would rather forget, but which was so much a part of what had shaped her.

Her grandfather had worked at the Foreign Office during the Seven Years War, and during that time someone was giving secret information to the French. No one could discover who was doing it, but everyone in the office was under suspicion.

The day came for their planned raid on St. Cast. It was to be a reconnaissance to lead the way for a full-scale invasion. Only a handful of men knew about the operation, but when the English forces landed, Monsieur d'Aiguillon, the governor of Brittany, was waiting for them with a band of volunteers. Three thousand Englishmen were killed and hundreds were taken prisoner. What was most humiliating to the Foreign Office was that the French volunteers were nothing more than farmers, yet they defeated a British army. The only logical assumption was that the French had known about the attack beforehand.

A few months later some letters from a Frenchman named the Duc de Romoulet were found in Lauren's father's possession. The man implicated her father by mentioning how helpful his information had been in the defeat of the British forces at St. Cast.

A sob caught in Lauren's throat and her eyes filled with tears, but she was unaware of the lonely picture she presented as the past wove its spell around her.

Lauren had been but a child, but she could clearly see her father's shocked face when her grandfather had accused him of treason. The fact that his father could believe the lies hurt more than the knowledge that he would soon be called a traitor by the country he loved.

Her grandfather finally broke down and ordered his son to leave before the military arrived to take him prisoner. He said that as much as he hated a traitor he could not allow his own son to hang.

All Lauren could remember of the rest of that horrible night was sitting in a dark coach as they raced through the deserted streets of London. She remembered hearing her mother's muffled sobs and her father's soft, comforting words. How could faith and trust be so lightly thrown away by all who knew her father for an honorable man? Never before had he given them reason to doubt him, but in his hour of need, all had deserted him and believed the worst.

They boarded a boat without being apprehended and sailed to safety, but there was no life in her father after that night. It might have been more merciful if they had caught him and hanged him because his heart and soul were still in England. He was but a shell of the man he had once been. Even her mother's love could not comfort him in his disgrace. He felt he was no longer worthy of her love.

He died a few years later, welcoming the release from the torment of being so unjustly accused and unable to prove his innocence. As he lay dying he told his wife that he should not have run as he did since that damned him even further as a guilty man. He should have stayed and fought against the lies. Yet Lauren's mother believed that he left because he wished to save his wife and daughter from harm and slander, which made him even more honorable in her eyes.

Most of Lauren's life was spent in exile, living in one country and then the next. Her father never found a place that gave him peace, so they were constantly on the move. After his death they settled in a convent in France, but with its rigid rules that life was not a happy one for Lauren.

When Lauren was older, her mother admitted that she believed Rodney had something to do with her husband's disgrace. She had tried to tell her husband, but he had refused to listen, saying that Rodney was a hero and heroes were not traitors.

When her mother died, Lauren knew she was tired of running and hiding from the past. She would either clear her father's name, or at least make peace with her grandfather, for she knew that was what her father would have wanted. For too long the past had been held inside her, growing and festering like a terrible wound that would not heal. How could she get on with her life when there were so many ghosts to haunt her? How could she bury a past that was so much a part of her?

"Flowers, my lady? Flowers?" an old woman chanted close to her, and Lauren jerked back to the present. She refused the beautiful blossoms and rose to her feet.

As she walked away, she wondered what she was going to do. She had not a farthing to her name and no place to call home. Her head was down and her thoughts were on other things when she stepped into the road. She was unaware of the carriage careening wildly toward her until she felt someone grab her sleeve and roughly haul her out of its path. Her eyes widened in fear as she watched the coach rush past without the driver giving her a second look.

"What's the matter with you, goose! Are you trying to kill yourself?"

Lauren looked at the girl dressed in dark, somber clothing. Something in Lauren's pale face and wide eyes must have told the girl that she was very shaken, for she took Lauren's arm, pulled her over to a tree, and made her sit down.

"Is something wrong?" the girl asked in concern.

Lauren wiped her eyes with the back of her hand. "Everything!"

"Everything covers quite a bit of ground," the girl said with a hint of amusement.

Lauren looked more closely at the girl. She had dark red hair beneath a small cap and happy green eyes that crinkled at the corners. Her teeth protruded too much and a profusion of freckles sprinkled her nose and cheeks, something every woman tried to remove since pale lustrous complexions were all the rage. But Lauren thought the girl was pleasant to look at and her freckles became her, making her appear even friendlier.

"What's your name?" Lauren asked shyly.

"Molly. Molly Putnam."

Lauren gave her a weak smile. "My name is Lauren de Fanchon."

"Well, Lauren, why don't you tell old Molly what the problem is. I always say things aren't so bad if they're shared."

Lauren hesitated and Molly grinned. "You can say 'A pox on you! Go away!' if you want and I'll understand. It's just that everything is wrong in my life, too."

At Lauren's interested look Molly continued. "I was a lady's maid to a woman with more money than looks and a son just as ugly. I lost my position because he got a little too eager in his attentions and I thwarted his plans with the side of my hand to his face. Of course he didn't tell his mother he was after me like hounds at a hare, and she didn't believe my story—or didn't choose to—so out I went like a pail of dirty water. She wouldn't even give me a letter of recommendation after two years of waitin' on her hand and foot! She said she would spread the word of my 'disgraceful conduct' so no decent woman would let me in her house."

"How unfair!" Lauren exclaimed in outrage. "Why should her word be taken over yours?"

Molly shrugged unconcernedly. "I'm just a servant and servants don't matter. But enough about me. What's wrong with you? You need to watch your step or they'll be cartin' you off in a box."

"Perhaps that wouldn't be so bad," Lauren said as a wave of self-pity came over her.

"Oh, enough of that talk! Things can't be that bad."

Lauren glanced away. "I don't want to bother you with my troubles. You have enough of your own." She rose jerkily to her feet. "Thank you for your help."

As she walked away, Molly gave a resigned sigh. She watched Lauren for a moment as she merged with the crowd on the street and then started after her. Lauren did not know how long she walked or that Molly tagged dutifully along behind her like a watchdog at her heels. If she received an interested look from a man, Molly would instantly quell his attention with a dangerous glare. When Lauren eventually found a bench and sat down, Molly did likewise, groaning with relief as she rubbed her feet.

"I thought you'd never stop!"

Lauren looked at her in surprise, unaware that she had been following.

"Are you hungry?" Molly asked, and as if in answer to the question, Lauren's stomach gave a light rumble. Molly laughed and produced a piece of bread and cheese from her purse. "I learned young never to go out unprepared," she smiled as she split her meal in half and offered Lauren one part.

As they munched quietly on their fare, time passed and the sun began to sink in the sky, but still the two girls sat quietly on the bench, lost in their own thoughts.

Finally Molly broke the silence. "Have you anyplace to sleep tonight?" she asked.

Lauren vividly remembered the little room at the inn, the warm, filling food, the handsome face of a man and then the tangled sheets on the bed. She hastily thrust those thoughts aside. She had no money for a room.

"No," she said quietly.

Molly sighed. "Me neither." She laughed suddenly. "We're a fine pair of birds, that's for sure. We've known each other less than a day, and we'll probably die together while we clutch our empty bellies. They'll throw us in the same pauper's grave and we'll be together forever." She laughed again in mockery, but stopped suddenly at the muffled weeping coming from Lauren. "Here now! I was only funning!"

"You have a strange sense of humor," Lauren sniffed.

"Aye. That I have," she chuckled. "But you need one in this world, lovely, or life will break you." She looked sideways at Lauren. "I don't mean to be sticking my long nose in where it's not wanted, but you're a beautiful girl. I can't believe you're out on your own with no place to go."

"I thought I had a place, but I was turned away." A sob caught in her throat.

Molly's arm instinctively came around Lauren's shoulders. "Tell old Molly about it, me love. It ofttimes makes the load less heavy to bear, and I swear I'll never repeat it to a soul."

Molly's friendly voice and comforting hold were as necessary to her in that moment as any bread and drink. She felt a strange empathy with this girl from the streets, as if they had been brought together for a purpose.

Molly's eyes were clear and straightforward, her touch light and soothing, and her voice gave Lauren a strength she desperately needed at this moment. All the walls of restraint and distrust came tumbling down and she found herself talking about things she had never told another soul. It seemed right, somehow, this meeting on a cold, bleak day; this sharing of troubles and woes that would bring them even closer. If anyone would understand, Molly would, and being a stranger, perhaps she would not judge her father as harshly as those who were supposed to have loved him did.

"I came from France hoping to reconcile with my grandfather," she began hesitantly. "He disowned my father years ago for something he did not do. My uncle turned me away tonight without tuppence to my name."

"What a nasty bloke he sounds. At least I wasn't related to my old mistress! What's an innocent babe like you gonna do out on your own with no coin in your pocket?" Molly asked, lines of worry on her forehead. "Me, I can take care of myself if I have to, but I can't see you survivin' long on your own."

Lauren's chin came up at that. "I can take care of myself. As a matter of fact," she added, "I had an offer of marriage."

"Marriage?"

Lauren blushed. "I met a man my first night in London. He rescued me from two men and took me to an inn. I—I, well, I drank too much and—"

Molly held up her hand. "Don't say any more. I can guess. The dirty fellow had his way with you."

Lauren turned even redder. "It wasn't quite like that, but yes."

Molly uttered an expletive. "If men had as many brains in their heads as urgin's in their breeches, this world might not be such a bad place to live."

"I was not without blame, and he did offer to marry me." Lauren felt obliged to defend him.

"Aye, but that's probably because the buck has eyes in his head. You're a beauty, my girl, and he could see what a treasure you are."

"That's not exactly why he wants to marry me."

Molly turned a stern eye on Lauren. "You mean there's more to this story?"

Lauren quickly explained the reason Julian wanted to get married, and Molly snorted with laughter.

"Why, that's the most insupportable thing I've ever heard. The gent wants to get married so he won't have to get married?!" Molly guffawed with laughter.

"Well, he thinks I'll return to France when things are settled and it will be as if I never existed. He never wants to marry so it will not matter that he is legally tied to me."

Molly looked thoughtful. "The more I think about it, the more this idea has virtue. He sounds like a right handsome fellow the way you described him, and I can't blame the gent for not wantin' to marry some scheming greedy bitch. This could work out to advantage for you both."

"But I have always wanted to marry a man I love."

"Love don't put a roof over your head or food in your belly," Molly admonished. "Besides, you told me this bloke took your virginity. Men are funny about that little thing. They want women pure and untouched so they can go about touchin' you themselves. It never quite made sense to me, but that's a man for you. You won't have to worry about this gent being disappointed about you not being a virgin since he's the one what took your maidenhead in the first place."

Lauren found solace just in talking to Molly. Her warmth and honesty were soothing.

"If I agree to marry Julian, will you come with me?"

"Do you think he'll let you bring me along?"

"I—I don't know. I really know so little about him."

"You know the best part!" Molly grinned, unabashed by Lauren's red, reproving face.

"I'm sure he'll let you come with me if that's one of the conditions to us getting married." She paused, looking thoughtful. "This is really like I'm doing him a favor and getting paid for the service, isn't it?" Lauren mused aloud, trying to justify what she was about to undertake.

"How right you are! Cheer up, I think all our problems have been solved."

Lauren suddenly felt a great wave of melancholy wash over her. It was sad to face the truth, but the only one left in London she could turn to was a stranger.

Once Lauren agreed to Julian's marriage proposal, everything was swiftly put into motion. She and Molly were installed in a small but charming house near St. James's Park. It was a three-story brick furnished in impeccable taste in shades of cream and pale blue in the dining room and sitting room. A small, neat kitchen was at the back and upstairs was a bedroom, sitting room and closet on each floor. The main bedroom was furnished in tones of silver and apricot with a lovely carpet carrying the same colors as well as other pastel and muted jewel shades. In the bedroom, the huge four-poster bed was draped with apricot-embroidered muslin as was the dressing table. Several gilt mirrors were on the walls, flanked by gold sconces holding fresh candles. The adjoining sitting room was comfortable with several Chippendale chairs, a sofa and a small writing table.

Cook and maid were already in residence and Molly became Lauren's personal maid at a wage that shocked them both.

Three days later Lauren was still waiting to hear from Julian. Finding his silence unbearable, she nervously paced her beautiful new bedroom and wondered if something had gone wrong with his plans.

She picked up a bottle of scent and then put it down. She pulled back the curtain and glanced out the window. With a sigh she moved to the bed and fingered the new gowns that had arrived that morning. Molly watched her agitated movements for several seconds before she stepped forward with a brisk movement.

"Here! Let me put those things away. You're in no state to do anything."

"What's taking him so long to arrange everything?" Lauren demanded.

"These things take time," Molly said, gathering the dresses in her arms. "The banns have to be read in the village he's chosen and the reverend has to agree to perform the ceremony."

"I just hate this waiting!" Lauren cried.

"Are you that eager to be his wife?" Molly grinned.

"You know it's not to be a marriage like that!" Her nerves were frayed.

"I know nothing of the sort! I've learned a bit about Lord Keaton these last few days. He's a man from top to toe and if he don't get lovin' here then he'll get it elsewhere!" she stated with conviction.

"Been gossiping with the servants, have you?" Lauren's tone was curt.

"And how else was I supposed to learn anything?" she demanded, lifting her nose in the air.

"And what have you found out about our Lord Keaton?"

"Ha! I thought you didn't approve of gossip."

"I don't approve of gossiping with the servants," she said, using a disinterested tone.

"Then I can't tell you anything," Molly announced, placing the dresses in the armoire.

"Why not?!" Lauren asked sharply.

"Because I'm a servant and I don't want to go and upset your delicate sensibilities."

"Oh, Molly!" Lauren sighed. "What did you learn?"

Molly laughed and smoothed down her skirt. "He's a rich and powerful man. He's got a wicked reputation with the ladies, but then you'd have firsthand knowledge of that, not me," she teased.

At Molly's words, Lauren felt her first twinge of jealousy. "He's known lots of women?"

"The cook says he's a regular collector of lovely ladies!"

"I don't want to hear any more!" Lauren protested.

"I think you love him, but you've not quite been able to admit it to yourself."

"I do not!"

"There's nothing wrong with loving a handsome fellow like him. Why, I could see myself getting a bit hot and bothered by him."

"That's enough!" Lauren insisted, not liking the way Molly talked about Julian.

"Aye! If you don't love him, then you're simmering. It won't be long before you're cooked."

"I do not love him!" Lauren spat out each word.

"Suit yourself!" Molly shrugged as she walked to the door, but she could not resist one last thrust. "They say love is blind, but in your case it's deaf and dumb as well!"

The wedding took place in a tiny stone church outside London. The Reverend Howard's housekeeper and Molly were the only witnesses present.

Lauren wore a simple gown of peach satin and a feathered hat tilted at a jaunty angle over her dark curls. Julian's concession to the occasion was to trade the dark colors he preferred for a blue velvet frock coat and gray silk breeches and waistcoat.

Sunlight filtered down from a high window to cast a glow upon the altar while the empty pews stood behind them like silent guests.

Lauren had often dreamed about her wedding day, but she had never thought it would be this cold, loveless affair. Julian looked rather forbidding with his tightly clenched jaw and hard eyes. She could tell he did not enjoy what he was forced to do and her heart felt heavy. How differently this could have been if they had loved each other, she thought sadly. As she looked into the reverend's smiling eyes, she wanted to cry out, "This is wrong! You cannot marry me to a man I do not love," but she held her tongue and tears filled her eyes.

The Reverend Howard saw the shimmer in

her eyes and thought they were tears of happiness. The groom looked stern, but then some men found it difficult to show their feelings. He thought they were very much in love.

As Julian solemnly began to repeat his vows, his voice echoed in the dimness of the church and in the hollowness of Lauren's heart.

Julian's hand shook as he placed the ring on Lauren's finger. She was amazed that such a small band of gold could place such a burden on her spirit. Finally it was done. They were married.

Julian was relieved the ceremony was over. It had been the hardest thing he had ever done, even though he knew it was very necessary. He had forced himself to remember that it would not be an authentic marriage, though the wife standing beside him was very real.

After they signed the marriage papers and thanked the reverend, Julian escorted Lauren and Molly back to the house. He claimed he had urgent business to attend to, but he really wanted to apprise Monica of his marriage and put an end to her threats. He left Lauren to enjoy a small supper that had been set out along with a bottle of champagne.

Although Lauren knew their marriage was not a real one, she wished Julian had stayed long enough to share their wedding feast. She felt very sad, sipping champagne alone on her wedding day. It should have been the happiest day of her life, but Lauren felt like crying.

Molly prepared her bath and then Lauren dismissed her, saying that she could dress herself for bed.

Later that night, as Lauren sat in a large tub of soapy water with her dark hair piled high on her head, Julian quietly entered the room. Her back was to him and several tendrils of hair had escaped and clung sensuously to the slim contours of her damp back. She was bending forward, soaping one long leg as she hummed a soft tune. She looked so beautiful and tempting that he felt the heat course through his veins, bringing the hunger of desire to the surface once again.

He had known she was lovely, but tonight she looked even more so. The sweet scent of lilacs teased his nose and he closed his eyes, thinking he was dreaming the lovely scene before him.

Julian moved forward, kissed one exposed shoulder, and immediately found a large cloth slapped across his face as Lauren cried in outrage.

"Get out of here!" she screamed, scrambling out of the tub, splashing water and bubbles everywhere in her haste. She grabbed her towel, quickly wrapping it around herself.

"Cease, woman!" he bellowed, wiping at the soap in his eyes.

"What do you think you're doing?" she asked angrily.

"I came to see my wife on our wedding night!"

"What?! You know as well as I do that today was a farce."

"We are legally married."

"Until enough time has elapsed to sever our relationship."

"Nevertheless, we are still man and wife, and I have every intention of claiming my rights."

"You never mentioned this when speaking of deals!"

"I thought you understood. I find you very desirable, Lauren. I would be a fool to ignore so lovely a companion when she is under my roof."

"And you're no fool, are you Julian!" she snapped. "But I obviously was!"

Julian's earlier desertion fired her anger. He now wanted to claim her as bedmate, but he had not had the time to share their simple wedding fare.

"I don't see what the problem is. This outraged-virgin act is a little hard to understand since I know that is no longer the case."

"That is not the case because you took my virginity."

"Are you going to constantly throw that up in my face? What's done is done; can't we now get on with more pleasurable pursuits."

"I'd rather sleep with a reptile than share your vile attentions."

He folded his arms across his chest. "I can assure you that my bed is not the hive of iniquity you imagine. I make love much like any other man. I do not enjoy the perverted pleasures you seem to think. Remember, you found no revulsion in my arms before."

"I was not responsible for my actions! I had too much to drink and it stunned my emotions."

"Tsk-tsk! You enjoyed that night as well as I did. Why not admit it."

"That's a lie!"

"It's the truth! Even now I can feel you in my arms, moving so delectably against me." His eyes rested possessively on the quivering fullness of her lips. "I know you think me the villain of this piece, but I have no intention of leaving you tonight."

"I think I would rather be thrown to the wolves than let you take me. You tricked me!"

"Not intentionally. I really thought you understood. And as for being thrown to the wolves, you are much too delicious for them."

"You would rather gnaw on my bones alone?"

He grinned. "I admit that I do not like to share."

"Well, sir, I am no toy to be given at a moment's whim. I was not designed for your pleasure!"

"But you must have been, my dear, for how else could I find such enjoyment in just looking at you. You tempt me and weave a spell about me that I find impossible to ignore."

She was unaware of how lovely she looked with her shining voilet eyes and her ebony curls escaping to frame her face. She looked rather wanton, like some mysterious gypsy woman, promising all and well able to deliver.

"You seek to seduce me with honeyed words," she murmured huskily.

"There is more between us than words. Something about you draws me, beckons me like a wisp of whimsy that must be followed or else forever felt as a loss."

"There is nothing between us but a deal."

He moved swiftly, catching her in his arms, and his mouth possessed her with a hunger that made her feel as if she were caught up in some magnificent storm. She clutched at his shoulders as the only solid thing in her world, and when he released her lips, her eyes remained closed and her mouth softly parted.

"Tell me now that you do not feel the pull between us. Passion is a very powerful lure, Lauren. Are you sure you can turn away from the bait? After all, you are human even though you look like a confection designed for the gods."

She gave a weak protest, but her eyes were glazed with desire and her breasts were heavy with longing.

"You are my wife, regardless of how it came to be," his voice was deep and husky. Suddenly, with one fluid movement, he picked her up and carried her to the bed.

"The covers will get wet," she protested as she was laid on the bed.

"To hell with the bed," he muttered, and then his lips stopped all talk and his touch wiped all resistance from her mind.

Their short first night together had been like a dream to Lauren, but she knew this was reality as his hands and body sent all thoughts flying into oblivion. She was only aware of the sleek powerful body beside her as her hand restlessly touched the smooth gray velvet of his coat.

He stood up and quickly removed his clothes and Lauren looked away in embarrassment. "Look at me," he ordered, and her head lifted as a blush stained her cheeks. "I am no satanic specter here to torment you. I am a man with needs only you can satisfy."

Julian's skin was like warm honey and his manhood was ripe and ready. She looked away, but then her eyes were again drawn to him almost against her will. He really was beautiful, reminding her of some mystical pagan beast she had imagined as she read mythology as a child. His chest was tightly muscled, stomach lean and flat, and his legs and chest lightly covered with dark curling hair. She suddenly longed to run her hand over him and explore all the mysteries of his body.

As if aware of her thoughts, he came down beside her, covering her with his body, warming her with his needs.

"Touch me," he said huskily, and she stiffened beneath him.

"I—I can't," she moaned, biting her lip.

"You can. I want to touch you. Don't you want to touch me?" He gently placed his palm over the peak of her breast and she jerked beneath him as if a hot brand had scorched her. A moan escaped her as he fondled her and then his mouth replaced his hand and the sensation of pleasure was so intense that Lauren could actually feel the shape and texture of his lips as they moved over her. He smiled against her skin and she gasped as tiny tremors shook her body.

Slowly, oh so slowly, her hand lifted and touched his chest, feeling the crisp hairs as they clung to her fingers. Her hand traced lower, feeling the concave of his abdomen before she found what she had been searching for and took it lovingly in her hand. Julian stiffened and he gasped slightly, making Lauren smile to herself as she realized she was not the only one caught in this spell that washed away all feeling of guilt.

"Oh, lady," he whispered. "You tempt and torment me until I fear I shall go mad."

He nipped lightly at her breast and her breath was raspy as she replied, "It is you who torments."

"Gently, Lauren," he soothed, watching her with burning golden eyes, enraptured by the sight of her so lovely and eager for his possession. He was dizzy, intoxicated by her smooth flesh as she moved against him. She was everything he could desire in a woman—everything that was beautiful and bewitching.

Julian's lips moved down her stomach until he was at the mound of Venus and then, slowly, with his lips and fingers, he brought her alive until her body was literally pulsing with emotion. Lauren was so dazzled with desire, that nothing mattered but the here-and-now and finding release from the waves of heat that rippled along her nerve endings.

Her hand tightened on him and then his voice tickled her ear. "Stop," he whispered, "unless you want to know the full measure of my need."

She released him and curled her hands around his shoulders as he parted her legs, entering her so fluidly that they seemed to merge like two streams. What had begun gently soon became urgent as they arched eagerly against each other, reaching higher and higher for paradise. The tension was so powerful that Lauren dug her nails into Julian's back, urging him on, demanding with her body that he release her so she could spiral upward into the clouds like some tightly coiled spring bouncing into the heavens.

Suddenly they seemed to explode, their bodies writhing spasmodically, and Lauren felt everything open inside her like a flower welcoming the sun after a pelting rain. She felt so warm and soft, like velvet, and her mind floated out of her body on a cloud so high that she never wanted to come down.

When she opened her eyes, she could feel the beat of Julian's heart against her breast. His breathing was deep and strong. She smiled as she moved her hands down his back, feeling the tiny drops of moisture on his sleek skin. He was like some beautiful animal that was only half tamed, with his lean strength and his overwhelming control of her senses.

Lauren forgot that she had married him only to fulfill a bargain. Nothing seemed important right now except staying warm and secure in his arms. She had not had anyone of her own since her mother died, and now she realized how much she needed Julian to keep the harsh world at bay.

"I still have a craving for you even though my body is replete and my mind is at ease."

"And I for you," she admitted. "You breathe a life into me that I have never felt before. You give me the stars I did not know were within my reach."

His fingers lightly traced her face, lingering on the gentle curve of her lips that tasted like ambrosia to his hungry mouth. "I never thought I'd hold such wanton sweetness in my arms. You learn quickly, *ma petite.*"

"You teach well, sir," she grinned.

"Have I paid for my earlier behavior?" he asked with a teasing grin.

"Aye," she cooed. "You can pay me anytime

you want." She gave him a saucy grin and wriggled delightfully against him.

"Anything the lady desires," he responded, and his hand slipped between her legs to play a strange, irresistible magic on her.

The world outside ceased to exist as the shadows lengthened and their bodies snuggled close to each other in sensual completeness. Finally, Morpheus gave a satisfied smile as he threw his blanket over them, leaving them in peace.

A knock at the door awakened Lauren and she sat up, pulling the covers around her. Molly peeped around the corner, carrying a tray, but Lauren silently waved her away. Molly gave a knowing grin and winked before she departed.

Lauren trailed a finger down Julian's spine and he immediately rolled over and pulled her down to him, burying his mouth in her neck, breathing in her sweet clean fragrance.

"Come kiss me, woman," he said, his golden eyes twinkling.

"It is morning and time to get up," she said, pushing the covers aside as she tried to rise, but he caught her and rolled her onto her back.

"I am already up."

"Are you trying my patience?" she grinned mischievously.

"No, I'm trying my best."

She shook her head. "We don't have time, Julian. Aren't you hungry?"

"Yes, but my hunger is for the sweet meat placed so temptingly before my palate."

"Surely your appetite demands something more substantial."

He shook his head as his lips hovered close to her own. "You quench any thoughts for the meager fare on the table. I only desire the delectable taste of your body beneath mine. I grow hard and mean when I am denied."

"Something does indeed grow." She laughed. "What a saucy one you are. I have a minx for a mistress."

Her fingers curled against his chest and she tugged lightly. "I never knew it could be like this between a man and a woman."

"That is the best combination."

"I still feel as if I dreamed last night," she whispered.

"Then I shall have to make the dream a reality."

His body merged with hers in one swift motion that had her lips parting with a gasp. She could see his pulse throbbing in his neck, and she placed her fingers on the spot.

Neither moved for a time and then he rubbed his rough cheek against hers.

As if savoring the feel of her, Julian's movements were slow at first, but soon Lauren clutched feverishly at his shoulders, urging him to increase his urgency. Faster and faster they rode until they crested on a wave of feeling so intense they thought they would die from the pleasure. Shudders shook them and when Lauren opened her eyes it was as if everything were intensified, placed under a microscope to make it larger than life. She could see every pore in Julian's face, and even the golden color of his eyes seemed brighter, more glowing. The rasp

of skin against skin and their breathing echoed
faintly in the room.

"I think I have to sleep again," Julian said
with satisfaction. "You wore me out."

"Then sleep."

"I must go home, for my sister and her husband know nothing of our wedding."

"Are you going to tell them?"

He looked impatient. "Of course not. I told
you that no one is to know. Felice would be something of a problem if she knew about you."

"What do you mean?" Lauren reached for her
robe lying across the foot of the bed.

He shrugged. "It's a long story."

"You had better go then." She sighed.

He watched her as she slipped into the robe.
"I much prefer you without garments."

She lifted an inquiring eyebrow. "And pray,
what would the servants say if I were to parade
around the house in my altogether?"

He chuckled and rose to his feet. She tried
not to watch as he dressed, but her eyes kept
returning to him. Julian was adjusting his cravat when his eyes met hers in the mirror and
they exchanged an intimate smile. He leaned
his hip against the dresser as he watched her
brush her long, silky hair.

"You make me want to stay here all day and
say to hell with the rest of the world." He did
not look as if the idea pleased him, and indeed
Julian was beginning to wonder about the hold
this girl seemed to have over him.

"There is always tonight," she said, giving
him a sultry look.

He laughed, forgetting his momentary apprehension.

"So there is, and I shall be here without delay."

"I will be waiting," she said softly, and Julian gave her a brief hard kiss before he left the room.

She heard him whistling as he went down the stairs and Lauren smiled to herself, feeling happier than she ever had in her life.

Man is no star but a quick coal of mortal fire.
—George Herbert

Chapter Four

Felice Taylor idly drummed her pale oval nails
on the dining table as she waited for Julian to
come down. She threw a glance at her handsome
husband as he sat across from her, eating his
breakfast with a robust appetite, and smiled
warmly at him, releasing a sigh of contentment.

Brendan's thick blond hair and good looks had
made her fall in love with him immediately, and
six years of marriage between them had forged
strong feelings of security and happiness within
her.

"It's been nice visiting Julian, darling," she
murmured, reaching out a hand that he quickly
captured in his own. "I'm glad you agreed that
our estate could do without you for a while."

"I know how close you are to your brother,
love. I do not begrudge sharing you with him."

Their estate was in Kent, but every now and
then they came to London to shop, view the
entertainments, and to see Julian, whose pri-
mary residence was on the outskirts of London.

Felice shook her head in exasperation. "Julian's never at home anymore! His bed hasn't

been slept in in weeks, and I only see him in passing as he goes out the door."

"He obviously has some diversion in town that is keeping him very busy."

"Whatever could it be?" she asked with a furrowed brow.

Brendan laughed. He gave her a teasing look and she blushed at her naïveté.

"A woman?"

Brendan grinned. "Don't sound so shocked. You know your brother has never been accused of having monkish ways."

She looked away in confusion. "I know he has women, but he has never been like this. Even with his women he's always had time for us. Now it's as if he can't get away from the house soon enough." She looked up with a startled expression in her eyes. "You don't think it's Monica, do you?"

Brendan shook his head. "No. I know for a fact that she's in France. She left over two weeks ago."

Felice looked thoughtful. "I wonder how Julian did it? I didn't think Monica was the type to give up quite so easily."

"Julian's very industrious, but I think I would have kept her around for a while."

She threw him a pouting look as she poured a fresh cup of tea. "You sound as if you would like to have a woman like that!"

Brendan cleared his throat, a smile hovering at the corners of his mouth. "Certainly not, my dear! You know you are all I need. I was just referring to Julian."

"I'm sorry now that I pressed Julian to marry

her. I never really cared for Monica, but she seemed the closest to getting him to the altar, and he does so need a wife. I had heard gossip that some people believe she might have had something to do with her husband's death in order to get his money. Do you think she could have done such a thing?"

"Oh, she might indeed have killed him," Brendan commented, leaning back in his chair.

"You really think so?" Felice asked, opening her eyes wider in anticipation.

Brendan nodded. "With that body she could kill any man."

"Brendan!"

He chuckled. "Well, you must admit she is a fine-looking woman."

She turned up her nose. "She was never good enough for Julian. I see that now."

"That is up to Julian to decide," he replied, unperturbed by her words.

"And he has decided, hasn't he? He's obviously found another woman that intrigues him more than Monica ever did. And she's probably much more suited to be his wife."

"Are you now suggesting Julian might marry this *fille de joie?*" Brendan asked warily.

"Why not?"

His lips narrowed. "Men don't marry their mistresses, Felice."

Her blue eyes grew cold. "If they're good enough to bed then they're good enough to wed."

"You really are desperate for Julian to marry, aren't you?"

She folded her arms on the table and leaned closer to Brendan in a conspiratorial manner.

"He smiles all the time of late and is seldom in one of his grumpy humors. I've never seen him like this."

"He does indeed put a great deal of wear and tear on the road between here and London. I'm not doubting he's smitten, but that doesn't mean he's thinking of marriage. Be reasonable, Felice. He has a definite loathing of the institution."

"Shhh! Here he comes."

Felice folded her hands in her lap and looked serenely toward the doorway. Julian paused as he entered the room. He lazily straightened his cravat and smiled at the scene.

"You look decidedly guilty about something, Felice," he remarked. "Are you contemplating stealing my silver?"

"Don't be ridiculous, Julian. I am not in the mood to suffer your odious behavior this morning."

He grinned. "I thought I was being most pleasant." He glanced at Brendan. "I was just telling Felice a few weeks ago that you have spoiled her, Brendan."

Felice frowned and Brendan laughed. "True, but I have enjoyed doing so."

Julian chuckled, and then there was silence as he filled his plate and sat down at the head of the table. Felice kicked Brendan under the table, and at his inquiring look she nodded at Julian.

"Hum—er, how have things been going, Julian?" he asked.

"Very well," he drawled. "Very well indeed."

A suspicious smile hovered about the corners of his mouth.

"I saw Lord and Lady Birch the other day while I was shopping. Lord Birch said he hasn't seen you at the club lately. You must be keeping very busy since you are constantly traveling to town."

He looked from Felice to Brendan with narrowed eyes and said, "Yes, I have been keeping busy."

Felice nervously cleared her throat, knowing that Julian would tell her nothing unless he desired to do so. "I—I saw Pamela Rawley yesterday. She said you have not been attending the routs and affairs about town."

Julian continued to eat. "I've had more important things to do."

Felice and Brendan exchanged knowing glances. "You haven't forgotten about tomorrow night, have you?" she asked lightly, lifting the delicate china cup to take a sip of tea. Julian lifted his eyebrow inquiringly and Felice grimaced. "You have forgotten!"

"Forgotten what?" he asked calmly, looking from Brendan to Felice.

"We are going to Vauxhall Gardens and you promised you would attend with us and Pamela Rawley."

"Damn!" Julian muttered, looking angrily at his meal. He had suddenly lost his appetite. "Are you sure I promised to go to that? You know how I hate those affairs."

"Yes, you promised, Julian. Pamela is looking forward to it."

"More of your damned matchmaking, little

sister?" he growled, but relented at Felice's
flushed face. "Very well," he conceded grudg-
ingly. He was supposed to take Lauren to the
theater and out to dine, but he would have to
get out of it even though he would much rather
spend his time with her.

"I won't be back until tomorrow anyway," he
stated to no one in particular.

"You're spending an inordinate amount of
time away from home," Felice said. "Is everything all right?"

"It's fine." His answer was abrupt. He had no
intention of revealing his relationship with
Lauren to Felice and Brendan. It was still too
new and precious. He wanted to keep her to
himself without the gossip and speculation that
would occur if she were discovered; Julian was
very circumspect with her, more so than with
any woman other than his sister. He took her
to places where she would not be commented on
and he kept her away from his friends; he did
not want them to pay attention to her due to a
devilish jealousy that had surfaced since meeting her.

Julian quickly finished his breakfast and rose
to his feet. "I'm sorry I can't spend more time
with you, but I must be off to London."

"But you just arrived!" Felice exclaimed.

"I have some things to attend to if I am to
take you to Vauxhall."

"And you will be nice to Pamela, won't you?"

Julian gave her a rueful smile. "When will
you stop this infernal matchmaking of yours,
little sister?"

"When you are happily married," she said with tight lips.

"You should choose your words with more care, Felice."

"How so?" she demanded.

"The words happily and married are a contradiction in terms."

"Brendan and I are happily married," Felice insisted. "Aren't we?" She threw the words at Brendan, as if daring him to dispute her claim.

"Of course," he answered with a wink.

"But then there is always the exception to the rule," Julian returned calmly as he strolled toward the door. "Enjoy your own marital bliss, Felice, and leave me to my own happiness."

After he was gone, Felice turned to her husband. "How dare you treat our marriage like some joke," she fumed.

Brendan threw up his hands in innocence. "I didn't. I agreed with everything you said."

"I know, it was just the way you agreed."

He laughed. "Men must act so, love, but only among themselves. You know you make me the happiest of men."

Her frown continued for a moment, then she gave him a bewitching smile. "I'm sorry I was so angry with you, dear. Julian just tries my temper so that I have to lash out at someone. I'm sorry it was you."

"I understand, Felice, but I think we've worried enough about Julian's love life for one day. Since we have the house to ourselves how about a private tête-à-tête in our bedroom?" Brendan asked, lowering his voice suggestively.

She blushed. "In the middle of the morning?"

"Why not?" he asked with a glimmer in his eye.

Suddenly she wanted nothing more than to lie in her husband's arms and know his wild lovemaking. "Why not indeed?" she grinned, placing her hand in his as he helped her to her feet.

Lauren was so happy as she rested against the velvet seat of the coach. The interior was dark and intimate and while she could not see Julian clearly, she was very aware of him sitting only a breath away; he had such a pleasing scent and she had quickly learned to recognize it as his. It was slightly musky and mixed with the faint scent of brandy that he usually drank after his meal.

She was a little afraid of how happy she was, having learned at an early age that most happiness was fleeting. But nevertheless she looked forward to their intimate suppers where they discussed everything under the sun and then made wild, passionate love into the wee hours of the morning, when Julian would rise and return to his home. She found a strange contentment in just being with him, sharing a glance across the room or engaging in love play that sent her senses spiraling out of control. Lauren never tired of his warm embrace, and when he left she could hardly wait for his return, eager to capture every moment of happiness she could.

Julian was a very private man and had been loath to talk about himself, but slowly he was letting down his barriers, showing her the gentle, intelligent man he was. He shared his views with her on everything from raising stock to what the King might do about the colonies. They were growing close in both body and mind. But when Lauren was honest with herself, she realized she was a little afraid of Julian's hold on her. She had never felt so strongly about anyone or anything; she wanted things to stay as they were forever, though she knew that Julian viewed nothing as permanent, and that frightened her. She sighed and Julian's hand covered hers.

"Is something wrong?" Julian asked in a warm, deep voice.

"No," she said softly, turning toward him in the darkness.

"You are so quiet and pensive tonight. I thought something might be troubling you."

She shook her head, smiling when she realized he could not see her. "I'm just so happy."

He reached for her. "I won't be able to see you tomorrow night. I have to escort Felice and a party of friends to Vauxhall."

Her fingers gently stroked his chin, lingering on the cleft in the center. "I hate to share you, but your sister does deserve some of your time."

"You are so sweet," he whispered into her ear. "You are so warm and open, like no other woman I have ever known."

His hands explored the slender, curved body until she was panting in his embrace, pulling his head down so he could plunder the sweetness of her lips.

"I love the smell of you," he groaned, feeling the heat rise up in his body. "No one smells like you." He laid her on the seat, placing his lips on the tantalizing swell of her breasts above the fine Mechlin lace of her dress. "You taste so delicious that mere food seems dull and bland when I imagine the creamy satin of your skin beneath my lips."

Lauren was aroused to an aching pitch by his words. She had thought his hands worked magic, but his low, husky tones were also making her hunger for the joining of their flesh. When he pushed her voluminous skirts up, sliding his hand along the silken length of her leg, she arched convulsively, as if he had touched the secret core of her being.

Julian was breathing deeply. "You open so trustingly to me, with none of the coy games women usually play. You want me and I want you."

When he entered her, she gasped, unaware that he had unfastened his breeches. The velvet seat of the coach was warm and soft as she felt herself pressed down and Julian took her with a gentleness that brought tears to her eyes.

Their moans mingled and their bodies rose and fell in unison. The motion of the carriage only intensified their response until Lauren felt herself straining higher and higher toward that plateau where Julian always took her. When they reached that wondrous ecstasy, stars seemed to light up behind her closed eyelids and she released her breath with a heaving sigh, knowing that she would always find heavenly pleasure in his arms.

"You are a witch, Lauren," he growled, totally satiated.

"And you are a devil, my lord," she grinned.

"Did I torture you so sorely, my lady?"

"Aye! I was truly on fire for you!"

"But did I quench the flame?"

"Yes, but only until the next burst of heat."

When they reached the theater and stepped out of the carriage, the driver could detect nothing of the heated scene that had just taken place within the confines of the carriage, for they were both impeccably groomed with cool expressions on their faces.

Rodney Warwick tossed and turned, thrashing about in his bed as he again experienced the terrible nightmare that had gripped and controlled him for years. Drops of moisture beaded his forehead and upper lip, and he felt he would be burned to a cinder.

The heavy drapes billowing in the windows brought a coolness to the bedroom that he could not feel, so lost was he in his troubled slumber.

He was in a tiny room that was hot, so hot! It was June in India and the room felt like a furnace, while all around Rodney were bodies, crowding in on him, suffocating him until he beat at the mass of flesh and he screamed like a madman. The air was thick with the stench of sweat and human remains.

Above him was the only source of relief—two small windows; he knew that he could survive if he could just get to one of them and breathe sweet air again. But then, everyone had the same idea, and they fought and gasped like a pack of wild animals after a bone, each intent on destroying the other if necessary.

Rodney had never thought he would be reduced to such a state when he had put on the red coat and gone to Calcutta to join the company of men at the fort. The second son of the Earl of Naylor, he had not minded that his brother Stephen would inherit everything; he was young and healthy and had heard that there were riches to be gained in India if a man was smart and ambitious.

A mere month had passed since he'd been at the fort, when word came that Siraj-ud-daula, the nawab of Bengal, was attacking the city. The British forces were nothing against the prince's large army and the city was taken. It was then that they were led at bayonet point into a small cell only fourteen feet wide and eighteen feet long, with only two small windows for light and air.

Later, Rodney would be told time and again how lucky he was to have survived when only a handful of men had lived through the ordeal. But Rodney knew it had not been luck. He was alive through sheer determination and a will to live that was even stronger than he had suspected. He was alive, but at the cost of the others.

As long as he lived he would never forget that dark hole and the way the moonlight came through the windows, outlining the suffering humanity wailing away like lost souls. The men did not sound human, but by then Rodney no longer felt human himself as he gasped and clawed to the top of the cell, not caring that one man's face was a step on the ladder toward that window that offered life and breath. All he could think about was himself; country and brotherhood came in poor seconds next to the basic needs of the moment. He vowed that if he lived, he would never worry about making a living or serving some country that was powerless to help him. He made his own luck, and in the end he would be one of the survivors.

When they came the next morning and opened the cell door, it appeared as if all were dead, but after sorting through the heap of bodies they found twenty-three survivors out of one hundred forty-six men.

They called Rodney a hero when he returned to England, saying what a fine soldier he was. But he knew he was not good or brave and the thought nagged at him, reminding him how cowardly he had really been. He also knew that he had changed. Before being imprisoned he had not minded being a second son, but now he knew he was tough enough to oust his older brother from his favored position.

Stephen was kind and virtuous, always caring about others before himself, and Rodney saw that as a weakness. He had not shown mercy in that black hole and he had lived. It was the weak and meek who had died that night. Stephen had everything, including a lovely wife and a pretty daughter; he was his father's blue-eyed boy, getting everything without effort. Rodney's brother had been riding about the estate, attending balls and parties, dancing until dawn with gaily dressed women, unaware and uncaring that at the same time Rodney lay in some black pit struggling for life.

Something happened to him in that hole that

magnified and grew in the days and weeks that
followed.

While on the outside he remained the same
urbane, charming gentleman everyone had always known, something bent and twisted Rodney on the inside. If he seemed a little quieter,
a little more thoughtful, then people assumed
that was due only to his terrible experience.
They couldn't see the bitter hatred that was
eating at his soul, couldn't sense the red fury
that swept over him whenever he heard his
brother's name.

And so Rodney had plotted and connived and
soon he was in a position to ruin Stephen. He
had no qualms about destroying his brother, just
as he had gotten over his guilt at being a sur-
vivor. Life was to be lived to its fullest and if
he had to scheme and ruin a few people on his
way to enjoyment of that life, then that was
their hard luck.

But now, as he lay tossing and turning on his
bed, he knew that the horror was still with him.
The dream came often, especially when he was
doing something particularly low and despicable. He was now in the process of buying a
bawdyhouse to be filled with young girls fresh
from the country, ready to sample the life of
London without the benefit of money and position. His partner was a woman named Lynell
Houdan, recently arrived from France with a
troupe of young eager girls.

When Rodney finally awakened it was the
middle of the night. He was panting and heaving as the sweat ran down his face. Over the
years he always had virtually the same night-

mare, though sometimes his dream made him remember Stephen's daughter's eyes and the way they had seemed to condemn him, as if she could see into his soul where no one else had access. No matter how many times he told himself he was being fanciful, he couldn't forget those eyes of such an unusual hue and the way they had watched him the whole time Stephen was declaring his innocence to closed ears.

Rodney rolled out of bed and walked over to the washstand, where he splashed his face and neck with cool water. The nightmare slowly began to recede from his mind, but he knew it would be back, slithering like some evil snake into his sleep, giving him no peace.

He reached for his shirt and pulled it on, knowing he would not sleep again that night. He found his breeches and waistcoat and dressed without his valet, it being the wee hours of the morning. The ticking of the clock, the creak of the stairs, the closing of the door as he left, were the only sounds that told of his restlessness.

As he walked along the dark deserted streets, he knew that something had to be done about Lauren. If she should ever meet his father then she would be welcomed into the family, and that was something he could not allow. She suspected too much, even though she had no proof. She made him nervous with her straightforward talk and accusing eyes, and her presence just might cause him to make a fatal mistake. He had schemed and worked too hard for his position to let anything put it in jeopardy.

As he walked, his thoughts grew bleaker. He had thought his position secure after all these years, and then that slip of a girl had to come prying her nose in where she had no right to be. An accident might be just the thing to get rid of her and keep his father from finding out about her return to London. It was a good thing she was using the name de Fanchon, having shunned the use of her real name. No one would question the appearance of her body when it was found and no one could trace her back to him and his family.

He smiled and took a deep breath. He was already beginning to feel better as he made his way to his partner's house.

Rodney's destination was a brightly lit building that was obviously a bawdyhouse. As he approached he could see men and women through the windows and hear their laughter and loud talking. He passed the front entrance and went around to a side door. He let himself in with his own key and went up some dark stairs to a private sitting room where he rang for a maid.

"Tell Madame Houdan I'm here and I must see her," he told the girl.

The maid turned away and Rodney sat down to wait.

Lynell Houdan was not in a good mood when her maid woke her from a sound sleep and informed her that Rodney wanted to see her. She forced herself to rise and fumble through the porcelain jars, searching for her beauty items. She splashed essence down the front of her gown and then repaired to her bed, pushing back the embroidered curtains so Rodney could see her as soon as he entered the room.

Lynell had once been a beautiful woman, but time and the life she lived had taken their toll. Initially beauty and determination had lifted her out of the Paris low-life to which she'd been born. She had become a celebrated courtesan with some of the most important names in France for lovers. At the height of her popularity one of her lovers had become so jealous and possessive that he had ordered her to quit her profession. She had only laughed at him, and in a vicious rage he had cut her face, marring her most valuable asset.

She then started a house of joy, employing beautiful young girls from the country who came to Paris to seek their fortunes. She did very well until her attempts to rid some girls of unwanted babies resulted in their deaths. The police threatened to arrest her until a good friend and one-time lover, the Duc de Romoulet, offered to send her to England. It was he who had put her in touch with Rodney Warwick.

Rodney had proved a valuable contact, finding the building she now lived in and helping her gather a group of girls for her business. Personally, Lynell found Rodney a bore, but she needed him and found that it was profitable to be nice to him. And he did not find it repulsive to share her bed despite her disfigured face. Lately, however, she was becoming more mother than mistress to him, listening with increasing boredom to his trials and tribulations.

When Rodney was admitted into her room, he was aware of the heady, mingling scents.

Lynell was rather flamboyant, using rich, bright contrasting colors, as evidenced by her purple and yellow boudoir with red velvet chairs and intense green curtains. Her hair was a rich brown with golden highlights, her eyes were wide and direct, but her lips were too full for beauty. Rodney found her fascinating even while he loathed what she was, not minding the large, puckered scar that ran from the corner of her mouth up to her temple. She was a large woman with big breasts that quivered when she moved, and Rodney found her fleshiness exciting, preferring it to the slimness of other women.

"What is it, Rodney?" she asked. Her voice was deep and husky, its undertone able to curl Rodney's toes.

"What makes you think something is wrong?" he asked idly as he fiddled with the jars and boxes on her elaborate dressing table.

She laughed. "It's barely light and you show up at my door demanding to see me. Is that reasonable? Something must be wrong."

He sighed and took a chair. "You're right. Something is wrong. My niece has suddenly appeared after all these years."

Lynell lifted one shoulder in a careless shrug. "So? What does that have to do with us?" She had learned everything about Rodney's past one night after he was tortured by his dream; she had comforted him, and he had confided in her.

"She confronted me a few weeks ago, saying that she knew I was responsible for her father's disgrace. I laughed it off, but I'm worried. What if she pursues this and resurrects all the old doubts my father had when Stephen was accused?"

Lynell sat up angrily, throwing him a look of distaste. "It is a little late to worry about that now! Why didn't you tell me earlier of this girl. We could have taken care of her."

"I sent her away and thought she would leave. I told her to go back to France, but I don't think she did."

"Where did she go?"

"I don't know."

"Fool! You had her in your hands and let her slip away!" Lynell scorned.

"What if she tries to contact my father again? He's been trying to find her for years, hoping to appease his guilty conscience." He gave a snort of laughter. "It seems that in his old age he regrets dismissing Stephen so easily. He hopes to make amends by taking in his widow and daughter, but Stephen's wife is dead."

"Let the old man have his dreams. I doubt the girl will come back if you have successfully scared her off."

"I don't know if I scared her off or not. You have ways of getting rid of people," Rodney added eagerly.

"For a price, my dear, for a price."

Rodney jumped angrily to his feet. "I pay the bill on this house and bring in plenty of customers. Surely you can do this for me!"

"I do many things for you, Rodney, for which I do not charge. I think I am within my rights to ask for more when murder is involved."

"Don't say that!" he stormed, pacing back and forth across the room.

She gave a gruff laugh. "Why is it so hard for you to speak the truth? Must your cowardly soul always give a false name to your misdeeds?"

"At least I'm not some madame of a whorehouse!"

"I prefer to be called a sybarite, and you should not look down on my profession, *mon ami,* for it doubles your money without your having to dirty your hands!"

He shoved his thin hands into the pockets of his coat and stared moodily at the woman lying so wantonly on the covers.

Her lips lifted in a slight smile. "Don't look so angry, Rodney. I have not asked for your soul. It would not bring much on the market, for the devil is a hard one with whom to bargain."

"I made no pact with the devil!"

"Ah, we both made a pact with him and that is why we wear his stamp of ownership."

"Stop being so damned philosophical! I'm not in the mood tonight. Besides, you're just talking nonsense."

"Oh, *mon ami,* I make much sense; it is just that you don't wish to hear." She ran one finger down the scar on her face, lingering where it touched the corner of her mouth. "The devil put his mark on me here, but he scarred you much deeper when he took your soul. I think he wants you much more than me."

Rodney felt a fine dew of perspiration on his brow and his fingers began to tremble. "Stop talking such witchcraft, Lynell. Will you do it or won't you?"

She gave a feline smile. "Let's wait awhile. Perhaps the girl has sense enough to stay away."

She lifted one shoulder in a shrug. "If not, then we can think about sending her on her way in a more permanent manner. Agreed?"

"Agreed. But there had better be no mistakes!"

Lynell held out her arms. "Come to me and I'll make you forget all your worries."

Rodney smiled his satisfaction at this turn of events as he pulled off his coat. Yes, he would forget all his worries in her arms.

If it were done when 'tis done, then 'twere well
It were done quickly.

—William Shakespeare
MacBeth

Chapter Five

It had been some time since Julian had seen
Pamela Rawley, so he was unprepared for the
outrageous way she flirted with him. She had
been a child the last time he saw her, but now
she was definitely a woman. Her parents had
spoiled her all her life, and the young men she
knew seemed to sense this and were always eager to fulfill her every wish, treating her like a
beautiful, treasured princess. In return she had
allowed a few stolen kisses to those who pleased
her the most.

Pamela had heard gossip about Julian, and
being rather curious, she wondered what it
would be like to kiss a man of Julian's reputation when all she had known were the chaste
pecks of boys. That he was proving very resis-
tant to her charms only heightened her need to
make him aware of her, and so she caught his
arm whenever possible as they strolled through
Vauxhall Gardens. She smiled at him through
her lashes in a way she had practiced before her

mirror, and whenever possible, allowed her breasts to brush lightly against his arm.

The more Julian looked on in amused indulgence, the bolder she became, wondering what she was doing wrong. She did not want him to act like some doting uncle, immune to her charms; she wanted him to beg for her favors and hunger for her lips. Pamela was used to getting what she wanted, and the thought that tonight she might not made her almost desperate.

Pamela wanted to get away from Felice and Brendan, and she sought a suitable excuse.

"Lord Keaton," she murmured softly, batting her eyelashes. "I need something to drink. My throat is parched from all this walking."

"Certainly. I could use something to drink also."

Felice watched in exasperation as Julian led her away. She turned to Brendan after throwing a scathing glance at the receding couple.

"Pamela has grown up since the last time we saw her."

"She's certainly changed," Brendan agreed with a teasing grin. "I don't remember her being so, er, well developed."

"I'll have to talk to her mother about her behavior tonight. She'll find herself in trouble if she doesn't settle down."

"I think she intends to settle down with Julian and that's why she's all over him."

Felice sighed as they walked over to a bench and sat down. "To be honest, I was thinking she might be right for Julian, but her behavior tonight is appalling. She's acting far too boldly for a properly-brought-up young lady."

"My dear, Julian likes bold women."

"As mistresses, but if I know him as I think I do, he'll not tolerate such behavior from his wife."

Brendan gave a laugh of pure amusement. "I think you're right. There's nothing worse than a married rake. He'll be forever looking under the bed."

Felice looked demure. "You should know. You had a rakish reputation before we married."

"Ah, but you've quite cured me of my jealous nature."

"You have no need to be jealous. As long as you don't stray, then neither shall I."

"What's this about straying?" His brows came together in a frown. "Are you thinking about straying?"

She giggled. "Of course not!"

"Then why bring it up?" he demanded.

"To show you that your jealous nature is quite cured, of course."

The frown eased from his face and he chuckled, pulling her closer. "You scheming rogue!"

"You adorable rascal!"

"Let's leave as soon as possible," he whispered close to her ear. "I want to show you what a dutiful husband I am."

"And I'll show you what a dutiful wife I can be, with the right scoundrel!"

He glanced around. "Where do you think Julian and Pamela have disappeared to?"

Felice looked worried. "Oh, dear, I fear we

have left them alone far too long. The way Pamela has been acting, anything could happen."

"Julian wouldn't seduce such a child," Brendan said.

Felice waved away his words. "It's strange. I'm usually worried about Julian, but tonight it's Pamela who tries my patience."

"We'd better find them then. Come on," he urged, pulling her to her feet. "The sooner we find them, the sooner we can leave." He gave her a hungry look, which she returned with a smile.

"Then lead on, conquering hero. I'm right behind you."

As they started down the walks, they were unaware that at that very moment Pamela was indeed trying all her wiles on Julian. They were hidden behind some shrubs, sitting on a bench, and Pamela was running her hand up his sleeve. At first he just smiled, but then his indulgence turned to impatience. He took her fingers and forcefully removed them.

"Enough, Pamela. I think the man who finally weds you will have his hands full. You're quite a minx!"

She moved away haughtily, looking at him with angry green eyes. She was a lovely girl with rich auburn hair, but she did not move him.

"Do you not find me attractive?" she asked, looking at him out of the corner of her eye.

"You're very lovely," he replied smoothly.

"And are you tempted by me?"

He laughed. "You're a child, Pamela."

Her head jerked up and her eyes flashed angrily. "I'm not a child! I thought you were supposed to be famous as a hellion with women, but obviously the gossip is wrong."

He grinned, unperturbed by her words. Her temper came to the fore. "Surely it's not a woman who holds you constant."

An image of Lauren flashed into his mind and he gave a slow, satisfied smile without being aware of it. Pamela saw the look on his face and grew even angrier, thinking that some common woman held him in sway while she, an aristocrat, could not move him.

She dropped her cloak and smoothed her hand across her throat, knowing that the low neckline of her white gown revealed her lovely shoulders and the tops of her breasts.

"I thought no woman would ever trap the elusive Julian Grey," she taunted softly.

His expression hardened, but he did not reply.

She leaned forward slightly so he could see the display of her rounded flesh. "Perhaps you can no longer hold another. Has this woman turned you into a eunuch as far as other women are concerned? What fetters has she placed upon you that bind you so fast?"

Her words were but an echo of Julian's thoughts. He was becoming afraid that Lauren did indeed hold him enthralled, wrapping him in her silken web of sensual scent and feeling, so that no woman could hope to compare. Of late, no other female had drawn his eye, or his lust. He was a slave to his desires as far as Lauren was concerned, finding that no other woman awakened them when he had such a fascinating female already in his bed.

Pamela watched the enigmatic expression on

his face and pushed harder, thinking that she might have touched a nerve. "She has put a ring through your nose and soon will lead you about like a tame pet. Will you jump at her every command?"

If Julian had been thinking straight, he would have known that he was being baited and that Lauren was nothing like the person Pamela was describing. But he was remembering how Monica had tried to trap him, how women seemed to want more than he could give, and suddenly he suspected that Lauren might desire that same end.

Julian looked at Pamela with dark eyes and realized that he had indeed become something of a eunuch where other women were concerned.

Pamela was a beautiful girl, a willing girl, and only a besotted fool would turn away from her blatant offer. Only someone helplessly in love would resist her. He did not love Lauren— he would not let himself.

Without another thought, he reached for Pamela, pulling her into his arms as his mouth claimed hers. She pressed ardently against him and he increased the pressure, finding no pleasure in the embrace, no soaring of the senses, as he did in Lauren's arms. He tried to pull away, realizing that this was a mistake, but Pamela wrapped her arms tightly around his neck, holding him to her like a leech.

Lazily, Lauren flipped through a book until, with a bored sigh, she threw it aside and rose to her feet. She stretched, reaching for the ceiling, and then with a satisfied smile she walked over to her dressing table, picked up the gilt-backed brush that Julian had given her and slowly began to brush her hair, hearing it crackle with every stroke.

She smiled secretly and a giggle escaped her. Placing her fingertips to her lips, Lauren could almost feel Julian's touch. How much she had changed since meeting him; she was more sure of herself now that she'd discovered she was someone who could be loved. How many times had she wished for someone to want her and care for her as she watched her mother dwindle away knowing that soon she would be alone— so alone.

Suddenly she needed to see Julian. It was an unbearable ache to know that he would not be coming to her tonight. She was patiently waiting for the day when he would announce to the world that they were truly man and wife and there would be no more separations, no more lonely nights when she craved him as an opium addict craves his oblivion. But tonight her patience seemed to escape her.

With a wide smile she rang for Molly, knowing what she had to do. Julian would be at Vauxhall Gardens tonight, and she had no intention of interfering with his party, but she did want to see him; she simply wanted to watch him, knowing that he was hers.

As Molly laced her, she felt a flutter in the region of her heart and felt so gay and light-hearted that she wanted to sing, dance, shout with joy, but she contained all these emotions behind a quiet façade. Molly slipped a lovely iridescent gown over her head. It had been a gift from Julian and she had not yet had occasion to wear the beautifully colored dress. It shimmered like turquoise one minute, but when she turned it seemed first almost yellow and then rose-colored. Fine Mechlin lace bordered its low neckline and elbow-length sleeves. She added an opal necklace and earrings as Molly fashioned her hair into curls on top of her head.

"It's not a good idea to go out alone at night without an escort," Molly intoned while Lauren sat quietly under her skillful hands.

"I'll be quite safe. Besides I shan't be unescorted; I'm taking you with me."

"That's not the same thing and you know it!"

Lauren gave her a wicked grin. "I love the way you answer so obediently. It's no wonder your last employer dismissed you."

"Oh, I was right enough with the lady, but I gave that son of hers a tongue-lashing he'll not soon forget." Her lips smiled at the memory. "I'll always hold that as one of my dearest memories."

Lauren laughed aloud and Molly joined her. "I'm glad you're more friend than servant." Lauren reached up and took Molly's hand, bringing a tinge of embarrassment to her servant's cheeks. "I don't know what I'd have done without you, Molly. It was providence that led you to me that day."

Molly turned away, blushing even brighter. "Oh, don't go on so. It's I who should be thankin' you. You put a roof over my head and food in my belly. You don't work my fingers to their bones, and you pay me generously."

Lauren's light tinkling laugh made Molly

smile. "Enough of our mutual admiration society. I think it's time we visited Vauxhall. I've heard it's an interesting place."

Lauren moved under one of the arbored walks and pulled her cloak closer as another inquiring glance came her way. She could not understand what gave the men the license to stare so boldly at her, and she was rather frightened by their admiring looks.

"I told you it was foolishness!" Molly whispered into her ear. "The sooner we get home, the better!"

Lauren lifted her chin petulantly. "I'm not leaving until I find Julian."

"He could be anywhere! All these walks and acres of gardens are good for trysts, not for finding someone."

Lauren moved on, ignoring Molly's words though she knew they had the ring of truth. She did not want to admit to herself that she had been a fool to come here alone and she was beginning to feel lost and frightened. She needed to see Julian now more than ever.

Molly lifted her shoulders in defeat. "Well, at least let's get a cup of Vauxhall punch. I've heard it's rather tasty."

They were standing away from the lighted path, drinking their punch, when three young blades, obviously in their cups, approached.

"Now here's two pretty maids without a man!"

"T-two for th-three," another one stuttered. "Th-that seems p-pretty e-even."

"Oh, be off with you, you drunken louts!"

Molly ordered, standing in front of Lauren to shield her from their scrutiny.

The third lad reached behind Molly and pulled Lauren forward into the light. Her cloak fell back and their mutual gasps were very audible.

"She's a vertible Venus! T'ain't seen the likes of her in quite a while, eh fellows."

"You let her go!" Molly insisted, taking Lauren's arm and pulling her away from the youth.

Three pairs of bleary eyes settled on Molly's outraged face. "You're not a bad one, but after seeing her, I think she's more my type!" one said.

At that moment a group of women came by, their spreading skirts rustling softly as they attracted the men's attention. They turned, smiling inanely, and Molly and Lauren took the opportunity to duck behind the shrubs and make their way down one of the darker paths. They had reached the end where a small bench was hidden in an alcove, and were about to turn and retrace their steps when Lauren heard a giggle followed by a deep voice that she immediately recognized. She stood still, thinking she was mistaken, but then he laughed and she knew it was Julian.

Like a thief, she flattened herself against the shrubbery and moved forward until she could see the couple sitting so close together upon the bench. Lauren's mouth gaped open as she watched Julian pull the girl into his arms, and lift her mouth to his.

She wanted to scream, but the sound stuck in her throat and she watched, horrified, as Julian worked his practiced charm on the young girl. Lauren felt sick and wanted to retch. She had to get away from this scene that was burning into her brain like acid.

Turning away, she tripped, uttering a soft curse as she fell. The couple broke apart and looked in her direction. Feeling like an idiot, Lauren tried to regain her composure before she turned to face them. Her glance went from Julian's surprised expression to the unbuttoned bodice of his companion. One ripe breast was in danger of escaping its resting place, and that pale flesh taunted Lauren as visible proof of Julian's infidelity.

Julian stood up, holding out his hand as if to explain, but Lauren wanted no explanations. With a muffled cry, she pushed past Molly and ran down the walk, refusing to stop at Julian's order.

He caught her when she had almost gained the safety of the crowd. She fought him like a wild animal, kicking out at him and mumbling incoherent, angry words, but he wrapped his arms around her and stilled her furious struggles.

"Y-you beast! You despicable louse!" she shrieked.

"I can explain," he said, but Lauren laughed harshly.

"Don't tell me. It was your sister!"

"No, but my sister is here with her husband. I came with them and Pamela."

Lauren began to struggle again but slumped weakly against him when he refused to release her. "Go back to Pamela! I'm sure you'd rather be with her than me!"

"For God's sake, Lauren! It was just a kiss!

You're acting like you caught me with my breeches down." Now he was becoming angry, not liking the role she was forcing him to play. He never explained his actions to anyone, but now Lauren was making him explain and he did not like the feeling.

"It's too bad you couldn't have found a quieter setting, for then I'm sure it would have been more than a kiss I interrupted."

"You're starting to sound like a nagging wife!" he thundered, becoming incensed at her behavior.

"That's because you're acting like an unfaithful husband!"

His face turned stony. "Do not try to put chains on me, Lauren. I told you before how I loathe them."

"I put no chains on you!" she raged. "I only want you to honor the vows we spoke."

"Those vows were a necessity at the time. I thought you understood that they were not to be taken seriously."

Lauren gasped and stepped back. "You mean it was all a façade? All those times spent together, you were just conveniently passing the time with a willing woman? That makes me no better than a whore!"

His hand came out to slap her, but he stopped himself in time. "Don't talk like that," he said tersely.

"Why not? I thought now was a time for truth! Let's get all the silly little lies out of the way!"

Julian began to notice that several couples were becoming interested in the noisy scene. He took her arm. "We can't talk here. Let's go somewhere where it's quiet."

"Get away from me!" she screamed, jerking from his grasp. "Don't touch me! Don't you ever touch me again!" she sobbed.

Seeing Molly standing before her like some safe harbor, Lauren ran right into her arms.

Julian tried to take a step toward them, but his eyes met Molly's over Lauren's head and she slowly shook her head, warning him that now was not the time or place to settle anything. He nodded and his outstretched hand dropped in defeat. There would be time to explain later. He would make her understand.

But as he turned away Julian wondered *what* he would make her understand. That he was already beginning to feel trapped by his need of her and that feeling scared him more than anything else in the world? What could he make her understand when he was floundering in the depths of confusion himself. Tonight had only magnified his consternation—now he knew for certain that Lauren was more to him than he wanted her to be. Julian refused to admit to himself that he loved Lauren. He didn't want to need her—and that was the crux of his problem.

He saw Pamela standing at the end of the walk and shrugged resignedly. The sooner he got it over with, the sooner he could go to Lauren, and he knew he would go to her; it was inevitable.

"Who was that woman, Julian?" Pamela demanded, hands on her hips.

Oh Lord, he thought, save me from suspicious women.

He wanted to bare his soul and tell Pamela that it was his wife, but he could not find the words. They were locked behind walls of restraint.

"Someone I know. I don't wish to discuss it."

"But Julian—" she began.

"Let's find Felice and Brendan. They can escort you home." And without giving her a chance to say another word, he stalked off in search of his sister, leaving Pamela to hurry behind him like a forgotten puppy.

As soon as Felice saw Julian she knew that something was amiss. He had a fierce scowl on his face, and his eyes glowed with a golden light. Pamela was no longer the flirting woman, but looked like a reprimanded child.

"Whatever has happened?" The words were out before Felice could stop them. Perhaps it would be better if she did not know.

"Leave it, Felice," Julian thundered, stalking past her.

Felice, Brendan and Pamela followed in his wake, hurrying to keep up with his long, angry strides. Once they were in the carriage, a heavy silence filled the interior.

Brendan noisily cleared his throat. "Felice and I saw quite a few old friends," he said into the strained atmosphere.

Felice took up his lead, hoping to dispel some of the tension. "Yes, Lord and Lady Richmond were there. You remember them, don't you Julian? Their lands in Kent are quite near our estate."

Julian did not reply, staring broodingly out the window.

Felice nervously twisted her hands together. "Do you know the Richmonds, Pamela?" she asked in a high voice. It sounded unnaturally loud to her own ears.

"Yes," Pamela's voice was sullen.

Felice lay back against the cushion and closed her eyes, knowing that the conversation would go no further. As the carriage bumped along the road, all the occupants were caught up in their own thoughts and did not again disturb the silence.

After they reached Pamela's home and deposited her in her parents' care, they started for home. They had not gone very far when Julian leaned forward, ordering the carriage to stop.

"Where are you going, Julian?" Felice asked indignantly. She was hoping that once home she could get some answers from him.

"I'm quite grown, Felice," he said, glowering at her. "I don't have to account to you for my movements."

"She's just concerned about you, Julian," Brendan interrupted, but Julian only glared at him.

"Continue home. I have some things to do."

Without another word, he slammed the door and they watched with open mouths as he started down the dark street at a brisk pace.

"What was that all about?" Felice wondered aloud.

"I don't know, but he is certainly in a hurry to go somewhere."

"What do you think happened between Pamela and Julian?"

"Whatever it was, I don't think it was what she wanted."

Felice shook her head. "Julian has been acting most peculiar of late. I think something is going on that we don't know about."

Brendan laughed drily. "Very astute, my dear, and if Julian's behavior tonight is anything to go by, I'd advise you not to pry too closely into his affairs. I think whatever is wrong does not concern us."

"I only want to help him," Felice's voice was distressed.

Brendan placed an arm across her shoulders. "I know, darling, but some things a man has to work out alone, and I don't think you can help him this time."

Lauren angrily paced the floor of her bedchamber, kicking the long, loose robe away with every step she took. She wanted to rant and rave, scream, throw something, but all she did was pace back and forth as hot, angry thoughts rushed through her head. She wished Julian were there so she could vent her fury.

The door opened and Molly's head came around the corner.

"Would you like a cup of hot chocolate?" she asked in a meek voice.

"No!" Lauren snarled, turning on Molly like a small whirlwind. "I don't want anything! Leave me be!"

"Don't you think—" she began, but Lauren cut her short.

"Oh, I think many things, but I've been told ladies aren't supposed to use words like those."

"Lauren," she said tentatively, wanting to help ease some of her pain, but not knowing exactly how.

Lauren threw out her hand in a dismissive gesture. "Go away! Just go away and leave me alone!"

Molly complied, although reluctantly.

Lauren moved moodily over to her dressing table and stared sightlessly at all the little bottles and porcelain jars that littered the top. Her eyes burned from the effort of holding back the tears that she refused to let go. She would not give Julian the satisfaction of tears. He deserved her contempt and her hatred, but never the tender tears of a wounded heart.

Her gaze locked with a pair of wild, violet eyes, and she stepped back, unaware for a moment that she was looking at her own reflection in the mirror. Never, never had she felt this bitter, not even when her father was so unjustly accused of treason, when her mother died a poor, broken spirit no longer wanting to walk the earth. The fervor of her feelings shocked her, and she feared she would be unable to control them. It was as if a demon had been let loose within her and all she could think of was life's cruel fate.

With the motions of a sleepwalker she picked up a book that rested on the edge of her dressing table. She slowly turned it over until she could read the title and a cold sneer touched her soft lips. Poetry! Words of love and longing. Silly prattle for silly minds! She hated poetry now, almost as much as she hated Julian, and she threw the book through the window, smashing the pane. Lauren watched in a kind of fascinated detachment as the glass that was once whole splintered into tiny fragments, falling to the carpet like shattered stars.

"Was that really necessary?"

Lauren whirled around at the voice, and glared at Julian like a tiger at bay. He stood there so confidently in his evening attire, looking like the king of all he surveyed. Again Lauren felt like throwing something, to hit him and hurt him as he had hurt her.

"What are you doing here?" Her voice was hard and cold, and she felt it did not really belong to her, but to some wounded animal.

He smiled grimly. "I didn't want to wait until tomorrow to settle this thing. I knew you would exaggerate everything all out of proportion unless I convinced you what a fool you're being."

"You don't have to tell me what a fool I've been." She gave a harsh laugh. "I know only too well what a gullible fool I am." Hostile eyes watched him—eyes that had once held only trust and tenderness.

Julian shook his head. "How can sweet lips spout such nonsense?" he asked, taking a step forward, but she moved back warily.

"So you think the dawning of reason is nonsense? Well, honeyed words will not move me tonight, Julian," she taunted. "Why aren't you in her bed? Isn't that where you'd rather be?"

He lifted a hand toward her but she looked away, refusing to be drawn by the warm look in his eyes.

"I know what you saw tonight looked damning, but there was nothing to it. Pamela is a friend of the family."

"An *old* friend of the family, didn't you say earlier? She didn't look so old to me. If she's old, then I'm positively in my dotage!"

"Would you let me explain?!" he growled. He had never seen Lauren like this. He had thought it would be so easy to make her forget her anger, but now he saw that he would have a fight on his hands even to make her listen.

"There's only one way to make you see reason," and he took her in his arms in one swift motion. She twisted and turned, trying to scratch him, but his lips found hers. He bent her over his arm, trying to kiss her into submission, but when he lifted his head she was staring at him with cold, empty eyes.

"Such potent passion," he said in a wry tone.

She had felt a small stirring in her body at his touch, but she beat the demon of passion down, knowing that it would consume her if she gave in to it. All reason would be lost if she let that dark desire gain control.

He moved away, finding that her coldness frightened him. He had never bothered with women when they were in their moods, but now he wanted to have his loving Lauren back, and her lack of response shook him to his core.

He cleared his throat. "I told you I was taking my sister and some friends to Vauxhall. The kiss you saw was nothing." Even to his own ears it sounded thin, but how could he explain something he did not understand himself?

There was no sound from Lauren, but her

eyes blazed at him, accusing him until he felt
guilty when he knew he was innocent. His eyes
lowered—well, almost innocent. There had been
a moment at Vauxhall when he wondered why
he was not interested in Pamela's advances, and
that had bothered him. But now, facing Lauren,
he knew he had simply been afraid of his growing need of her.

"I saw you pawing her like some lovesick calf!
How many times have you sought out other
women while I thought I was the only one?"

"You know you are the only one! I *told* you I
was going to Vauxhall. If I had been planning
such a rendezvous then I wouldn't have told you
where I was going."

"You're very clever, Julian. You embellish
your lies with half-truths, hoping I'll play the
dupe again, but no longer! Save your lean lies
for someone else! I'm not so deficient in judgment that you can utter a few banalities and
I'll rush into your arms again, forgiving everything."

"Pamela and I have known one another for a
long time. You happened upon us in an entirely
innocent moment."

She placed her hands on her hips and her hair
flowed wildly about her shoulders. She looked
like some pagan princess standing before him
in her long, flowing white robe, with her breasts
heaving in anger. He wanted nothing more than
to take her into his arms and carry her to bed,
but he knew she would not yield in this mood.
He had to convince her of his innocence.

She gave a slightly hysterical laugh. "Innocent? You forget I know you, Julian." Her voice

lowered suggestively. "If there's a woman anywhere in the vicinity then your intentions are not innocent; you'd act like the lusting stag that you are. Innocent is not a word you should use. It is sullied by your lips. In fact, everything you touch is soiled."

His eyes flashed and a glow began to burn in their depths. Unconsciously, Lauren stepped back, knowing that she had angered him beyond the point of return.

His hand came out and cruel fingers wrapped around her wrist, jerking her toward him until she was crushed against his hard chest.

"And what of you, my sweet pretty witch?!" His voice was dangerously quiet. "Has my touch sullied you?" His eyes raked over her frightened face, and then down to where her gown parted, revealing the smooth swell of her breast. "You don't look so abused and dirty to me."

"I-I am! I'm dirty and tainted! Your touch has ruined me, for no other man will want me now."

His mouth lifted in a sneer. "That's good, for no other man could have you even if he so desired. You are my wife."

"I am no wife! I was but a tool to be used and then discarded when my usefulness was done."

"You are my wife!" he shouted, amazed that he wanted to state something that before he had been loath to admit.

"And you are my husband, but you do not act as a husband, do you?" she asked, her breath catching in her throat as his eyes scorched her. He was so close that she could see the tiny pores on his face and smell the slight scent of wine that lingered on his breath.

"I thought I acted the part admirably," he said, a smile smoothing over the hard shape of his lips.

"In bed! You make a fine stallion, my lord, but there is more to marriage than rutting like an animal!"

His grip tightened and it took all her will-power not to cry out. She bit her lip, closing her eyes at the blazing anger in his eyes.

"Then you 'rut' as you say, admirably, my dear, for I feel the urge to 'rut' with you right now."

She flinched at the coldness in his eyes that had once burned so brightly. She saw the purposeful intent in their depths and knew she had to stop him no matter what the price. She could not bear it if he touched her now in anger, when once they had touched so sweetly.

"If you touch me, I'll kill myself!" she threatened in a wild, breathless voice. She hated herself for lying, but she would hate him more if he tried to make love to her now.

His grip loosened for a second, but that was the only sign that her words had any impact.

"I don't think I could touch you tonight if my life depended on it!" he said cruelly, watching in cold amusement as the color left her face. He threw her away from him as if she were something dirty, and indeed she had never felt so tainted and ugly in her life. "There are other women who can please me more than you." His eyes speared her, moving over her with insulting slowness. "No, I want a woman tonight, a real woman, something you are a long way from being."

"Go to Pamela!" Lauren threw the words at

him and immediately regretted them. She didn't really want him in any other woman's arms.

"I think I might," he smiled, but his smile held no humor.

The look on his face increased the anger in Lauren and she had no control over the next words that came out.

"Perhaps you should find some young virgin to ravish as you did me? I'm sure you would enjoy ruining some other girl's life!"

His fists clenched at his side and a pulse throbbed in his temple with the effort to keep his hands off her. "I'm sorry I did not deny myself that night. It would have saved us both a lot of trouble." He turned away and walked to the door. When his hand was on the knob he turned, and there was a bleakness in his eyes. "But never tell me that you regret the times after that, for I know you enjoyed our lovemaking as much as I did. We shared some memorable moments."

"We shared nothing!" she stormed, refusing to let him play the tender strings of her heart.

His eyes were steady. "I'll leave you alone for now. I was wrong to come tonight. You need time to calm down and so do I."

"Yes! You'd like me to calm down. You want some meek little woman to say 'Yes, Julian,' and 'No, Julian,' and never question your actions!"

She got one last look at his hard profile before he left, closing the door so softly that she could not believe he was really gone. She stood for a moment in silence wondering if this might be the last time she would ever see him.

Impulsively, Lauren ran to the door, throwing

it open as she rushed out to the landing. She clutched the smooth banister, so hard and cold beneath her fingers, and looked below to see Julian already on his way out the door.

She held out a hand in mute appeal, agony in her eyes. She wanted to call him back, tell him she did not mean what she had said, beg him not to leave her, but the words died with the click of the door on his retreating figure.

Her hand slowly fell to her side. She knew her stubborn mind wouldn't allow her to speak the words which had trembled so temptingly in her heart.

"You have done nothing to regret," her mind insisted. "He is the one who should be sorry. Vile deceiver that he is, he should be on bended knee begging *your* forgiveness.

"But I love him!" answered her helpless heart.

Then she thought again. "Loved! That is past. He killed all feeling, took all trust tonight."

Lauren shivered as if a strong north wind blew by her. It seemed as if all the music in her soul was gone and there was only the lonesome howl of the wind echoing through the pained chambers of her heart, uttering a mournful cry like some lost soul shrouded in agony.

Lauren wrapped her arms protectively around her waist and bent over, rocking back and forth like a ship tossed on stormy waves. She heard the strange mewling of some tormented animal, unaware that it was her own crying until Molly came to her, gently leading her back into the bedchamber.

Lauren's eyes were fixed, staring off without seeing anything. Molly slowly put her to bed and covered her. She stood back, shaking her head sadly. She never wanted to be in love like this, she thought as she bent to blow out the candle. People like Julian and Lauren loved too deeply and consumingly. They wanted all or nothing; she would just settle for something safer.

Through a mist of despair, Lauren heard the door close behind Molly and then she rolled over, watching as the moonlight streamed across the floor. She didn't want to retreat into the shadow of pain but it beckoned her on. She wanted to be soothed and stroked, but there was only emptiness in her bed tonight. She felt so raw, so exposed to all the hurt, as if her skin had been pulled back, letting everyone see all the private emotions that made her what she was.

Her hand lifted and stroked the pillow that was Julian's, but when she realized what she was doing she jerked upright. There seemed to be no defense against all the memories that crowded in on her, haunting her with the hours she and Julian had spent together.

She lifted the pillow and could smell him as surely as if he were in the room now. A sob escaped from her as she crushed the pillow to her bosom. The bitterness of their argument had left an acrid taste in her mouth that was slowly finding its way down to her heart.

Lauren could see her life stretched out before her like some barren plain. She had hugged Julian's love to her like a precious jewel, but now it crumbled like dust in her hands.

She did not want to feel this pain, but somehow she felt she deserved it. She had given her-

self too fully to a man who neither wanted her
love nor needed it. He had seemed like some
knight on a white charger and she had let him
into her heart, but instead he had plunged his
lance into the very center of her being, ravaging, pillaging and destroying all love and trust.
Worst of all, Julian had taken her self-respect.

Lauren clutched the pillow closer and fell to
the bed. Mixed with intense feelings of anger
and remorse were vivid memories of the passion
between them. A picture formed in her mind of
her and Julian entwined in tangled sheets. They
were so warm from their lovemaking that they
had sought to kick the covers from their naked
flesh. Now the sheets were cold, so cold. She
whimpered softly, but the image would not disappear. She could almost feel Julian's strong
hand as it touched her back, traveling so temptingly down her spine, drawing her toward him.

She jumped off the bed as if it were on fire.
How could she lie on this bed? she asked herself.
How could she sleep here, knowing that all the
times she had slept with Julian, his arm across
her, were now confined to memory, never to happen again.

Lauren could almost hear the creak of the bed
as they made love and she covered her ears to
shut out the sound. From somewhere in time
past she heard herself giggle and Julian laugh
huskily. They were whispering, sharing secrets
like two children. She had placed everything in
Julian's hands—all her dreams, all her hopes
for the future.

She turned away and left the room; she could
not bear to stay in the bedroom another minute.

Downstairs she lit a candle and then dropped listlessly into a chair in the sitting room.

Seeing the brandy decanter, she remembered the last time Julian had poured a drink. He had been laughing at a story she was telling, and when he turned to her there had been so much joy on his face. Her heart had soared as she realized that she was responsible for his happiness.

Lauren closed her eyes, but still the memories kept crowding in on her. There was Julian calling her to the breakfast table and smiling down at her as he held out her chair, Julian indulging her in a present, and Julian holding out his arms as she ran so eagerly into his embrace that she thought she would surely die from such intense pleasure.

She wiped away a tear that clung stubbornly to her lashes. How was she going to keep him from haunting her? Suddenly Lauren was burying her face in her hands as the tears refused to be held at bay.

She knew she could not stay here in this house that held so many memories. She rushed up the stairs.

"Molly!" she screamed. "Molly!"

Molly came through her door in a minute, looking concerned. "What is it? I thought you were being murdered in your sleep!"

"Get your things together. We're leaving!"

Molly looked astounded.

"Leaving? But where will we go?"

"Anywhere! Nowhere! I won't stay in this house!" She was becoming hysterical.

"All right, love. We'll go, but we have to have

some place to stay. We can't go off half-cocked into the middle of the night."

Lauren's mind raced feverishly. "We'll go to my grandfather's."

"But I thought your uncle turned you away."

"He did once, but he won't this time," she stated with confidence. "I'm through letting men take advantage of me. I'll not play the meek maid any longer. The least he can do is offer me a roof over my head. This time it won't be so easy to get rid of me!"

"Are you sure? I mean, Lord Keaton—" she began.

"Don't ever speak his name again! Go now and pack only what is necessary!"

When Molly was gone, Lauren ran to her armoire, throwing it open with one hand while the other was already reaching inside. She pushed aside all the beautiful silks and satins that Julian had bought her, searching for one serviceable dress to wear. She would leave all the jewels and gifts, and bring nothing that would remind her of Julian.

As she turned, hugging the dress to her chest, her gaze lingered once again on the bed sitting so innocently in the middle of the room. The tears and heartache of the last few hours overshadowed everything, making all that had gone before unbearable.

She had thought Julian was all hers, but their love had been a sham. Now there were only the dry useless bones of distrust.

As she closed the door behind her, Lauren knew she was closing the door on her dreams. Once she had thought herself a cherished lover, but now she knew she had been but a convenient whore. Never again would she give so whole-heartedly of herself. Never again would she set herself up to receive so much pain and heart-ache. Once was enough.

When she left the house Molly was with her, refusing Lauren's offer to stay behind.

As dawn painted the sky, lifting the darkness, Lauren still felt hollow and empty, as if the night would always be with her and the day would never come again.

All love, all liking, all delight
Lies drown'd with us in endless night.
—Robert Herrick

Chapter Six

Lauren nervously wiped her palms down the sides of her dress before she lifted the knocker and let it fall. She looked over her shoulder at Molly, waiting at the bottom of the steps with their belongings at her feet. It seemed ages before the heavy oak door opened and an imposing servant stood before her.

"I wish to see Lord Rodney Warwick," she demanded, putting a trace of hauteur in her voice.

"He is not at home," the servant intoned. "If you would care to leave a message I will inform him that you called."

Lauren felt her hackles rise. She was certain Rodney was home at this time of the morning, and thought he had just left orders that she was to be denied if she should call. She pushed past the servant, startling him. "Tell him I want to see him now!"

Molly gathered their possessions and quickly climbed the steps to follow Lauren inside. She cringed at the outraged expression on the servant's face, but Lauren was too angry to care.

"Now see here, young lady!" the servant said.

"I want to see him now!" she repeated, marching toward the stairs, but the servant stepped in front of her, blocking her path.

"I shall have to remove you bodily unless you leave immediately!"

"What seems to be the problem, Baxter?"

Three pairs of eyes flew to the top of the staircase where an old, bent man stood, viewing them all with keen gray eyes. His white hair was brushed back into a queue. He wore a long blue brocade dressing robe.

"I'm sorry we disturbed you, your lordship, but this female refuses to leave without seeing Lord Rodney. I told her he was not here."

"That is quite right, young lady," he assured her. "Rodney has not returned this morning from his night out." His head went forward like a turtle as he strained to get a better look at her. He pushed the glasses up on his nose and started down the stairs. "What is your name?"

Lauren was standing with her mouth open, realizing that she was in the presence of her grandfather and he did not know her.

"My name is Lauren Warwick."

She saw him blanch and stagger for a moment before he closed his eyes, pressing his hand to his chest. Without stopping to think, she was around the servant and up the stairs helping to support him as he leaned weakly against her.

"Come and sit down," she begged, leading him down the stairs. The servant helped her lead the old man into the sitting room. When he was comfortably placed in a chair, he waved the servant away with a frail hand.

"But your lordship," he protested, not liking the idea of leaving him alone with this girl. "Are you quite sure? Just because she bears the same last name—"

"Go on, Baxter," the old man cut him off. "I will call you if you're needed." His voice was weak.

Jonathan Warwick, Earl of Naylor, rested his head wearily against the back of the chair and closed his eyes. After a few moments he opened them again and he seemed to have regained some of his strength. He fixed Lauren with piercing eyes, studying her intently, and then shifted so he could see Molly standing hesitantly in the doorway.

"I see that you didn't come with your mother. Is she waiting to hear if I will accept you?"

Lauren hung her head, realizing that her grandfather knew nothing about her. Rodney had not told him of her visit.

"She's dead, my lord. She was buried in France."

He shook his head sadly. "I heard of your father's death years ago and tried to find you and your mother, but you had effectively disappeared. It was impossible to trace you."

"We went to a convent in France where my mother had friends."

He nodded. "At least they took good care of you." He sighed heavily and shifted in his chair. "I know this will not make me appear kinder in your eyes, but I did suffer after Stephen left. I found it hard to believe he could betray his country."

"You found it hard to believe because you knew that he was incapable of such treachery."

"Child, child," he murmured. "The evidence was there before our eyes. There were those letters sent from France. They said he had informed them of the proposed invasion of St. Cast."

"There could have been a hundred letters found in my father's bedroom and still I would have believed him innocent. All those years, as we moved from one country to another, one town to the next, he talked of nothing but wanting to clear his name, but the way to achieve it eluded him. Can you imagine how he felt? Ostracized by family and country, and forced to wear the unearned name of traitor? He was a decent and honorable man unable to disprove the lies." She looked accusingly at him. "He was your son! He loved you! How could you believe he was capable of treason?"

Suddenly he looked very gray, revealing how heavy a toll the burden of Stephen's supposed guilt had taken on him. "He was my son and my heir. I loved him so much—perhaps too much. When he left, it was as if a part of me had gone with him."

"How could you have believed the lies when he told you of his innocence?" she asked again, needing to know how father had so easily turned against son.

"I might not have believed it except that he was married to Angelica. She was French and he loved her so much. He might easily have been swayed by that love into betraying his country."

Lauren angrily shook her head in denial.

"Never! Mother would never have demanded so terrible a price for love. She told me that when she married my father she became English, turning her back on her family and friends, who had wanted her to marry a Frenchman."

"But she went to France after Stephen's death! If this had really been her home she would have come here!"

Lauren laughed bitterly. "How could she return here? This is the country that sent her away in disgrace. She went back to France, not because she was guilty but because the convent offered her a haven from the world. Once Father was dead she had no need for the outside world. Even I could not lighten her days."

Lauren paused, and when she continued tears were on her cheeks and there was a catch in her voice. "My mother and father never laughed or enjoyed life after we left England. There were too many sad thoughts that blotted out the joy of living. Father finally died, wasting away with misplaced guilt and the longing for an England he would never see again." She wiped away her tears. "Sometimes I think he wanted to come back and face hanging just so his tortured mind could rest, but he had a wife and child to care for. He would not turn his back on us and take the easy way out."

Her grandfather slowly rose to his feet and walked to the window. He stared out over the gardens and woods that he had once planned to give to Stephen. Now they would go to Rodney, and the thought brought a sadness to his eyes. He knew that Rodney did not love the land as Stephen had; he just wanted the money it would put in his pocket. Rodney did not care for the tenants who farmed it generation after generation; he only cared that they brought in a good harvest.

"I cannot take back the past no matter how dearly I might desire it, but I can give Stephen's daughter a home." He turned to her and tears filled his eyes. "Will you stay, Lauren?"

Lauren's smile was small. "I had come to ask for shelter so I will accept."

"It has been a long time since this house had youth and beauty in it. I can't remember the last time that I heard laughter here. You see, Lauren, it was not just your father who suffered. I have suffered also. I know it is much to ask, but can you forgive me? I cannot ask it of Stephen since he is gone, so I ask it of you."

Lauren looked away, wondering what her father would have done. In a flash she knew, almost as if he had spoken to her. She crossed the room and stood within inches of him. "I forgive you and my father forgives you. The suffering has gone on long enough, and it is time for peace of mind."

His thin hands came out tentatively and Lauren moved into his embrace, wrapping her own young arms about his frail body. He shuddered in her arms and she knew that he was crying. A tear slipped from her own eye, sliding down her smooth cheek until it dropped to his shoulder.

They were unaware of the door opening behind Molly. Rodney stood in the doorway, regarding the scene with a sneer.

"How touching!"

Self-consciously they broke apart.

"Ahem," her grandfather cleared his throat. "This is Stephen's daughter, Rodney. She has returned to us."

Rodney realized that Lauren had not apprised his father of their previous meeting, so he decided to pretend it had never occurred.

"How wonderful!" he said, and only Lauren and Molly were aware of the sarcastic edge to his words.

"I'm sure Lauren is tired. Rodney, would you see that a room is made up for her and her servant. I want you to be very happy here, my dear," he said softly to Lauren.

Lauren looked sideways at Rodney and said with a smile on her lips, "How could I be otherwise with such charming company."

After they were shown to their quarters, Molly prepared a bath for Lauren. She slipped into the warm, welcoming water; bubbles overflowed the tub and the sweet scent of lilacs filled the air. She glanced around the room, noticing the splendor. The bed was large with billowing drapes that could be drawn to keep out the cold.

Unbidden came the thought of crawling between the covers, drawing the drapes and being welcomed into warm, strong arms. The arms led up to a muscled chest and then she was looking into a familiar pair of golden eyes.

She sat up, splashing water over the side of the tub. She was hot with embarrassment. How could she think of him? Her hand gently traced the curve of her lips and she could almost feel his touch. Angrily she shook her head, calling herself a fool. She found a large brush and began

to wash her back. Next she wet her hair, scrubbing it vigorously to keep thoughts of Julian at
bay. Molly appeared with a pitcher of water and
Lauren leaned back as the water flowed over
her. It was so warm that she was again reminded of supple fingers on her skin, bringing
delicious little shivers of pleasure.

"Stop it!" she said aloud, and Molly stood back,
looking at Lauren in surprise.

"I've finished," she said, holding the empty
pitcher.

"Oh, I—I didn't mean you," Lauren stammered in embarrassment.

"Are you all right?" Molly asked.

"Yes." Lauren bent to retrieve the brush. "Yes,
I'm fine."

Molly shrugged and left the room.

Lauren finished her bath and then put on the
one dress she had brought with her. Her grandfather had promised to order her some new
clothes and the fittings would take place tomorrow.

Exhausted, Lauren rested on the bed. She
tossed and turned, but after a while she drifted
off into forgetfulness to sleep the day away.

On her way to the dining room, she saw the
study door open and Rodney appear. He crossed
the marble foyer and stopped at the bottom of
the stairs, smiling up at her with a particularly
nasty look in his eyes.

Lauren was not ready for a confrontation with
him, but it seemed she was not to be spared.

"Pray allow me to escort you in to dine," he
offered, extending his arm.

Lauren could not resist asking, "Surprised to see me?" as she allowed him to lead her across the floor.

"You look like the cat that has swallowed the bird, dear niece," he said, opening the door to the large dining room. "I pray you won't get indigestion."

"Oh, I have a remarkable constitution."

Her grandfather was already at the head of the table and he stood when they entered.

"Ah, Lauren. It is so nice to have a lovely face at the table. I have missed feminine companionship."

"It's entirely your own fault," Rodney mumbled rather bitterly. "You have refused to have any parties or balls, locking yourself away like some mad hermit."

The Earl smiled humorlessly. "I didn't think it was appropriate to have parties when there was nothing to celebrate." He gave Lauren an appraising glance. "But now that Lauren is here, I think I shall remedy that. I plan to give a ball and invite all the *beau monde*. I want to show her off to all the eligible young men who will surely envy me my beautiful granddaughter."

Rodney's lips tightened. "How generous you are."

"I don't want a ball, Grandfather. I would just like to remain here quietly and get to know you. I'm not interested in being received by society."

"We shall see, we shall see," he said gruffly. "First you need time to feel at home, and then there is the matter of suitably attiring you."

"It is not necessary..." she began.

He held up his hand. "Allow me this whim.

It would give me great pleasure to see you assume your rightful place as my granddaughter. If I could turn back time, I would, but since that is impossible, I want to indulge you as much as I can."

"Do you feel like a princess, dear niece?" Rodney murmured, relaxing back in his chair as the servants brought out the dishes of steaming food. "Is it not odd to find yourself in the lap of luxury after all this time?"

"I am most fortunate." She demurely dropped her lashes.

He lifted his fork, toying with it for a moment before his glance again speared her.

"What *have* you been doing all this time?"

"She buried her mother and came to us, Rodney," her grandfather supplied, not realizing that Rodney and Lauren both knew she had been in London well over a month.

Lauren continued to eat, letting her grandfather's words hold Rodney for the time being.

"Of course. But what have you done for funds?" he persisted.

"I sold my mother's jewels, and it was enough to make the trip."

"Ah, so you come to us penniless? How sad, but how fortunate for you that we are not short of money."

"Leave off, Rodney!" the Earl thundered. "She came to us because she's family, not because she expected payment. I think you're beginning to confuse her greed with your own."

Rodney averted his eyes from his father's and then the fresh salmon placed before him took over his attention.

After dining, Rodney left them. He had some things to do in London, which was but a few miles from their estate. Lauren and her grandfather retired to the sitting room, and in the ensuing silence Lauren was unaware of the sad, wistful expression on her face.

"You seem so sad, child, as if life has no more dreams to offer you. I assure you that is not the case."

"Dreams are such elusive things, Grandfather."

"That I know. But we are nothing without our dreams. They are what set us apart from mere beasts."

Lauren sighed, coming to her feet. "I think I'll retire for the night. I'm suddenly very weary."

"Sleep well. And I do intend to give you a ball, Lauren, so please don't resist. It's time I brought a little magic back into this house, and music and laughter are just the things which might accomplish that."

Later, while Lauren lay in bed, she was suddenly glad that she had found her grandfather again. She was sure her father would have wanted her to forgive him, as he had forgiven him years ago. The Earl was a lonely old man whose wealth had not brought him happiness, and she was a young girl whose happiness had been fleeting. Maybe she could change both their situations.

Julian stood outside the house he had shared with Lauren and stared up at the dark windows. He had been here many times in the fortnight since she had left, each time in the hope that she might have returned. But always the house was dark, no light showing within to welcome him home.

Slowly Julian mounted the steps and went in the house. He glanced around idly, trying to disregard the heavy feeling in his chest. He walked into the sitting room to stand in the middle of the floor with one hand in the pocket of his coat. The room looked neglected despite its cleanliness, and he knew that Lauren's presence had made the room seem warm and elegant. She had imposed her personality upon the house, making it a home—a place where he had felt comfortable and at ease. He turned and went upstairs, listening carefully as if he might hear her voice as she talked to Molly.

The door to the bedroom stood open and he let his gaze wander over the furniture, his eyes lingering on the bed. He sighed, knowing he would never put another mistress in this house. There were too many memories of Lauren here, particularly in this room. He moved toward the neatly made bed, his fingers gently touching the sheer hangings. With his eyes closed, he could almost see her lying provocatively on the covers, holding out her arms to him as she gave him a seductive smile.

"Damn you to hell, Lauren!" he said aloud. "Damn you to hell for tormenting me like this!"

How had she entered his soul? He had vowed to let no woman master him, no woman chain him. But with silken arms and whispered words she had bound his heart and now no other woman tempted him, no other woman made the heat rise up in him like some wild tide. He wanted no one if he could not have Lauren.

He twisted away from the bed, uttering a curse. There! he thought. Finally he had admitted his need of her. But it was too late; she was gone and he did not know where to find her. He had searched high and low for her until he thought he would go mad. What was happening to her? Did she need him? He would often wake from a nightmare in a cold sweat, with a feeling of utter helplessness, for Lauren had called out to him in his dream and he was unable to go to her.

Julian had tried to forget her. He had become blazingly drunk and had found a woman who did not demand too much, but settled for what he was willing to give. The long night in her arms had brought no release; it had only increased his hunger. He had found the girl's voluptuous figure slightly repellent after Lauren's sleek curves, and her bright red hair had seemed garish when he compared it to the thick dark silk that he had once stroked so lovingly with his fingers.

That night he had damned Lauren to hell because it was where he wished he were. Since then he had not tried to bed a woman again; he knew that no matter how lovely, and no matter how temptingly they displayed themselves, other women were useless to him because they were not Lauren.

Julian turned toward the bed and flung himself down into the silken covers. He could almost smell her scent. Wild, sweet violets came to mind and he groaned as he rolled over, staring at the far wall.

He spied the gilt tub in the corner, and he smiled at the memory of Lauren resting back in it, liberally soaping her arms as she hummed softly. Julian had scooped her into his arms and carried her to the bed, falling with her into the covers as her smile faded and she began to breathe deeply and rapidly.

And now his smile faded, and he rolled from the bed. Walking with purposeful steps to the armoire, he threw open the double doors, the bright silks, satins and velvets seeming to taunt him with their gaiety. He slammed the doors, but one refused to close, swinging open again as if to mock his anger.

The sight of all the jewels he had given Lauren lying carelessly upon the dressing-table made him bitter. Julian wished she had taken them with her instead of nobly leaving them behind. It would have made him feel better to know she had some way with which to support herself.

Where was she now? he wondered. Was she some man's mistress? Was some man lying with her now, even as she had lain with him?

"No! Never!" he said as he looked down at his clenched fists and impatiently turned away. Why did he keep coming here, tormenting himself like this? He was beginning to think he was going mad, and he knew Felice and Brendan were worried about him. These visits to Lauren's former home at first seemed a comfort, but ended up tormenting Julian.

He hurried down the stairs and out the front

door, having decided to go to his club, where he knew he could escape for a while the thoughts that haunted him night and day. He needed a drink, or may two.

Lauren stood in front of the mirror, holding before her the ball gown she was to wear in a few days' time. It was a beautiful white silk with Venetian lace lining the bodice and two rows of lace on either side of the wide skirt, which revealed an underskirt of the palest lilac. Along with white satin slippers came a pearl necklace and a length of jewels which were to be entwined in the darkness of her hair.

"You'll look just like a queen," Molly breathed, touching the hem of the silken garment.

"I wish this were over!" Lauren announced impatiently. "Grandfather just wouldn't listen when I told him this was unnecessary."

"You should be delighted! I'd give anything to have a ball given in my honor! Just think of all the handsome young men who will be begging to dance with you."

"The few men I have met lately leave much to be desired. They are either callow youths or doddering old men!"

"If you compare them to Lord Keaton, then they'll all come up lacking."

Lauren threw the dress to the bed. There was a belligerent expression on her face. "I don't compare them to Julian. In fact, I don't even think about him!"

"Sure you don't," Molly teased, picking up the discarded garment. She pushed back a wispy strand of red hair. "And I don't think of eating except under a full moon!"

"I'm going downstairs. The company is more convivial!"

"I'm sure, if that uncle of yours is nowhere to be found."

Lauren left Molly to put away her new dresses. The foyer was deserted so she went into the library. She was scanning the vast shelves of books when a sound alerted her to someone's presence; she turned to find Rodney leaning against the door jamb.

"Seeking knowledge, dear niece?"

"No, just passing the time."

He moved into the room and thoughtfully rubbed his chin.

"You never did tell me where you stayed all those weeks in London."

"I don't think it's any of your concern." She tilted her head. "Why are you so interested, Uncle?" She used the same sarcastic intonation that he used when he called her "niece."

He watched her covertly. "I was just wondering. Why didn't you go back to France?"

"I had even less there than I did here."

He leaned one hip against the desk and she noticed how thin he was, reminding her of a wiry weasel.

"If you should decide to return to France, I will supply you with the funds necessary to keep you in comfort for a long time."

"I don't wish to leave."

He straightened angrily, dropping his veneer of friendliness. "I don't know what you hope to gain here, but let me tell you that I am the sole heir to my father's estate. I intend to foil any efforts you might make to find a place in that inheritance."

She gave a hard laugh. "Money is very important to you, isn't it?"

"It is important to everyone."

"I agree that it is important to have enough to live comfortably and eat well, but you have an obsession with money."

"You speak so glibly, having come to us a pauper."

"You speak so forcefully, knowing that *your* inheritance would have been my father's until a strange piece of evidence took it all away from him."

Rodney picked up a pen and began to twirl it between his fingers. "It *was* most unfortunate." He shrugged. "But then, traitors deserve what they get."

"Do they?" she demanded, pushing a book back into its place with a vicious motion. "Then I'm sure you'll get your comeuppance one of these days!" She turned her back to him.

Lauren felt her arm taken in a hard grip and she was spun around to face Rodney.

"Enough of these innuendos! You have no proof for your lies. Besides, it was a long time ago and nobody cares anymore."

"*I* care!" she rasped angrily. "My father went to his death caring!"

His grip tightened until he could feel the fragile bone beneath his fingers, but she did not wince and her eyes did not waver.

"My father will only be tormented by mentioning this again. If you know what's good for you, you will cease this endless prattle about your wronged father."

"What about wronged brother! You're his flesh and blood, but the thought of him being exiled forever didn't bring a tear to your eye. In fact, things worked out quite well for you, didn't they?"

"Enough!" he ordered tersely. "Keep your prying nose from things better left alone. Stephen's dead and gone. It will only hurt his memory to bring up the past."

"It will only hurt his memory if he is not cleared of all guilt!"

"What's going on in here?" They turned startled eyes toward the door where Lauren's grandfather stood.

"Nothing, Father," Rodney slowly released her arm. "We were just having a discussion."

"It appeared to be more like an argument."

"Never mind, Grandfather," Lauren found her voice with difficulty. "It wasn't important."

He looked as if he were about to disagree, then changed his mind. "When you're through here, I'd like to see you in the study, Lauren."

"Very well. I can come now," she said, brushing past Rodney.

Before he turned to follow her, the Earl gave Rodney a level look. "Don't try to harm her, Rodney."

His smile was cold. "She's concealing something from us and I mean to find out what it is."

"You had best look to your own behavior without worrying about everyone else!"

Rodney lifted one eyebrow. "And what is that supposed to mean, dear Father?"

"It means that I want you to leave Lauren alone!"

"I shall be a doting uncle, Father. Never fear." He gave a satisfied laugh as his father angrily left the room.

Lauren's back was to her grandfather when he entered the room. He stood for a moment, watching as she gazed into the empty grate of the fireplace.

"I want you to have something, Lauren," he said, breaking into her thoughts.

She turned and a gasp escaped her as he held out a lovely strand of diamonds.

"They're lovely! But I can't take them."

"Yes you can," he said with satisfaction, placing them into her hands. He closed her fingers around the necklace. "They were your grandmother's." His eyes grew wistful. "You remind me of her with your violet eyes and dark hair. You even have her fine nose."

"Is that her?" she asked, nodding toward a small portrait that rested on the table beside the sofa.

"Yes," he murmured, gazing longingly at the picture. "It was painted the year Stephen was born. For years we thought we would have no more children, and when we had virtually given up, Rodney was born. He took a toll on her since she was quite a bit older than she had been when she'd had Stephen. She died six months after Rodney was born."

"You must have missed her very much. It's not easy to raise children without a mother."

His face grew troubled. "I suppose I'm to blame for Rodney's selfishness, although he was not always so. I spoiled him much more than I did Stephen, because Rodney always knew it would be Stephen who inherited the estate."

The Earl poured himself a drink and held the sherry decanter for Lauren in invitation, but she refused.

"Well," he continued, "when Stephen returned from France with the lovely Angelica on his arm, I could see that Rodney was jealous. Ah, she was a beautiful woman, with so much life and vitality."

"I carry a different remembrance of her," Lauren whispered.

"Yes." The one word was filled with unspoken understanding. "Well, in any case, it was right after your father's marriage that Rodney joined the army and was sent to India."

"Why are you telling me all this, Grandfather?"

"Let me continue," he begged. "I think you'll see in a moment. Anyway, Rodney was boasting before he left about the fortune he would make in India. He planned to come back a rich nabob." He chuckled and set the glass down with a clink. "He did come back, but not with wealth. He returned a shadow of his former self."

"My father told me about the Black Hole and how my uncle survived it."

"Ah, but did he really survive it?"

Lauren looked confused. "I don't understand, Grandfather."

"Rodney has never forgotten the treachery of

his imprisonment in India—nor will he let anyone else around him forget."

"He does seem to be a very bitter man," Lauren said.

"Aye, bitter and greedy." His eyes lingered on Lauren's troubled expression. "I just wanted you to understand that any unpleasantness between you two is probably a result of his bitterness over the past. Don't let him upset you."

"I don't think he wants me here," Lauren said.

"But I want you here, and that's what matters." He saw her brow wrinkle and he grinned. "Your grandmother used to wear just such an expression. Go now, and rest. In a few days you will outshine all of England's society."

She moved forward hesitantly. "About this ball, Grandfather," she began.

"Yes? Are you getting excited, little one?"

"I don't think it's a good idea. You'll overtax yourself with all these arrangements."

"It's been good for me! My doctor says I have never been in better health. I owe it all to you, Lauren. You've given me a reason to enter the world again. You've given me a reason to live."

"Oh, Grandfather," she cried, throwing her arms around his neck to hug him. "There's so much about me that you don't know. There's so much I can't tell you."

"You're here with me now and that's all I need to know. You're Stephen's daughter and that makes you very precious to me."

He patted her on the shoulder as he eased her away. There were tears in her eyes, glistening like tiny diamonds. "Go to bed. Things will look better in the morning."

"Are you sure about this ball?" she asked one last time.

"You'll enjoy it," her grandfather said. "You've been looking far too pale and wan of late. Some music and dancing is just what you need."

"Very well." She gave him an impish grin. "But I really think you're the one who wants to dance."

His eyes twinkled mischievously. "You could be right."

He kissed her forehead as she bid him goodnight.

In secret we met:
In silence I grieve
That thy heart could forget,
Thy spirit deceive.
If I should meet thee
After long years,
How should I greet thee?—
With silence and tears.
                              —Lord Byron

Chapter Seven

The ballroom floor was polished to a satiny
sheen. Along with the mirrors lining the walls,
it reflected the myriad flashing colors of satins,
silks and velvets worn by the couples that danced
past. Chandeliers glowed with more than a
thousand flickering candles, creating a picture
of elegance. The whole room reflected the es-
sense of the society gathered.

Julian stood in the entrance and gave the
scene a passing glance. Felice watched as his
brows went together in a scowl and she noticed
the lassitude in his eyes.

Despite his expression, she thought her
brother looked magnificent tonight in his black
French frock and black silk breeches. His waistcoat was white embroidered silk and his dark
hair had a light dusting of powder since he refused to wear a wig. She could not understand

him of late; he seemed to have everything a man could desire, and yet he was tormented by a strange restlessness.

Fits of anger seemed to be the only outlet for whatever was troubling Julian. He had been an absolute beast to the servants, snapping their heads off at the slightest annoyance, until they learned to walk warily when he was around, which was not very often. He would lock himself in his study after dining, and spend the entire evening with only a bottle of brandy for comfort.

Felice found herself forbidden from entering his den of despair; whatever was bothering him was not something he intended to share with his sister. That, more than anything, hurt her. They had been so close, but now there seemed to be a gulf between them that she could not cross until he was willing to let her. He had not wanted to come tonight, but she had insisted, thinking he needed the laughter of a crowd instead of the solitary silence of his study.

"I hope you mind your manners tonight, Julian," she said with a smile. "From the look on your face I don't think you intend to have a good time."

"How could I not enjoy myself among this bacchant crowd?" he asked with a light hint of sarcasm.

She turned to Brendan for support. "I think we shall all have a wonderful time tonight, don't you?"

"With the most beautiful woman of them all on my arm, how else could it be?" he returned with a charming smile. "It seems that we are the last to arrive and the dancing has already begun. Shall we join them?"

Felice looked anxiously at Julian, but he waved away her concern. "Go on, little sister. I shall manage quite well on my own."

Julian watched them until they blended in with the other dancers and then he accepted a glass of champagne from a passing servant. He took a sip and let his eyes roam casually over the dance floor.

He only intended to stay for a short time. He was in no mood for laughter or gaiety. Very little pleased him lately. He considered leaving before anyone noticed his presence when, suddenly, he saw Lauren.

She was dressed in white like an angel, floating across the floor in another man's arms. Julian covered his eyes with his hand, sure he was hallucinating. When he looked again, she had disappeared into the brilliantly dressed throng of people like an elusive mist.

With shaking hands, he raised his glass and sipped the drink, trying to regain his composure. He had hungered so long for the sight of her that now he was imagining things, thinking he saw her where she could not possibly be.

He turned away, and moved on across the room toward the balcony. He needed some time alone without eyes prying into his secret thoughts. He needed some fresh air to clear his foggy brain.

Lauren was dancing with a nice young man, but she could only vaguely recall his name. It seemed as if her mind, as well as her heart, had deserted her. As they went through the paces of the dance, she had no idea how lovely and desirable she looked to Richard Attenby, the son of a marquis. The white silk gown sliped off her soft shoulders, competing in vain with the loveliness of her skin. The light from the chandeliers caught the gleam in her dark hair, and the pearls stood out in perfect splendor like stars on a dark night. Richard had never seen anyone so beautiful, and he had seen many beautiful women in his time.

Lauren smiled and moved correctly. No one knew how callow she found all the young men when all she could remember were two golden eyes molten with passion. She laughed happily at Richard in an effort to forget, and was unaware of how she charmed him without even trying.

When the music ended, he was loath to let her go. He touched her arm and she looked inquiringly at him.

"It's warm in here," he said. "Perhaps you would like to go outside for a little fresh air."

She nodded her agreement and allowed him to lead her through the double doors. She leaned over the balustrade to view the scene below. She turned with a smile, but it died on her lips when she saw the hunger in Richard's eyes. Lauren put out a hand in denial, but he took her arm, pulling her closer.

"You are so lovely, Lauren," he groaned.

He saw the rejection in her eyes and stepped back. "You're right." There was regret in his tone. "I'm glad your prudence overcame my passion. But I dare to hope that I may soon convince you that I hold you in the highest regard."

"I will hold you in high regard if you would get me something to drink," she teased, hoping to lighten the moment.

He took the hint and bowed. "Anything you wish if it will redeem me in your eyes."

Once she was alone, she gave a deep sigh of relief. A faint sound came from the darkness and she turned, barely suppressing a scream as a man detached himself from the shadows, stepping into the light spilling from the outside sconces.

There was no mistaking that lean face or the perfection of his attire.

"You're surprised to see me?" he queried sardonically. "No more than I am at seeing you."

"W-what are you doing here?" she gasped. Her hand went to her throat where a pulse jerked madly.

"I could ask the same of you." One eyebrow lifted. "It didn't take you long to find someone to take my place, did it?"

She was baffled for a moment, but then it dawned on her that he assumed her to be Richard's mistress. "Go away, Julian," she said coldly. "We have nothing to say to one another."

"We have a great deal to discuss. You left rather precipitantly..."

"I thought my actions voiced my decision. Words were not necessary."

"Ah!" he grinned. "But you know what a persistent fellow I am." His gaze roamed over the enticing swell of breast above the laced décolletage of her gown, and he caught his breath. "I had forgotten how lovely you are. I thought you entrancing when you were no more than an urchin, but now you tease my senses with the woman you have become."

"How did you find me?" she asked, voicing the question that was nagging her.

"You overestimate your charms if you think I've been looking high and low for you," he lied. "I happened to see you when I was dancing, and thought I'd pursue our brief but memorable acquaintance."

"Go away and leave me alone, Julian," she begged. "There are things you don't understand, things that don't concern you."

"You concern me!"

"Why me? Why must you torment me when you say there are others more willing?"

"You are my wife," he stated simply.

She gave a hard laugh. "Oh no, Julian. Let's not make that an issue. I was never your wife— merely a paid companion. The vows meant nothing to you and even less to me." She had to convince him to leave and never bother her again.

He shrugged, trying to hide the fact that her words stung. "I've missed you. Haven't you missed me?"

"Am I really missed, Julian? What of your other women? Can't they satisfy your whims?" Her voice was cold.

"You are a tantalizing memory. I constantly compare you to other women and that is something I don't like. I want you, and I mean to have you until I have purged myself of your spell!"

She stepped back at the flare of anger in his eyes, but she quickly regained control. "You only want me because your male ego was wounded when I left you! Ha! Quite an experience for the high and mighty Lord Keaton. You're always the one to discard lovers and now you don't like the feeling when it happens to you!"

"My ego is not so easily dented. In fact your elusiveness only heightens my desire."

"Oh!" she stormed. "I'm not some hare to be chased through the woods until caught!"

He moved swiftly, taking her in his arms. "But capture is sweet. Don't you remember the way your passion joined with mine and how the world ceased to exist?" Julian's voice was soft and seductive, playing wildly on her nerves. She could smell the clean warmth of him, and wanted to reach up and smooth a curl away from his forehead, but resisted the temptation, looking away in restless confusion. When his lips touched her neck it was like a jolt of lightning, igniting all the passion that had lain dormant the last few weeks.

Lauren felt feverish and wondered at how easily he led her astray from all her good intentions. She wanted to push him away, to do something to show him she did not want him, but instead she found her head turning and her lips lifted to his.

When he claimed her mouth, it was as if time had rolled back and they were alone again in their bedroom, laughing and loving the afternoon away. She was floating on a tide of feeling that made her arch against him until she could feel her legs snugly next to his. She wanted to be closer, much closer. Heat beat through her body, making her ache with desire.

"Did you really think you could escape me so easily?" he murmured huskily into her ear.

The words brought her back to the present and she angrily pushed him away, blushing to her roots as she realized how easily he had manipulated her.

Before she had been burningly alive, but now she felt as cold as ice, ashamed of the way she had responded. She vowed it would never happen again.

"Lord Richard will return in a moment and I don't want him to find you here."

Julian rested one hip negligently against the banister. "A callow youth like that will bore you in a week." His voice was deep and mocking.

"Then he will entertain me longer than you, for you bore me in less than a minute."

He laughed in genuine amusement. "What a quick little tongue you have, Lauren."

"Thank you." She started past him, but he moved to block her exit.

"Why are you running away?" he taunted.

"You flatter yourself, Lord Keaton. I'm not afraid of you."

"So formal!" he mocked. "Perhaps I should remind you of the intimacy of our relationship when you quite often moaned 'Julian' in the sweetest tones."

"Go away!" she said through gritted teeth. She stamped her foot as she looked up at him. "That's the past and I wish it dead and buried!"

His hand cupped her cheek and one finger lazily traced her angry lips. "But the past is not dead, my dear, and thus it cannot be buried. It lives in your eyes and the way you respond to my touch."

"Damn you, Julian! Leave me alone!" She tore away from him, stalking into the ballroom where the light and laughter could dispell the images Julian had conjured up in her mind.

Lauren saw Lord Richard talking to her grandfather, so she made her way across the crowded room to his side.

"Ah, there you are my dear," he smiled. "Richard was just telling me that he was taking you something to drink!" He frowned at the flush on her cheeks and the wildness in her eyes. "Is something wrong, my dear?" he asked in a concerned voice.

She shook her head, forcing a light laugh. "Of course not! I'm having a wonderful time, Grandfather. I must thank you for this ball."

The worried creases left his face as he patted her arm. "It gives me pleasure to give you pleasure."

The music started and Richard requested the honor of another dance. Lauren was grateful for something to do and she accepted.

She was unaware of Richard talking until he frowned.

"Am I boring you?" he asked in a petulant tone.

Lauren started at his words, remembering that Julian had predicted that very thing. As if the thought of him held some sort of magic power, her eyes flew to the far side of the room and she saw him leaning against the wall. Her eyes widened, dilating in fear as she realized how handsome he was. He had quite spoiled her taste for any other man.

She jumped guiltily as a finger traced the lines on her forehead. She looked at Lord Richard, having forgotten for the moment that he was there.

"Are you ill?" She shook her head. "No? Then what's wrong?"

Lauren laughed shakily, forcing her gaze away from Julian. "Nothing is wrong. For a moment I thought I saw a ghost from my past."

He snorted humorously. "You're too young and innocent to have a past."

Her eyes were wide and violet when she looked at him. "Everyone has a past. Some more than others," she declared softly. "You really know very little about me." Unwittingly tears welled up in her beautiful eyes and her lips began to tremble.

"Lauren," he said with concern in his voice, and she noticed the way her fingers trembled as he took them in his hand. He pulled her away from the dancers and over to a sofa against the wall. When she was seated, he sat next to her, retaining his hold on her hand.

"Something is the matter, isn't it? You can tell me, for already I am devoted to you for life."

Finding comfort in his kind eyes, she gave him a gentle smile. She was about to say something when a shadow fell across them. Julian stood before them like some avenging god with anger in every line of his body and his eyes glowing fiercely. Then suddenly Lauren's grandfather appeared, beaming a look of pride on her.

"Ah, darling. The Duke of Dornay has requested a dance with you. He said that my granddaughter is the loveliest woman here tonight."

Julian had gone strangely quiet and Lauren found it too painful to look at him. She rose to her feet, extending her hand to her grandfather. "It would be my pleasure," she murmured before she walked away, leaving Julian to brood.

"Quite a beauty," Richard said to Julian. "And being the Earl's only grandchild means that she's probably worth a small fortune."

Julian gave the younger man a glare of distaste before he walked away, and Lord Richard felt he had been suitably snubbed.

Lauren spent the next few hours trying to avoid Julian. She was reasonably successful, not realizing that Julian was following the same tactic, waiting to choose the right moment. It was when Lauren was standing by the refreshment table that Julian approached. She jumped nervously when he took her arm between his hard fingers.

"This dance is mine," he insisted, and Lauren could not dispute his words without causing a scene, for several curious glances were thrown their way.

She went into his arms, but they maintained a stony silence. Felice was standing across the room with Brendan, and noticed the set expression on Julian's face as well as the mutinous one on the face of his partner.

Brendan glanced around. "I haven't seen Julian in a while, have you, Felice?" He was unprepared for the shortness of her tone.

"He's dancing."

"Dancing?!" He scanned the dancers. "Julian rarely dances."

"I know, and he's obviously said something to upset his partner. I knew he wouldn't behave himself tonight! He's been in a foul mood for weeks!" She paused, watching with narrowed eyes. "I wonder who she is," she murmured. "She's very attractive."

Brendan looked down at his wife and grinned. "Attractive isn't she? We must have missed her introduction since we were late in arriving. I suspect that's the Earl's granddaughter."

Felice lightly rapped his knuckles with her fan. "I thought she might catch your attention."

Brendan finally saw Julian and a laugh escaped him. "What's the matter with the fellow? He's dancing with the most presentable woman here—besides you, my dear," he hastily amended at her frown. "And he's holding her like he's dancing with a broom."

"Yes, and his expression is quite fierce. What can the problem be?"

"I don't know." Brendan watched thoughtfully as the couple disappeared through a doorway. "But I think Julian is planning a discreet tête-à-tête by the way he just successfully danced her out of the ballroom."

"Oh! How dare he create a scene here!" Felice fumed.

"I don't think he's planning on creating it here. That's why he just went into the library."

Felice's startled eyes met Brendan's amused ones. "What can he be thinking? He'll ruin her reputation for sure, and then what will I do? I can't disown him! He's the only brother I have."

She frowned angrily. "He's obviously lost all sense." She thought for a moment, then said, "I'm going in there." She started for the door, but Brendan detained her.

"To what purpose?" he asked.

"What purpose?! Why to keep Julian from ruining that poor girl!"

"She looked more than capable of looking after herself. Leave them alone for a few moments. I don't think anyone else saw them leave."

"I'll give them until I've had a glass of punch, but that's all!" Felice promised, and Brendan raised his eyes heavenward.

Lauren shivered as Julian closed the door, shutting them off from the noise of the ball. She turned away, wrapping her arms protectively around her waist. Her senses were so heightened that she could smell the leather bindings on the books, and she distinctly heard the ticking of the clock in the corner of the room.

Lauren was more afraid of herself than of Julian; she had longed so to be with him that the incident with Pamela no longer seemed important. Only being with Julian mattered.

"Quite a change from a wharf waif to the granddaughter of an Earl."

She faced him, lifting her chin defensively.

"Why were you roaming the wharf that night like some stray cat?" he demanded. "And how did you explain your brief sojourn with me?"

"My grandfather knows nothing about you. I thought it would be best."

"Best for whom? You or me?"

"Both of us. It was a mistake to stay with you,

but I'm thankful for your help when I needed it."

"I don't want your damned thanks! I want to know why you lied to me."

She looked away. "I-I didn't exactly lie. I wasn't sure if my grandfather would accept my return or not."

"And why wouldn't he accept his grand-daughter?"

Lauren hung her head. She had not wanted Julian to know of her father's disgrace for fear he would judge her father as everyone else had. She could not bear it if he turned away in disgust without giving her father the benefit of the doubt.

"My father left England branded a traitor, and my Grandfather disowned us."

"And was your father a traitor?" he asked, and she smiled at him for asking.

"No. The evidence was heavily against him, but he swore his innocence to us long after he had any need to do so."

"Does your grandfather know we're married?" he asked in a hard tone.

"No. I'll never tell him unless you want me to. I gave my word that no one would know and I'll keep it." She looked restlessly away from the golden eyes. "We should go back to the ball-room. People will talk if they discover us gone."

"I have never let the speculations of gossips concern me."

"I don't wish to hurt my grandfather. He's been very kind to me."

"And what of me, Lauren?" he asked softly. "You hurt me when you left without a word."

Her eyes locked with his and her breath was short. She ached to touch him, finding the lean planes of his face so dear and familiar. More than anything she wanted to be able to call him hers without fear of losing him. She swallowed a lump in her throat. "It hurt me to leave."

Julian's eyes softened as they rested on her upturned face, and one finger came out and touched the hollow in her throat where her pulse was frantically throbbing. Her violet eyes grew misty and then her lashes dropped as his fingers traced lower until they reached the creamy mound of one breast. His strong hand flattened and cupped her softness, causing her to moan as his hand slipped inside her bodice and captured the hard peak.

She knew she should feel affronted, but she didn't. Lauren wanted him to touch her and she reveled in his possessive grasp. Julian's free arm came up and encircled her, bringing her closer before his lips touched her eyelids. She raised her mouth in silent supplication and with a soft oath his mouth came down, crushing the moist sweetness of her lips. His tongue darted in, meeting hers in a hungry battle.

Julian hated the way he seemed to need her— the way his body responded to hers. "You wanton witch," he murmured against her mouth, his fingers tightening painfully on her breast, making her cry out and pull away from him.

"You hurt me!" she breathed in distress.

"I wanted to hurt you all those nights you were gone and I didn't know where to find you."

"I thought you'd be glad to see the back of

me. You never wanted to be married. I was more mistress than wife."

"You're right. I didn't want a wife and I still don't want one."

"Was that why you went to Pamela?" she asked bitterly, saying the one thing that still had the power to hurt him.

"You judged me too hastily."

Her mind flew back to the scene in the park and she had to admit that she had been ready to find Julian guilty without having heard a word in his defense. She had acted like all those people who had condemned her father.

As she met his cold stare, she saw no tenderness or passion, only an inscrutable expression. She was unaware of how her deep, languorous, violet eyes made him want to take her in his arms again. Only his anger seemed apparent; his hands clenched into fists at his sides. Lauren wanted to go into his arms, but this remote stranger did not appear touchable. When she spoke there was a slight tremor in her voice.

"What do you want of me?"

"What do you want of me?" he demanded.

They watched each other in wary silence. She did not want to leave him and he did not want to lose her, but everything seemed to be pulling them apart.

On an impulse she decided to speak the truth. "I just want you," she said huskily.

"Lauren," he murmured, and she sighed heavily as he reached out, gathering her into his arms. She protested weakly, knowing that they could be discovered, but then his lips silenced her and all she could do was taste him, feel him, drown in the intoxicating nearness of his warm body. Her arms encircled his neck and she felt the heat of his smooth skin before her hand slid slowly up through the thick darkness of his hair. It was crisp beneath her fingers and she moaned deep in her throat, pressing her lower body intimately against his. She pushed the paniers of her dress back until she could feel his arousal, firm and demanding through her thin gown. Suddenly, she was overcome by a hunger so intense that she wanted to strip off his clothes so she could feel the rasp of his hair against her swollen breasts. She wanted to feel him move within her, to show her more effectively than any words that this was no dream, but reality—sweet, sweet reality.

Julian thrust his hands ruthlessly through her hair, dislodging her pins, and his mouth grew hungry with desperation. Her mouth was swollen and tender, but the pain was welcome as he brought her to dizzying heights. Soon Lauren forgot they were surrounded by hundreds of guests that might find them at any moment. She forgot that Julian wanted no wife. She forgot everything but the sheer bliss of being in her lover's arms once again.

A slight cough and "Ahem!" effectively cooled their ardor. Julian reluctantly released her, taking several deep breaths before he turned to the intruder.

Lauren wanted the room to fall in around her and cover her shame at being found out. She turned her back, unable to face the visitor.

"What do you want, Felice?" There was an

edge of irritation in his voice as he faced his sister.

Felice cast a speculative eye at Lauren, watching as the girl nervously tried to restore some order to her tumbled curls.

"Are you quite out of your mind?!" she demanded.

He shrugged negligently. "So it would seem."

Felice gasped at his unconcern. "You can seduce all the whores in London for all I care," she stormed. "But leave innocent girls alone!"

"You don't know what you're talking about, Felice." His voice was bored. "Go back to the ball and leave me alone."

"Already the tongues are probably curling with malicious amusement. Don't you care?"

"Not particularly. They're always intent on ruining someone's reputation so why shouldn't it be mine?"

"And what of this girl?" She threw her hand out at Lauren. "Don't you care about her?"

"No one saw us come in here, Felice."

"I saw you!"

"True, but then you have always had the maternal eye trained on me in case I should err."

"E-excuse me," Lauren stammered. "I must go."

"Stay, Lauren!" Julian ordered, but she was already out the door without a glance at Felice.

Julian heaved a sigh of disappointment and crossed his arms across his chest. "Don't ever treat me like a recalcitrant schoolboy again, Felice," he said in a tone so cold that she took a step back.

"B-but how could you? I know you've been

different the last few weeks, but I never thought you would take a well-born girl and seduce her at such a gathering of society. Julian, you're acting like a fool!"

"So I believe, but I can't seem to help it," he said quietly.

Felice stumbled back and her eyes widened in shock. "W-what did you say?"

"I said I was a fool. Didn't you want me to agree with you?"

"B-but, but—I don't understand," she wailed, torn between being outraged and distressed.

He nodded. "True. You don't understand— yet. Say nothing of this to anyone. I'll explain everything in due time."

"Leave her alone, Julian," Felice said stubbornly. "She's no match for you."

He shook his head. "No? Don't let her fragile air confuse you. She can take care of herself."

Felice opened her mouth to question him further but he held up a hand. "Later, Felice." He walked past her, holding open the door so she could pass through it, a confused expression on her face.

Outside, they quickly parted company and Felice eagerly made her way to her husband's side.

Brendan lifted one eyebrow at his wife's flushed face. "Are you feeling ill?"

"I don't know what I'm feeling," she said mysteriously. Brendan looked perplexed. "I want to tell you everything, but I think it should wait until we're alone. I don't want anyone to overhear me."

He was intrigued. "Does it have anything to do with Julian and that girl?"

"Yes," she affirmed. "Something's going on. I don't know everything yet, but I will soon." All was not right, that much was sure. She shook the feeling away and decided to enjoy herself.

Julian searched the ballroom for Lauren, but could not find her. He finally approached her grandfather and asked where she had gone.

"Oh, I think she had to tidy herself. You know how these young girls want to look lovely at their balls."

"She is quite lovely, my lord!" Julian said, sipping his champagne.

"Yes," the Earl beamed. "I thought I would never see her again after her father left England. I was so surprised to find her on my step one night. She had come from France."

Not quite from France, Julian thought, but he said only, "It was a tragedy about her father."

"Yes." The Earl shook his head. "I suppose you heard the story? It was bandied about enough in the early days."

"No. I haven't heard it, but I would like to."

The Earl saw no harm in telling Julian because the affair was common knowledge among his peers. He told Julian everything, even his own doubts about Stephen's guilt.

"Of course," he finished, "there was no one else to blame."

"I believe there was a brother," Julian interjected, and the Earl looked uncomfortable.

"Rodney had served faithfully in India. He was above suspicion as far as everyone was concerned."

"Yes," Julian murmured, excusing himself as he saw Lauren enter the room.

She was claimed by a young man before he could reach her, and he thought he saw relief in her eyes. He mingled with the other guests, but his eyes never lost sight of his quarry.

Lauren was very careful this time, refusing to be alone so as to prevent Julian from coming to speak intimately to her. Her grandfather had suffered enough scandal in the past and she didn't want to do anything to bring pain to him again. Julian, however, was relentless and finally cornered her, requesting a dance in the presence of her grandfather, who eagerly gave his consent.

Again they danced in silence, Lauren holding herself stiffly away from him as they went through the movements of the dance. It was almost over before Julian said anything, and then his words shocked her.

"Meet me tomorrow."

Her eyes flashed. "Certainly not!"

"Are you afraid?" he taunted.

"No, it's just that I know what a devil you are!"

"And it is a devil you know very well—the devil of desire!"

She looked away from the fire in his eyes.

"Would you have me hurt my grandfather?"

"What he doesn't know will not hurt him. No one need know."

She lifted a cold shoulder. "I don't trust you."

Julian laughed. "I should hope not!"

A smile tugged helplessly at her lips, but she refused to give in to his demand.

"Come, Lauren," he said with honeyed sweetness. "What harm will it do to meet me?"

"No!"

His lips tightened. "Has respectability taken away all your fire?"

"I have merely come to my senses as far as you are concerned! You poison all my good intentions and turn me into a wanton! I want nothing to do with you!"

His arm tightened around her waist. "You liked being in my arms once!"

"If you were a gentleman, you wouldn't bring up so delicate a subject to a lady."

He laughed shortly. "I never said I was a gentleman, and I much prefer your not being a lady. At least then you were warm and inviting."

She dropped her eyes. "Leave me alone, Julian. It's over." When the dance was finished, she pushed away from him and walked to her grandfather.

Julian wanted to go after her but knew that it was not the right time.

"It is far from over, Lauren," he murmured under his breath.

Now I know what it is to have strove
with the torture of doubt and desire.
—William Shenstone

Chapter Eight

Lauren urged her horse forward, enjoying the
peace and quiet of her solitude. For three days
now she had remained indoors to avoid any encounter with Julian, and although she had
physically escaped him, his hold on her mind
seemed stronger than ever. She dreamed of him
every night, waking in a cold sweat as she imagined his hands on her, sharing a shuddering
ecstasy. Always, she woke with an unfulfilled
yearning inside, knowing deep down that she
was incomplete without him.

She had planned a leisurely ride, but her tur-
bulent thoughts soon made her push her horse
to a wild gallop across the grassy slopes. She
kept riding until a fine perspiration formed on
her brow and her heavy blue velvet habit grew
warm. When she saw a small lake enclosed by
tall oaks and smaller shrubs she decided to rest.

Lauren dismounted and stretched lazily. She
tethered her horse to a bush before she sat beneath a shady tree and rested her head against
its broad, gnarled trunk.

The chirp of birds and rustle of leaves on the

low-hanging branches eased her nerves and she soon drifted into a light sleep. How long she remained thus, she did not know, but when she awoke, she felt hot and sticky. Glancing idly at the lake, she though how inviting it looked.

The area was secluded enough and the trees and shrubs protected her from prying eyes. How lovely it would be to cool off in the water, she thought. She sent another glance around and then began to unbutton her jacket. Her skirt and chemise were next, and soon she was submerged in the cool clear water. As she lazily floated around she felt a moment's misgiving about the impulsiveness of her behavior, but consoled herself with the fact that this was private property and it was unlikely she would be disturbed.

Back and forth across the pond she went, slicing through the water as it cooled her warm body. The leaves overhead swayed gently in the breeze and off in the distance she could hear the faint barking of a dog. She turned and floated on her back, closing her eyes as the peace and serenity of the place washed over her, forgetting everything but the gentle lap of the water against her and the warmth of the sun as it touched her face.

A smile curved her lips as she wondered what Julian would think if he should happen upon her. She allowed herself several delicious daydreams and lost herself in the fantasy.

"What the hell do you think you're doing!"

The angry voice shattered her mood and she slipped beneath the surface in surprise, only to rise spluttering and choking on swallowed water.

Julian, astride his horse, was leaning forward with his hands crossed on the reins. He watched her with narrowed golden eyes and the frown on his face made her realize that she was not dreaming this encounter.

Her wet hair had fallen across her face and she pushed it back, blinking the water out of her eyes. Julian looked so proud and arrogant sitting there in judgment of her that she felt her temper rise and forgot her embarrassment. Moments ago she had wanted to see him, but now he was just an irritant to an otherwise enjoyable day.

"Go away and leave me alone," she called, treading water.

"Get out of there right now!" he ordered imperiously.

"I'm not some servant to be ordered about."

"I'm well aware of that fact," he snapped back.

"Then you'll understand when I don't jump at your every command."

"Stop acting like a child. Get out and get dressed."

"Make me!" She knew she was indeed being childish but something made her want to shatter his control of the situation.

He sighed impatiently. "I'm not in the mood for games."

"How did you know where to find me?"

"I've been watching the house for days. When you didn't appear I decided to visit. The servant told me you had taken the horse out."

"You've been watching the house?" she asked innocently. "Whatever for?"

"I've been waiting for the mouse to come out of its hole."

"So the mean old cat has been made grouchy by his elusive prey?" she taunted.

"I don't have time to bandy words with you. Get out. Now!" he demanded, swinging out of the saddle in one lithe movement.

"I don't think so. It's rather pleasant in the water." A mischievous smile curled her lips. "You should join me."

"Very well," He inclined his head sardonically and then his fingers went to the buttons on his riding coat. He deftly removed the garment and had begun to unfasten his waistcoat when she found her voice.

"What are you doing?" she asked tremulously.

He did not answer, but now his hands were at the fastening of his breeches and the smile he gave her sent shivers of anticipation down her spine.

She felt frozen and unable to move as she watched Julian shed the last vestiges of civilization and then stand before her as naked and proud as a savage. He walked slowly into the water until it was deep enough to cover him, and with sure strong strokes he started toward her.

Lauren came to her senses and forced her paralyzed limbs into action, but she was too slow and he caught her hair as it floated out behind her like dark seaweed.

"Let me go!" she cried, trying to swim away from him.

"Isn't the cat allowed to toy with the mouse before he closes in for the kill?"

She turned to face him and her eyes widened.

His derisive smile slipped from his face to be
replaced by something much more dangerous.

"Come here," he murmured, gently pulling
her hair until she floated before him.

As her breasts touched his chest, their tender
peaks swelled and hardened, making her breathe
rapidly as the shock echoed through her slender
frame. Her hands came up to grasp his muscular
shoulders as she treaded water. His dark hair was
curling in damp ringlets on his forehead, giving
him the look of a gypsy. Golden eyes skimmed
across her face before they dipped to where the
water lapped tantalizingly around her breasts.

She felt desire curl in her stomach and to ease
its hold on her, she kicked him, twisting away
and swimming out of reach. They warily watched
each other and then Julian moved forward, but
Lauren cupped her hand and splashed water in
his face. Julian shook his head, the droplets
showering her like a light mist, and then suddenly he had her, drawing her to him until she
could feel the hunger in his body.

As Julian molded his hands around her soft
flesh, he knew that his craving for her had not
lessened. He was addicted to her and to live
without her was agony. She had captured his
passion from their first night together, and then
she had invaded his mind, driving him insane
with need. Now, looking at her floating so
temptingly before him, he felt her pull on his
heartstrings, luring him ever closer to that elusive emotion of love. The thought made him
angry, for he did not want to love Lauren; he
did not want to offer himself on that altar of

agony. Suddenly he stiffened and pushed her away, then turned to swim to the shore.

Lauren remained in the water and wondered what was wrong with Julian. One minute he had wanted her and the next he had rejected her. When he reached for his breeches to put them on, Lauren left the water. She wanted him so much, and she might never again have this opportunity to be with him so intimately. If she was to spend the rest of her days without Julian, then she must have this moment.

When her fingers touched his back he jerked, but she was not deterred. Her hands lightly traced the ridge of muscles on his back and then moved to stroke his neck. Her fingers slid up into the darkness of his hair. She placed her lips on his shoulder and let her tongue move down his spine. He groaned and turned, intending to push her away, but the sight of her standing in front of him with her wet dark hair clinging to her breasts stopped him. Moisture was beading her face and her eyes were alight with a hunger he easily recognized.

His needs grew stronger and stronger as he felt the blood rushing to his head. She placed her fingertips on his chest and pushed him back until they were kneeling on the ground. When she bent toward him, his mouth was eagerly awaiting the touch of her pale lips. He did not touch her, letting her make all the advances.

He lay back and she followed, placing her slim limbs against him. She lifted her head and looked into his eyes, telling him without words that she wanted him. Her hand lightly traced his face, lingering over his lips, before she placed one finger in the cleft of his chin.

Julian shifted restlessly beneath her gentle caress and she smiled softly, knowing that his hunger was building. She lifted his hand and kissed each finger while she held his golden gaze with her violet eyes. In turn, he placed his lips in the hollow of her throat where her pulse pounded, her head falling back with a whimper. Lauren released his hand and it cupped her breast, his skin dark against her paleness.

She could feel every muscle in his legs as they entwined with hers, and his hot lips slid down the throbbing cord in her neck to follow the taut line between her breasts. It seemed as if all her senses were heightened. She could even smell the sweet scent of grass beneath them. Her skin was hot and then cold as she shivered against him with a need as old as time.

She had started out as the seducer, but now they became as one, and each responded instinctively to the other's needs. Her hands spread across his chest and tangled in the dark curly hair, then moved lower, brushing against his manhood. That small, gentle caress made him groan with desire and Lauren reveled in her power over him. She wanted to make him remember this day for fear it would be their last.

Wordlessly she opened to him and they joined smoothly, like a sword being sheathed in a silken scabbard. His cries mingled with hers as wave after wave of ecstasy coursed through their bodies. Time was suspended in the glade; they were in perfect harmony.

Finally Julian rolled over, capturing her beneath him. He gazed down into her rapt face, still in the thrall of passion, and he marveled at her sensual beauty. There was no pretending in her response. She was as totally aware of him as he was of her. Their lovemaking was as natural as night following day and spring coming after winter.

His mind told him to push her away now that his carnal appetite had been served. He should not let her think that she meant anything more to him, but something deep within him made him draw her closer. He rested his chin on her head and breathed deeply the sweet fragrance of her. He could also smell the honeysuckle on the bush behind them, and without thought he reached up and plucked a branch to tickle her nose lightly.

With her he found a gentleness in his nature that he mistrusted. Barriers long erected were being threatened by this mere wisp of a woman. Julian did not understand himself in this mood of lightness and love.

He moved away, twirling the honeysuckle in his hand as he looked out over the countryside. She stirred and he turned, watching as she lifted her dark cloud of hair from her shoulders and let it fall about her like a silky cloak. Lauren sat up, bending one slim leg as she rested her elbow on her knee.

She gave him a wicked smile. "I've never made love outside before." Her voice was deep and her eyes slanted in an alluringly mysterious way. "I found it most"—she paused to stretch out a hand and rub it up and down his calf—"stimulating."

Already he felt the fire lick his insides and realized that he would never get enough of Lauren. She did not sate him as other women did. He was always eager to taste and taste again of her tempting body. Every caress was but a need for more. Every smile she bestowed upon him haunted him with its sweetness until he wished to see her smile more often. And he wanted to be the one to make her smile. With Lauren there was always the need for a tomorrow. Today was never quite enough.

"Come," she whispered, holding out her arms to him, and he gladly gave himself into her web of delight.

His eyes roamed hungrily over her and she grinned at his look. "You remind me of a wolf about to devour its dinner," she teased.

"Ah, but this is no meager fare placed before me. This is the very sustenance of life."

"Then partake of this sustenance, my lord, for it seems the more you take the more I have to give."

The shadows lengthened and the two lovers were aware that their tryst would soon end. Lauren clung desperately to Julian and wanted to beg him for a commitment, but she knew she could never force him. If he did not want a wife, then she did not want a husband, for to have him without his heart would bring only sadness.

They dressed in silence and each wanted to say something but could find no words. As Lauren mounted her horse, Julian held the reins and looked up at her with a tender expression.

"Will you meet me again?" he asked.

Her eyes filled with tears and her voice was

a painful knot in her throat. She could only shake her head.

"Please, Lauren," he murmured, grasping her booted foot in one hand.

She quickly whirled the horse and he lost his hold on her. As she rode away, he had the strangest feeling that he had let go of her in a way he did not understand.

He finally mounted his horse and left the small glen of happiness. Once on the road, he saw Rodney riding toward him and he stopped.

"Lord Keaton! Have you seen my niece?" Rodney asked. "Father has become anxious about her since she has been gone so long." His keen eyes went over Lord Keaton's less than immaculate linen before his gaze swept the countryside. He saw Lauren disappear over a hill and he turned back to Julian. "Has she been with you?" he asked suspiciously.

"Why don't you ask her?" Julian returned coldly, not liking the speculative gleam in Rodney's eyes. Without another word he rode off and left Rodney smiling at his retreating figure.

"I think my dear niece knows Lord Keaton better than a young lady should," he mused aloud. "I'll have to get Lynell to dig a little deeper and find out about her stay in London." A cruel smile curled his lips. "Yes, indeed," he continued. "I think my little niece is hiding something and that just isn't allowed between dear relatives."

Lauren reached the stable and dismounted, throwing the reins to a boy standing nearby. She hurried across the lawn to the house and hoped no one would see her. She knew she looked a mess with her hair falling about her shoulders and her riding habit stained with dirt and grass. She entered through the front door and heard her grandfather talking to a servant, so she quickly scurried up the stairs and into her room.

"Where have you been!?" Molly demanded, coming out of the bedroom with a dress over her arm.

She stopped at the sight of Lauren and her mouth formed an O. "Did you fall off your horse? Are you hurt? Let me see if there are any bruises." Molly's words were quick and worried, but Lauren brushed aside her concern.

"There's nothing wrong with me. My horse didn't throw me so stop fussing."

Lauren walked to the chaise longue and fell onto it. She pulled off her boots and dropped them languidly to the floor.

"Then how come you look like you do?" Molly insisted.

A smile formed on Lauren's lips and her eyes lightened. "I saw Julian."

Molly placed her hands on her hips. "I thought you were finished with that rascal. Didn't you tell me just yesterday that you never wanted to see his lordship again?"

Lauren's eyes misted over and she rested her head on a pillow, covering her eyes with her forearm. "He followed me when I went riding. I couldn't help meeting him."

Molly's mouth twisted in disdain. "And couldn't you help not keeping your clothes on your back?"

Lauren sat up with a jerk and glowered at

Molly. "And who said anything happened?" she demanded.

Molly threw the dress over a chair. "The look on your face and the state of your clothes told me all I needed to know."

Lauren blushed, knowing that Molly missed very little. "I can't seem to help myself when I'm around him!" Lauren moaned. "This desire eats at me like poison until I think I'll go mad!"

"You speak of desire. Are you sure it isn't love?" Molly asked shrewdly.

Lauren jumped to her feet. "No! I refuse to love him. He doesn't love me. He won't admit to the world that I'm his wife, so I'll not admit that he's my husband."

"It would be a simple thing to go downstairs and tell your grandfather the truth. He'll make Lord Keaton accept his responsibility to you once he knows the story."

Lauren sat down as if drained of energy. "I would never force Julian to accept me. I knew what I was doing when I agreed to his scheme and I'll honor the bargain. Besides, I want him to want me as his wife. If it was forced on him it would be no victory and he'd hate me for it."

"That sounds like love to me. You're thinking of him over yourself."

Lauren buried her face in her hands and began to cry. "I can't love him, Molly. He'll destroy me if I let myself love him. I don't think he has a heart."

Molly sat down beside Lauren and gently stroked her bent head. "Ah, love, we can't always rule our heart with our head."

* * *

Lauren took another bite of the delicious mutton and thought that the food tasted especially good after her ride in the afternoon. She was sipping her wine when Rodney gave her a twisted smile.

"I met Lord Keaton when I went looking for you this afternoon. I wondered if you happened to meet him."

Lauren almost choked on the ruby liquid, but her gaze was innocent when she met his calculating eyes.

"Why should you think I met him?" she parried.

Rodney shrugged as he toyed with his silverware. He noticed that his father looked interested so he pursued the matter.

"I saw you riding one way and he was riding the other. I just assumed you had been together."

The Earl glowered at Rodney. "Lauren has better sense than to dally with a man when she's unescorted." His eyes were indulgent when they rested on Lauren. "I wouldn't blame Lord Keaton if he was to take a fancy to you, my dear. You're very lovely. But I think it would be wise to tell you that he is not a suitable companion for you. His reputation with women is notorious and he has vowed not to marry. Any interest he should show in you would not be of an honorable kind."

Lauren dropped her head. What would he think of her if he learned that she had bedded the fellow on her first evening in London? What kind of a creature would he think her to be? How simple the truth could be and yet how damning. He thought of her as a child, and would find it hard to distinguish that child from the woman she had become in Julian's arms.

Rodney noted the blush on her cheeks and felt like rubbing his hands together in satisfaction. Something was going on between Lauren and Lord Keaton, and he was determined to know what it was.

"Father speaks in your interest when he tells you that Lord Keaton has no respect for womankind. He discards his mistresses at an unnatural rate."

"I'm so glad you're concerned about me," Lauren replied tartly.

"It's only right that your uncle should care for you, Lauren," the Earl added. "We want only the best for you."

"I thank you, Grandfather." The food which had looked so appealing now held little interest for her. "If you will excuse me, I think I'll retire now. The ride this afternoon made me weary."

"Of course," the men replied in unison, but where there was genuine affection on her grandfather's face, she noticed that Rodney's was mocking.

When she was gone Rodney threw his napkin to the table and pushed back his chair.

"Where are you going?" the Earl demanded gruffly.

"I thought I might go out tonight. I have the urge to do a little gaming."

The Earl frowned at his son and thought how different he was from Stephen. Rodney appeared to care about nothing, while Stephen had shown an interest in everything and everyone

around him. He shook his head in regret for all
the things past. More than ever, he hoped to
make up for it through Lauren.

"If you should ever need to talk, Rodney, then
I'm here."

Rodney looked surprised. "We talk all the
time, Father."

The Earl shook his head. "We exchange words,
Rodney, but we don't talk."

Rodney shifted nervously and then smiled
broadly. "Very well, Father. Should the need to
bare my soul ever be upon me, then I'll come to
you." The Earl nodded and Rodney left the room.

The old man sat alone, brooding over the past
and knowing that it would always haunt him.
He had nightmares of Stephen fleeing with his
family while he had watched, sitting in judgment. Now, through the haze of time, he could
see that he had been wrong. Stephen had needed
his love and his help in that time of despair, but
he, like an old fool, had turned his back on him.

He thought of Lauren, who was so like Stephen, and vowed that he would not let her down
as he had his son. He would not rest until she was
happy and content—no matter what the cost.

Rodney paced Lynell's room and ignored the
sounds of bawdy laughter coming from below.
He had slipped in the back way and was now
waiting for Lynell to appear.

The door opened and she entered, bringing
with her the strong scent of perfume.

"Rodney!" she said, extending her hand in
greeting. He ignored it and she frowned at him.
"What is it now?"

"It's that damned niece of mine! I wish to heaven we had finished her off before my father ever met her!"

Lynell languidly glided over to a chair. She spread her skirts and gingerly sat down, taking care not to wrinkle her silk.

"Well, we could have her taken care of now, if you wish," she said.

He snorted in disgust. "It would be too risky to do something to her now. The old man dotes on her."

She smiled at his tone. "Jealous, my dear Rodney?"

He turned on her with a savage expression. "I've never had his affection. When I was young it was always Stephen, Stephen, Stephen! I grew bloody sick of the sound of his name. Now that girl interests him beyond everything else."

Lynell stifled a bored yawn. "It seems to me that you've done very little to endear yourself to him."

"Ah, such a caring little whore! Do you think you have a heart of gold, Lynell?"

Her eyes glittered with anger. "I have clients below, Rodney. If you've come here for someone to kick, then I suggest you take one of the girls and get to it. If not, you'd better leave."

"I want you to do something for me," he said quickly.

She rose to her feet. "Is it something of the bedroom variety?"

"No," he sneered. "I want you to find out what my dear niece did while she was alone in London. She's very closemouthed about that time."

Lynell moved to the door and looked at him

over her shoulder. "I'll put my best man on it."
She lifted one eyebrow. "How soon do you need
this information?"

"As soon as possible. I think I might just have
the tool to rid myself of the slut."

"Are all women sluts to you, Rodney?" she
asked in a disinterested fashion.

"Of course." He looked surprised by her question.

Her eyes narrowed. "I thought so," she said
before she closed the door behind her.

Rodney pondered her question for a few moments then dismissed it as unimportant. He
picked up his hat and left the room. He wondered how long it would take to find a way to
get Lauren out of his life.

There was a tap on the door and Julian turned,
folding his arms behind him.

"Come in," he called.

Felice entered with a smile. "You wished to
speak to me in private?" she asked.

"Yes. Have a seat." He gestured to the chair
by his desk.

Felice's blue eyes were curious as she sat
down.

"There's a soirée being given this Saturday
by your good friend, Lady Buxley. I want you to
request her to invite another guest."

"Who it it?"

"The Lady Lauren Warwick."

"I'm not privy to your thoughts, but why don't
you invite her to our party tomorrow instead of
having Emily arrange it?"

He smiled wryly. "I fear she wouldn't come if she knew I had issued the invitation"

"What?!" Felice began to laugh. "Dare I hope that one female in England is immune to your charms?"

Julian did not find the idea amusing. "Will you see to it that an invitation is sent?"

Felice nodded. "I see no reason why Emily wouldn't want to invite the Earl's grand-daughter."

"Thank you, Felice."

She did not rise to leave, but instead carefully studied his face, noticing the tension about him. "You know I'll gladly give you my help, and if you should need to talk, then I'm always here to lend an ear."

"Some battles must be fought silently," he murmured, slipping one hand into his coat pocket.

Felice frowned. "Is this battle between you and this girl?"

"No. We all have battles that rage inside us. Some are mere skirmishes and others are large-scale wars."

"I would help you if I knew how."

He gave her an intimate smile. "This is one I must handle alone, although I appreciate your concern."

She rose to her feet with a rustle of satin. "Brendan wants to return home soon. He thinks we have overstayed our welcome."

"Never think that. If I have not been the perfect host then blame it on circumstances beyond my control. You know I like having you here."

Her smile was wistful. "I know, but things are changing. We are no longer two children

who cling to each other in a mutual need. I have
Brendan and you"—she paused for a moment—
"sometimes I don't think you need anyone, Julian. I know I shouldn't say this to you, but if I
don't then no one will have the courage. Sometimes you are like a man without a heart, but
I know this isn't so. Why do you shut people out
and maintain this stoic need to be alone?"

"There are things you don't understand, Felice," he said stiffly.

"Then *make* me understand! Tell me! I know
our parents' deaths deeply affected you, but that
was a long time ago. Let go of the past or you
will have no future!"

"As I said before, you don't understand and
I'm not in the mood for an exorcism tonight."

Felice moved forward and gently touched his
set jaw. "I love you. Never doubt that."

His hard eyes softened, but just for a moment:
With a sigh she turned, leaving him alone in
the shadow-filled study.

He moved slowly toward the brandy decanter
and poured a healthy measure into the crystal
glass. He swirled it, holding it up to the candle's
light so he could see the rich liquid. An image
of Lauren's laughing face appeared in the brandy
and with a satisfied sound he downed the drink,
as if he could consume her.

"What do I want?" he demanded of himself.
"Do I really want to live my life alone?"

He turned away from the decanter and paced
the floor until, with a savage gesture, he threw
the glass into the fireplace, where it shattered
against the bricks. The noise was unusually loud
in the quiet room and Julian angrily raked his

hands through his hair as he battled the demons within him.

Julian leaned against the wall and watched as Lady Buxley greeted her guests. Lauren was dressed in a pale green gown of watered silk and her hat had long silky green ribbons. She looked so young and beautiful as she entered the room on her grandfather's arm that he felt his heart lurch in his chest.

Lauren was smiling as she took a seat. She had not yet noticed him. Julian scowled when he saw that young puppy, Richard Attenby, place himself beside Lauren. He was about to move forward when Lady Buxley demanded his attention. He listened to her without hearing a word, his total attention on the two people seated on the sofa.

Lauren smiled. "Lord Richard. It's good to see you again."

"The pleasure is all mine, for my eyes have never beheld a more beautiful face," he said gallantly.

Her smile was warm. She liked him and found him safe after Julian's more demanding attentions. "Have you been here long?"

"Long enough to lose a tidy sum at the whist tables. I can only blame it on myself since my partner played admirably." He leaned his head to one side and studied her. "Do you play?"

A bewitching smile drew two dimples to her cheeks. "I much prefer backgammon."

"A woman after my own pleasures! Let's go in the other room and I'll show you how soundly I can defeat you."

She looked toward her grandfather, silently asking him if it was all right to go. He nodded and smiled at Richard, and Lauren rose and followed him from the room.

Julian's attention had been diverted for a few moments, and when he glanced back to where Lauren had been sitting, he was disconcerted to find that she was gone. His eyes flew around the room, but he could not find her.

"Excuse me," he murmured politely to Lady Buxley, and she gave him a gracious smile before she turned to another guest.

Felice came up behind him and touched his arm. "Would you care to play whist with me? Brendan seems to be occupied talking farming with a group of gentlemen."

He looked impatient. "Not now, Felice. I'm looking for someone."

She smiled demurely. "She's in the gameroom."

He glanced at her with a frown on his brow. "What did you say?" His manner was distracted.

"I said she's in the gameroom."

"Who is?" He still did not understand.

Felice looked innocent. "Oh, I beg your pardon. I thought you were looking for the Lady Lauren. It seems I was mistaken."

Julian gave a lighthearted laugh and held out his arm to his sister. "I think a game of whist is just what I need."

The first thing Julian noticed as they entered the room was Lauren and Richard bent over the backgammon board. They had intent expressions on their faces.

"You see," Felice whispered, "they're playing a game, nothing more."

"There are many ways to play a game. Come, I thought you wanted to lose some of Brendan's money."

She lifted her chin disdainfully. "I occasionally win, dear brother."

They passed Lauren's table, and although she was concentrating on her backgammon game, some signal within her made her lift her head. She caught her breath as her eyes looked into Julian's. He gave a mocking bow in acknowledgement and then moved away. She felt strangely breathless, as if her heart had dropped to her stomach.

Lauren felt a wave of jealousy rise up in her as she watched Julian solicitously hold the woman's chair. She could see the woman's back and heard her give a light tinkling laugh.

"Your move," Richard reminded her, and when she did not respond, he followed the line of her vision.

"It's strange to see Lord Keaton here. He rarely attends these affairs."

"Perhaps it's due to his companion," she responded more tartly than she had intended.

"Oh, I doubt it. They're very close but he does as he likes."

She nervously toyed with the dice box. "You say they are very close?"

"Closer than most brothers and sisters." Richard was studying the board and missed the look of relief that crossed her features.

Her grandfather came into the room a few moments later, and he frowned when he saw

Lord Keaton playing cards at a table. He glanced at Lauren and was relieved to see that she was engrossed in the game with Richard.

The Earl moved across the room and took a seat next to Lord Keaton.

"I believe I'll try my luck tonight," he informed the table at large.

"Julian's luck has been running well tonight," a stout, overdressed gentleman laughed.

The Earl glared at Julian. "That remains to be seen."

Felice was startled at the Earl's outright challenge and sent an anxious glance at her brother. Julian appeared unperturbed by the Earl's words as he continued to look at his cards.

As they played the stakes went higher and higher, and Julian continued to win. Finally the Earl threw his cards down in disgust. "It does seem that you have the luck of the devil, Lord Keaton."

"I prefer to have my own luck, and rarely depend upon others for it," he said smoothly. His eyes went to Lauren.

The Earl did not miss the action and he wondered about its significance. He knew Lord Keaton collected beautiful women like butterflies, but as far as he knew they had always been married or widowed. He had not thought Lord Keaton would be interested in an innocent maid like his granddaughter. Even as he watched, Lauren lifted her head, and he was shocked at the yearning he saw in her eyes when she looked at Julian.

He was suddenly angry and wanted to show

his lordship that he did not have a hope in hell of getting within a mile of his granddaughter.

"I have quite a bit of luck myself," he said with admirable calm. "Although it doesn't concern gaming."

"Really?" Felice inquired politely. "Pray tell us of your good luck."

"I have my granddaughter back with me and that's luck indeed, but I fear she'll not long be with me."

Julian's eyes swiveled abruptly to the Earl. "Not be with you?" his voice was low.

The Earl feigned a chuckle. "Young Attenby is desirous of her hand in marriage. He came to me the other day, and let me say that I didn't reject his suit."

Richard Attenby had indeed called on him, but as he had no wish to lose Lauren so soon after finding her, he had turned Richard away, bidding him to request her hand at a later date. He disliked having to lie, but he knew he had to do something to discourage Lord Keaton in his pursuit of Lauren.

The Earl saw with satisfaction the way Julian's fingers tightened on the cards. His face was a mask of indifference but the whiteness of his knuckles gave him away.

"And the Lady Lauren?" Julian asked woodenly. "What does she say about this suit?"

The Earl waved his hand expansively. "Over the moon, I dare say. You can see for yourself how well they get along."

Julian could not resist turning his head, and his lips tightened in displeasure as Lauren laughed and threw her companion a teasing look.

He felt like storming from the room or telling the old man that *his* wife would not marry anyone, but he restrained himself with effort.

"We must offer our congratulations to her," Felice intervened, seeing the wrath on Julian's face.

"Oh, say nothing yet," the Earl said in a rush. "Things have not progressed so far along that I want anyone to know."

Out of the corner of his eye, Julian saw Lauren rise and leave the room with Richard. He continued to play, but it was obvious that his mind was not on the game. When he won, he quickly left the table.

"Is Lord Keaton not well tonight?" the Earl asked in mock concern.

"He's fine, your lordship," Felice defended. "I dare say his mind is on his business ventures."

"And are they doing well?"

"Very well. Thank you for your concern."

The Earl smirked. It seemed to Felice that he had been deliberately taunting Julian. And although Julian could usually take teasing, tonight Felice had glimpsed a vulnerability that surprised her.

Julian found Lauren and Richard sitting on a sofa in a corner and he quickly made his way to them. Lauren glanced up at his approach and the smile died from her lips.

"It's good to see you looking so lovely tonight, Lady Lauren." His tone was light, but there was a hardness in his eyes.

"Thank you, Lord Keaton," she returned.

Richard looked uncomfortable when Julian's steely stare fell on him. "If you'll excuse me, I think I'll see if my mother needs anything," he said, quickly vacating the seat next to Lauren.

Julian stiffly sat down. "Quite the ardent beau," he sneered.

She stiffened her spine. "Richard is very kind."

"Kind! Huh! He's a boy."

"I think he's very nice," she returned indignantly. "And I don't wish to hear you defile him."

"Such staunch support for your husband-to-be! I doubt he would defend you so ably if he knew that you already have a husband and cannot take another."

Her voice held scorn. "I have no husband."

"What of the vows we made? What of the paper we signed?" he blurted out.

"Empty vows and a meaningless piece of paper!" she snapped. "You wanted no wife, only a convenience! Well, my time of convenience is past, so I consider everything null and void."

"I doubt society would see it as such!"

"Why are you doing this, Julian?" she whispered angrily. "You've told me time and again that you want no wife, and yet you constantly tax me as a wife. I filled your requirements and I've promised to tell no one. What more do you want of me?"

"I want you to tell me that Richard Attenby means nothing to you and that you don't intend to marry him!"

She was amazed. "Whatever gave you that idea?"

"Don't play games with me, Lauren," he hissed.

"You are the one who likes to play games with

people, Julian." She tried to rise, but his hand grasped her wrist, holding her down.

"Then you don't care for Richard?" he asked with a frown.

"He is amusing company—nothing more."

The lines on his face softened and his eyes, dulled once by anger, began to glow again. "I want to see you," he whispered.

"No!" she tried to rise again, but still he held her. "Will you let me go?!"

"Not until you've listened to me."

She subsided onto the sofa. "I'm listening."

"Come to the house we shared."

She shook her head, but her heart was madly beating.

"I want you, Lauren," he insisted in a low voice. "I need to see you."

"You're seeing me now," she said in a breathless voice.

His hand slowly moved up her arm and under the wide sleeve of her gown. "This is not enough and you know it."

Her breathing came quickly and her breasts rose and fell in agitation. She looked away from the persuasive power of his eyes. "I-I can't."

"You can! You must!" His voice grew seductive. "I can't sleep at night thinking of you lying alone and not in my arms."

"Take some other woman to your bed and let her ease your lust!" she said fiercely, but the words wounded her more than him. She could not bear to think of him holding another woman.

"No other satisfies me. It's you I want."

"You speak of wants and needs, but nothing of the heart."

"My heart is already carved upon a platter awaiting your feast."

She looked at him in exasperation. "You speak in jest of a thing I hold in all seriousness."

He shrugged. "The heart is a very overrated organ. Isn't it enough that I want you?"

"You don't want me to be your wife, but you seek me out as whore to your needs!"

He looked furious. "Don't call yourself a whore!"

"It's what you would make me!" She sadly shook her head. "Why, oh why can't I find it within me to hate you as I wish?" she asked aloud.

His face lost its harshness. "It's because there's so much between us. We share secrets which bind us."

"I thought you loathed links and chains of any kind," she taunted.

He grinned suddenly. "But we link most delightfully, do we not?"

A blush tinted her face. "I don't wish to speak of that again. It's over."

His grip tightened. "It's not over. Look at me, Lauren. Look at me!" he repeated when she still evaded his glance. "You still want me. Can you tell me that what we shared is no longer of worth?"

"It was of worth and I want to keep it that way."

"I don't understand."

She gave a tired smile. "I know. That's the problem." She sighed. "Accept that we had a time of happiness together but now it must end. Don't continue to seek me out. Let me get on with my life."

"And don't I have a place in this life of yours—

or is Richard Attenby my replacement?" he scorned angrily.

"Richard is a friend and nothing more. I have accepted your decisions in the past. Now please accept mine when I say that I cannot and shall not meet with you again."

"Lauren!" he said urgently as she tried to rise.

"Leave it, Julian," she said in distress when she saw her grandfather coming toward her. "Don't turn what we had into something sordid. Don't destroy my honor as well as my self-respect."

Julian released her and she stood to her feet. She was shivering after the scene, but her grandfather did not appear to notice.

"So we meet again," the Earl said stiffly, and Julian nodded curtly. "I think it's time we left," the Earl said to Lauren. "I'm too old to stay until dawn like you young people."

"Perhaps I will see you and your grand-daughter at Lady Randal's tomorrow?" Julian queried.

Lauren shook her head. "I don't think we'll attend. I find that I don't like to attend too many social gatherings. I prefer a quiet evening spent with Grandfather."

The Earl gave a satisfied smile. "We will bid you goodnight."

After they were gone, he stood staring at the empty doorway. He was unaware that Felice had joined him until she touched his arm.

"Are you all right, Julian?" she asked in concern.

"I'm fine, Felice," he said, but even as the words left his lips he knew that he was not fine. He did not understand the hollowness within him. He did not understand the urge inside his soul to be with Lauren. She might call it lust, but he knew there was more to it than that, or any woman would be able to satisfy the need within him.

Lauren had said he wanted no wife and he had once thought it was true. But now, deep inside, he was not sure.

Julian brooded over it a long time that night as he lay alone in his huge bed.

"Excellent, Lynell! Excellent!" Rodney was euphoric and he rubbed his hands together in satisfaction.

"I'm glad you're pleased," she said.

Rodney smirked. "This is quite a comedown for the high-and-mighty girl. She was Lord Keaton's mistress and might very well still be."

Lynell's eyes slanted like a cat's. "I don't think that's such a comedown, my friend. I've heard that Lord Keaton is a fine figure of a man and quite a catch for any woman."

"That's beside the point!"

"I think it's very much the point," she smiled maliciously, enjoying his anger.

"Are you sure this is the residence Keaton gave her?" he growled, waving the paper in the air.

"You've never doubted my reports."

"This is far too important for any mistakes."

She lifted one shoulder in a negligent shrug. "There's no mistake. I've had it checked out from several sources."

He gave a delighted laugh. "This will ruin her in Father's eyes! Lauren is just as disgraceful as her father."

Lynell laughed drily and patted her hair. "How accommodating your mind is, Rodney. Have you forgotten that Stephen was innocent of any wrongdoing? It was you who planted those letters."

"I don't want to go over that! It's done. But now I have the power to ruin Lauren as well. Ha! I can imagine the old man's face when he learns that his sweet, innocent granddaughter is the lover of the most notorious man in London."

"Don't forget that I expect to be handsomely paid for this information."

"As greedy as ever, eh Lynell?" he mocked.

"It's something you should understand," she said, walking over to her mirror. She adjusted the low neckline of her gown and then she fingered her scar. "The things we want do not come cheaply."

"You'll be paid and paid well, don't worry."

"I'm thinking of enlarging the house," she murmured. "Perhaps you could see about getting me some more girls."

"I brought you twelve not more than a month ago!"

She raised her eyebrow. "You know how rough some customers get. I have to give them time off to heal their bruises."

"It's a nasty business you're in, Lynell," he scorned.

"You should know."

But Rodney did not hear the sarcasm in her voice. He was already making his plans for exposing Lauren.

For I'm engag'd by word and oath
A servant to another's will.
                    —Anonymous

Chapter Nine

Lauren pulled a book from the shelf and idly flipped through the pages. Her mind was not her own today. She kept thinking about Julian and wondering if he had gone to their house, even though she had told him she would not meet him.

The door opened and she glanced up, her eyes widening when she saw Rodney enter. There was a smug expression on his face as he advanced toward her.

"Since your return to England, I have had nothing but bad luck. Like a dark specter from the past, you have haunted my days and nights, giving me no peace."

"If you've been haunted, then don't blame me." She lifted her chin. "Blame it on your own tortured conscience that knows you've done wrong and torments you because of it."

He laughed. "I must give you full measure for cunning. You've insinuated yourself into my father's good graces without any trouble." He cocked his head to one side. "He fairly dotes on

you, fool that he is. He's constantly singing your
praises, listing your virtues for all to hear."

"I'm also fond of him," Lauren said.

Rodney studied his fingers for a second, but
when he looked at her again, she saw the hatred
in his eyes.

"I'll hate to disillusion him about his dear
granddaughter, but then what else can I do?"
he asked, lifting his shoulders. "I wouldn't be a
dutiful son if I kept the truth from him."

"What truth?" she asked softly, eying him
warily.

"You might indeed ask what truth, for you've
told very little of it since you came here."

"I'm going upstairs," she said, moving past
him. "I'll not listen to you spout your evil."

He stepped in front of her and she stopped
abruptly.

"You've been a wicked, wicked girl, Lauren,"
he chuckled. "And I'm going to make sure that
Father knows all about it."

She swallowed with difficulty. "I-I don't know
what you're talking about."

"Oh, I'm sure you do. Did you really think
you could hide you filthy little affair?"

She paled. "What?"

"You heard me. I know all about it, you see."

"What's going on here?" The Earl stood in the
door and watched Lauren and Rodney with a
confused expression on his face. "What are you
saying, Rodney, to upset Lauren?"

Rodney turned with a flourish. "I was just
telling my dear niece that all has been uncov-
ered concerning her affair with Lord Keaton."
His face was alight with malicious amusement.

The Earl's voice was angry. "I'll not have you slander her so!"

"I speak no slander, but the truth! Ask her if I lie."

"I'll not shame her by asking. She can speak for herself if she has need to defend herself against your attack."

The Earl looked hopefully at Lauren and she knew that her guilt was clearly written on her face. Her grandfather swayed slightly and his skin turned gray.

"I'll ask her then!" Rodney snapped. "Tell him where you lived when you first came to London."

"I-I had no place else to go," she began.

"You could have come to me," her grandfather moaned. "You should have come to me from the very first and perhaps none of this would have happened."

Lauren looked at her uncle and was tempted to tell her grandfather how Rodney had refused her shelter, but she knew that her meeting with Julian had already happened and so she had no one to blame but herself.

"I did share a house with him," she whispered, bending her head. She could not bear to see the pain in her grandfather's eyes.

"Were you his—his—" he searched for an appropriate word. "Were you his mistress?" he asked hoarsely, praying that she would deny it.

"Of course she was!" Rodney thundered. "Why are you being so blind to the facts?"

Lauren gave Rodney a bitter look. "Yes, why doubt the facts," she said in an angry tone. "The facts spoke of my father's guilt, did they not?

Everything was very neat and tidy, so why should facts be doubted!"

"Enough of your sniveling about your father. We're talking about you and your guilt." Rodney's voice was contemptuous.

"Lauren?" her grandfather whispered. It was a plea for all this to be a lie.

"Why should I waste words? There are things you don't know and which I am not at liberty to tell you. It's clear that I've already been found guilty by you both." Her gaze scorched Rodney. "I expected nothing less from you, Uncle, and you have conformed to character." Her eyes moved to her grandfather and softened. "But you, Grandfather. I thought you had learned from the past and would not judge me so harshly. I am not able to explain, but that doesn't mean I am guilty." She turned away. "I shall leave at once," she said, but his voice halted her.

"Nay, lass. I don't blame you," her grandfather said softly.

Her eyes flew incredulously to his. "You don't blame me?" she repeated in amazement.

"I well know Lord Keaton's reputation with women. An innocent like you would have had little armor against the likes of him. He's well versed in the art of seduction, while you knew little of men and their ways."

"You judge Julian too harshly," she began, but he held up his hand, silencing her.

"Don't speak of that rogue! His name makes the blood rush angrily through my body."

He did look flushed, and Lauren feared for his health. "Grandfather, come upstairs and we'll discuss this another time," she begged.

"Do you need time to come up with a suitable explanation?" Rodney growled, not liking the way the conversation was going. He had expected the old man to toss her out, but the Earl seemed far from doing that.

"I owe you nothing!" she stormed.

The Earl held up his hand. "I've had enough of your provoking behavior for one night, Rodney."

Rodney cursed and turned on his heel, slamming out of the room in a fit of temper.

"Go upstairs, Lauren," The Earl ordered in a gentle voice. "I need some time to think."

"Grandfather, you don't know everything," she said, torn between keeping her word to Julian and wanting to take the cold, gray look from his face.

"I know more than you can imagine," he smiled wanly. He patted her hand as it rested on his sleeve. "Go upstairs and in the morning everything will seem better."

She looked at him with a worried expression and did his bidding. She slowly made her way up the stairs and when she entered her room, Molly was standing inside nervously.

"What was all the shouting about below?" Molly asked.

"Rodney told Grandfather that I had been living with Julian," Lauren stated bluntly.

"Oh, mercy!" Molly gasped. "That snake has been looking for a way to harm you in your grandfather's eyes." A smirk lingered about her lips. "I bet your uncle turned every color of blue when you told them you're married to Lord Keaton."

Lauren wearily shook her head. "I didn't tell them."

Molly's mouth dropped open. "You didn't tell them?!"

"No."

"But why not? It would have put a stick in your uncle's wheel and a feather in your cap."

"I can't tell them. I promised Julian I would guard the secret of our marriage. I can't break my word to him."

"He breaks the words of the ceremony when he doesn't take you truly to wife and have done with all this slinking about!"

"Whatever others do, I'll not break my word," Lauren insisted.

Molly marched to the door. "Then I'll tell him! I promised no such silence!"

Lauren jumped up, catching the hem of Molly's gown as she passed. "No, Molly! No! You'll do no such thing."

"I'll not have that uncle of yours getting off without a piece of my mind and I'll not have your grandfather thinking you're a woman to be bedded by every knave that passes."

"He doesn't blame me. He puts it all soundly on Julian's head."

Molly snorted. "Good! That's where it should be. But your grandfather will know that you're married or my name's not Molly Putnam!"

"Then your name must be Mary, for you'll tell no one!"

"But—!"

"I mean no one!" Lauren insisted. "Tomorrow I'll go to Julian and ask him if I can tell my grandfather. If he says nay then so be it, but I'll ask him first."

"I think you're a fool!" Molly scorned. "Lord Keaton has a hearty hatred of marriage. He won't want to acknowledge his fall into matrimony."

"We'll ponder this on the morrow. I'll hear no more about it tonight."

"Hmph! Very well," Molly agreed ungraciously. "It's your reputation."

"I'm very glad you realize that," Lauren responded calmly.

"And it's your decision," she added.

Lauren nodded.

"But if that fellow don't come clean with the truth, he'll hear a few truths from me, and that's for sure!"

Lauren could not help grinning. "I'm sure your lecture will straighten him out."

"Aye, it will or—"

"Or your name's not Molly Putnam."

"That's right!"

They both giggled and soon were in helpless laughter.

The Earl sat alone in the library for over an hour before he knew what he had to do. Then he took pen and paper and set to work.

Julian was dining with Felice and Brendan when a servant discreetly advised him that a message had arrived.

"Bring it in here," he said, turning back to his food.

"What is it?" Felice asked, lifting her wineglass.

He deftly speared an oyster and swallowed it. "I don't know. Some kind of urgent message has arrived."

A servant entered, bearing a white envelope on a silver tray. Julian took the letter and used a knife to slice through the heavy paper.

He read the contents in silence, but Felice, watching him, saw his fingers become rigid as he held the page.

"Is something wrong?" There was concern in her voice.

Brendan saw the glitter in Julian's eyes and was disturbed. "Is it bad news?"

"Jonathan Warwick, the Earl of Naylor, wishes to see me tonight," he said coldly.

"The Earl of Naylor? Isn't that Lauren Warwick's grandfather?" Brendan asked.

"The same," he said through clenched teeth. "Damn, but women can't be trusted! I thought she was someone I could depend on." He gave a harsh bark of laugher. "I'm indeed getting foolish in my age, for I let her lull me into such a state of illusion."

"What does he want?" Felice murmured.

Julian rose to his feet, knocking over his chair in his anger. A sense of *déjà vu* was coming over him as he remembered the letter Monica had written.

"Is there something we can do?" Brendan asked in a quiet voice.

Julian's eyes were cold and Felice felt herself shiver as they passed over her. "I'll deal with this myself." Without another word he left the room.

"I knew he would get into trouble over that girl!" Felice exclaimed.

"She's a lovely creature, but she's hardly the type Julian usually associates with." Brendan deftly folded his napkin. "Perhaps he has trespassed into deeper waters."

"What do you mean?" Felice turned angrily on him, concern for Julian making her short-tempered.

"The bait is always there, but sometimes it takes a more experienced fisherman to hook the really good catches."

"Are you saying that this girl is seeking marriage and hopes to push him into it?"

He shrugged. "I don't know, but I remember a similar look on Julian's face when Monica tried her line and he got away."

"But Julian appears to be doing all the chasing with this girl. She acts as if she doesn't want him to bother her. Could it just be a ruse to spur him on?"

"You know women better than I do."

She paused. "No. I don't think this girl is like that. There was something about her that I liked. There was a trustworthiness about her that Monica could never match." She pushed back her chair. "I must talk to him."

Brendan restrained her with a hand. "I don't think he's in the mood for advice."

"He needs me, even though he might not think so. I can't let him think he's alone in his troubles."

"Then don't be hurt if he spurns your help."

She gently touched his cheek. "Thank you for

your concern, but Julian is my brother. He wouldn't hurt me."

"He's angry and troubled, and will not want your interference."

"You're probably right, but I must try."

She left the room and slowly approached the study door. She knocked tentatively but received no answer. She took a deep breath and opened the door.

Julian was slumped in the chair behind his desk. He was reading the letter and his eyes looked over the page in displeasure.

"Go away, Felice!"

"I want to help you," she whispered gently.

"Stop trying to mother me just because you have no child!" he snapped angrily.

She turned away with a wounded cry, reaching blindly for the door. Julian expelled his breath on a curse, and swiftly moved to her side.

"I'm sorry," he said huskily.

When she looked at him she saw the troubled expression in his eyes. "I'm beginning to think I don't know you anymore. You are privy to my deepest desires and know how much I long to have a child. How could you use my barrenness against me?"

"I never meant to hurt you." He sighed heavily as he gently touched her shoulder. "You mean so much to me."

"I know you're hard when you're angry, but lately you've not been yourself. There is a distant feeling between us, as if another has all your thoughts." She paused delicately. "What is this girl to you?" she asked bluntly, thinking he would deny her importance, but she was wrong.

"She is my wife."

She gasped as the full import of his words hit her. "Your wife?" she squeaked.

"Aye!" There was a bitter twist to his mouth.

"But why has no one known? Why all the secrecy?"

"I didn't want a wife, but I needed a wife. Monica was becoming tiresome and Lauren's appearance seemed fortuitous. At the time I didn't know she was the granddaughter of an earl."

"And she agreed to this silence?" she asked in surprise.

"So I thought, but this letter from her grandfather demanding my presence tells me that the secret is out."

"Do you love her?"

"Love?" he laughed scornfully. "Why must women always use that word? Desire, want, greed, these are the words to use. Love is a word women use to trap men's minds and draw them into their web of pleasure. But once the pleasure is gone men find themselves locked into marriages with shrews for wives. Then a man must go seeking again for that panacea of all ills, called love, in the arms of another woman until she demands more of him than he can give and off he goes on a perpetual search for an illusion. I'll not be one of those silly seeking fools!"

"You're so cynical," Felice said sadly. "I know life has not always been pleasant for you, but don't say that love is an illusion. It exists." Her eyes were soft as they rested on his hard profile. "What has made you so bitter about love?"

He stiffened at her words. "Our dear mother made me thus."

Her eyes widened and her lips parted in astonishment. "Our mother? But our mother is dead."

He shook his head, regretting his outburst. "Never mind. I shouldn't have said anything. The past should be buried."

She moved after him, catching his sleeve and forcing him to stop. "What does our mother have to do with this?"

"You have kind memories of her. I don't want to ruin that image."

"If she is responsible for your cynicism and bitterness, then I want to know why!"

He poured a glass of brandy and drank it. "Shall I pour one for you? You might need it." His smile flashed and was gone.

"No. I want nothing to drink, only the truth."

"Please sit down." When she had complied he leaned against the corner of his desk, a somber expression on his face.

"The night before our parents died, I went to their room. They were arguing bitterly, so I hid behind the drapes so they wouldn't see me. Mother was telling Father that she was leaving him. She had met another man and was going away with him.

"Father was in tears, begging her not to leave, telling her he loved her, but she just laughed in his face. She said she hated being married to him, and that marriage was a trap of respectability forced upon her. She claimed that as far as husbands went she had had to make do with what was available at the time, and our father had been the best she could find. Mother had wanted to marry a duke but had settled for an earl; now, she told him, she had found a real man, a man who could make her happy."

"Mother said that? I never thought she could be so cruel," Felice said, her face pale with shock.

"You were but a child, younger than myself." Julian's voice was dry. "If you'll think back you'll remember she rarely had time for us. Occasionally she visited our rooms or allowed us to be brought before guests like prize dogs to be petted and then sent back to their place."

"I do remember her always being busy."

"Well, Father left and soon after a servant came with a letter for Mother. She started to cry when she learned that her lover had decided not to take her along on his journey. In despair, she started wailing and throwing things. She saw me behind the curtain and dragged me out, screaming at me. I was just like my father, she said. I suffocated her with my fawning adoration. Mother said she pitied the woman I would marry, for she would have a weak, spineless bridegroom.

"I ran from the room crying, and the next day they were both dead, released from a marriage that neither enjoyed. I vowed then that I would have no part of marriage and no woman would ever use me to elevate herself in society."

"Oh, Julian!" Felice cried in distress. "How could she have hurt you like that?"

He shrugged in unconcern. "She was hurt and angry at being discarded, just as she had discarded Father. She took her wrath out on me."

He grinned wryly. "I seem to have inherited that trait from her. I'm sorry I hurt you earlier."

"That's forgiven." She was stunned that she had never known the truth. "I wish you had told me earlier. All these years I've been kept in ignorance."

"I almost told you before you married Brendan, but you seemed so happy, so eager. I couldn't bring myself to be the one to ruin your happiness."

"But Brendan and I have been so happy. Didn't you think then that Mother could have been wrong about marriage?"

"I was surprised, but I thought your marriage was unique. There is an exception to every rule, I suppose."

"You married Lauren," she began hesitantly. "Did you perhaps think she might be different?"

He shook his head. "I married her to keep from marrying Monica, nothing more, nothing less." He suddenly remembered his first night with Lauren and a lump formed in his throat.

"Were you happy together? I remember a time when you rarely came home and when you did, you were eager to be off again."

He did not want to think of that time. "I might once have thought she was different, and in my foolishness I imagined a need greater than what it was. Now I know she is just like all women. She told her grandfather of our marriage and no doubt is expecting to take up her position in society as my wife. I gave her a weapon and she could not resist using it."

There was a sadness beneath Julian's anger, as if something precious had been taken from

him. Felice covered her eyes; she was beginning
to sense that she was intruding into her brother's personal memories.

"What will you do?" she asked.

"Do? If she wants to be a countess then she
shall be a countess, but she'll find no generosity
or warming of my heart toward her. I'll make
her wish she had never crossed me in this manner."

Julian seemed so violent when he talked of
Lauren that Felice could almost feel sorry for
her.

"Don't let Mother's bitterness be your bitterness or she will have won, don't you see?" Her
eyes were filled with tears. "Her disappointment in marriage has become yours and her
lack of feeling your lack of love. I'm not like our
mother, however, so she needn't rule your life.
Don't let her words forever haunt you and taint
your future happiness."

"I find it hard to believe in love." His voice
was quiet. "But there was a time when it seemed
so close." He closed his eyes, remembering in
pain. Julian felt he must not give in to his emotions; he would not let Lauren have his heart
as her plaything.

"Leave me alone now, Felice. I need some time
alone before I call upon the Earl."

"Of course." She gently kissed his cheek. "I
do love you."

"I fear it's not easy to love this bitter man,"
he said half-jokingly, but there was also an ele-
ment of sadness in his voice.

"Your bitterness is but a thin veneer—it only
needs a little stroking to vanish forever."

After she left, Julian sat at his desk, his face buried in his hands as Lauren's face floated in his mind's eye. He growled at the image.

"You want to make me weak with your wily ways," he said aloud. "And I was weakening. But you've played your hand too soon." He gave a sardonic laugh. "You have revealed your true colors. I was beginning to think you were an angel, but now I know what horns you hide!"

He continued to berate her, bringing all his ire to the surface, but still his heart ached. No matter what names he called her, there still lingered the picture of her smiling as she lay in his arms, giving herself so eagerly and lovingly.

When Julian arrived at Lord Warwick's he was immediately ushered into the library. He saw Lauren's grandfather sitting in a chair facing the door, but there was no sign of Lauren.

"I believe you wanted to see me," Julian said.

"Thank you for coming so quickly," the Earl returned, motioning for Julian to be seated.

Julian glanced around the room. "Is Lauren not to join us?" he asked expressionlessly.

"I sent a servant to bring her down. She's unaware of your visit. I thought it would be better if we talked first."

"By all means."

The Earl cleared his throat. "I have just learned that you and my granddaughter were living together before she came to me."

Julian smiled sardonically and inclined his head.

The Earl came to his feet, clenching his hands

at his side. "How can you sit there and calmly admit to seducing my granddaughter?"

Julian shrugged. "It's not difficult."

"I hope you intend to do the honorable thing!" the Earl growled. He had wanted to keep his temper, but the arrogance of the man was too much.

Julian lifted one eyebrow. "And what is the honorable thing?"

"Why—why, accepting her as you wife!"

Julian laughed out loud. "Of course! I'll take Lauren home with me as soon as she can pack."

The Earl looked dumfounded. "You don't imagine I'd let her go with you?"

"Why not? As her husband I do have that right."

"But not until the marriage vows have been repeated."

"I have no intention of repeating the vows!" he stated coldly. Once had been more than enough for him!

"Why, you—!" the Earl began, then the door opened and Lauren entered.

She stopped in surprise when she saw Julian and wondered what he was doing in her grandfather's house. She covered her surprise and advanced slowly.

"You wished to see me?" she asked her grandfather.

Julian stared at her like a hungry wolf. Just the sight of her set his senses spinning. He wanted to take her in his arms, but her grandfather's presence and the fact that she had tricked him held him in his seat.

"My dear," the Earl said, his voice gentle. "I

was going to give you to Lord Keaton as wife, but after his behavior tonight, I think you'd be better off without him."

Lauren blanched and sent a wild look at Julian. Had he told her grandfather of their marriage? His eyes revealed nothing.

"I'm happy with you, Grandfather," she said softly.

Julian came to his feet. "Enough of this foolishness. You asked me to take Lauren as my wife and I intend to do just that."

A stern look came over the Earl's features. "I'll not give her into your care! You've shown me what an unfeeling, arrogant man you are. Do you think I would entrust my most precious jewel into the care of such a one as you?"

Julian rocked back on his heels. "I don't think you have much choice. Lauren is mine."

"I think you give yourself rights that are not yet truly yours!" the Earl returned with heat.

"Lauren gave me the right!" Julian said coldly. He was not sure what was going on, but he had not expected to have to fight for Lauren. He had thought she would be eagerly handed over.

"Grandfather!" Lauren interrupted, not liking the way the two most important men in her life were snarling at each other. "Leave me alone with Julian for a few moments. We need to talk."

"I don't trust that young blade with you!" he growled.

"I'll be quite safe," she assured him. "Please wait outside."

The Earl gave Julian an angry glance.

"I won't rape her," Julian said blandly.

"Just make sure you don't!" the Earl said as

he stormed from the room, slamming the door behind him in a most undignified manner.

"What are you doing here, Julian?" Lauren asked once they were alone.

Julian laughed scornfully. "Don't try to pretend, Lauren. You know why I'm here."

A spark of anger brightened her eyes. "I didn't know you were coming. I didn't even know you were here until I entered the room."

His lips tilted. "And you didn't talk to your grandfather about us before he summoned me?"

She blushed her guilt. "We—we did discuss you."

"And I'm sure your grandfather was very enlightened as to our relationship."

She turned away. "I'm sorry he found out, Julian."

"Ha! Save your innocent act for a more gullible fool! You told him of our marriage when you promised you wouldn't."

She caught her breath and whirled to face him.

"I didn't tell him!"

"Then how did he come to know?"

"He doesn't know."

"Come, Lauren," he sighed his exasperation. "He sent for me and he told me I had to accept you as my wife. He must know!"

"I—I don't know how he could have found out about our marriage. I told him nothing about that."

"Then what did you tell him?" he sneered, clearly not believing her.

"Rodney found out we had lived together, and

he told Grandfather. When he confronted me with it, I told him it was true."

"And our marriage was never mentioned?" Julian scorned. "That pertinent piece of information never crossed your lovely lips?" She stepped back at the harsh expression on his face. "Don't tempt me to beat the truth out of you, Lauren."

"You lay a hand on me, my lord, and you'll regret it!"

"You're a very clever girl."

"Clever?" she asked, clearly puzzled.

"Stop playing the damned innocent! You planned this whole thing, didn't you? You wanted our marriage to become common knowledge."

"Of all the unmitigated gall!" she snapped. "You forced your attentions on me! You used me knowing that you could discard me at a moment's notice, and then you verbally abuse me because your carefully laid plan has gone astray!"

"You were never exactly unwilling, my dear," he drawled. "Everyone knows that token resistance whets the appetite."

With angry strides Lauren walked over to him, and raising her hand, she struck Julian across the face. When she tried to hit him again, he caught her hand, and pulled her roughly to him.

"Don't tempt your luck again, Lauren," he said through clenched teeth. "The mood I'm in right now, I could easily hit you back."

Looking at his cold hard face, Lauren could very well believe it, but it still did not appease her anger or the hurt she felt hearing his callous accusations.

"You're a complete idiot if you think I planned this!" she stormed. She started for the door, intending to put an end to the conversation.

"Just where the hell do you think you're going?" he asked in an abrupt voice.

"I have no intention of listening to you rage at me. I'm going upstairs to bed."

A muscle jerked in his cheek, but his voice was calm when he spoke. "There are things we must discuss."

She raised one eyebrow haughtily. "We have discussed too much as it is."

"I think my animosity is well deserved in the circumstances," he said with a taunting smile.

"And *I* think my innocence in this matter has been defiled enough."

"We could debate this all night and not come to an agreement," he returned grimly.

"As I've said, there's nothing left to be discussed." She placed her hand on the doorknob and he moved swiftly, catching her and spinning her around to face him.

"Leave me be!" she cried. "Oh, I wish it had been Lord Richard who found me that night on the docks! At least his intentions have always been honorable!"

His eyes darkened ominously. "And what is honorable?"

She lifted her small chin aggressively. She wanted him to know that other men desired her as a wife even if he did not.

"He's asked me to marry him."

Julian laughed angrily. "You don't need two husbands, Lauren. You can't even handle one."

"I would much rather handle Richard than you!"

"The hell you would!" he denied with sudden savagery. The picture of Lauren in another man's arms made him see red, and his grip tightened painfully on her shoulders.

She trembled at the rage on his face. "L-let me go!" She hated the way her voice quavered uncontrollably.

"Never," he muttered, meaning it from the bottom of his heart. "I'm taking you home with me to be my wife."

Her eyes widened with shock. "I thought you didn't want a wife."

He gave a mirthless laugh. "True, but I seem to have one. Wedlock tends to seek me out no matter what I do."

"I won't go with you under these circumstances," she insisted.

"You have very little say in it. You're my wife and a husband has certain powers. Besides, the tale is told and there's no reason to hide it any longer."

"I'm so sorry, Julian," she whispered and a little tear ran down her cheek. She did not want Julian like this. She had wanted him wholeheartedly or not at all.

Impulsively he bent and kissed away the tear. She gasped at his action and then, with a groan of impatience, Julian turned her mouth to his. Her lips blossomed beneath his touch and her hand lifted to slowly trail up his neck and then curl in the thick dark hair on his nape. Suddenly her legs were too weak to hold her and she melted against him.

"You have the temper of a shrew, the body of an angel, and make love like the very devil," he whispered huskily into her ear.

"You talk too much," she muttered, drawing his lips back to hers.

Julian restrained himself with an effort, and when he stepped back there was no love or warmth in his eyes. She shivered, feeling bereft of his masculine warmth.

"Surely you aren't suggesting we make love here?" he asked. "What if your grandfather should come in and find us?"

She paled at his words, feeling like a complete hoyden. Julian had that effect on her and he probably always would. He could make her forget everything but her hunger for his touch.

"I shall try to be a good wife to you," she said expressionlessly, trying to still her rapidly beating heart.

Julian gave a tight laugh. "That, my dear Lauren, is exactly what I don't want you to be."

She was shocked. "What? B-but I thought—" she began.

"Oh, I still intend to accept you as my wife, but I want you to be more mistress than wife. Wives grow boring with their domesticity, but a mistress is always eager to please."

Anger flared quick and hot within her. "Would you tie me naked to the bed and use me at your will?"

He rubbed his chin thoughtfully as his gaze roamed wickedly over her heaving bosom. "There's a thought," he mused aloud. "It would save me a pretty pence in dresses and other feminine fluff."

"You odious pig!" she hissed. "Satan surely spawned you!"

"And you with your sweet voice and soft ways would tempt the saints," he grinned, mocking her temper.

She turned once more to the door and threw it open. "Pack only what is needed tonight," he ordered. "I'll take care of everything else."

"I'm sure you'd like to," she threw over her shoulder. "A wife you might have in name, but don't expect to come crawling between the sheets of my bed! I know you for what you are now, and I'll not yield to you again."

"You should wait until you're asked before you act so outraged," Julian returned coldly. "Your bed holds no charms for me that I can't find elsewhere!"

"Good! So long as we understand each other I'm sure we'll live together admirably."

She marched past her grandfather and up the stairs, leaving both men to watch her in silence. When she was out of sight the Earl looked at Julian with contempt.

"You don't think I'll let her leave with you tonight, do you?"

Julian's face tightened in anger. "She's my wife and she goes with me. I think my rights are stronger than yours."

"But she's not your wife until the vows are spoken!"

Julian was very still. "What are you saying?"

"That I will not allow Lauren to go with you until you are legally husband and wife."

Julian felt a shaft of ice go through him. "You didn't know that we were already married?"

The Earl's startled face was answer enough.

"Already married?" He was shocked by the news as much as he was by the fact that Lauren had not seen fit to communicate it to him. When Rodney was slandering her, she had not defended herself. "I didn't know!"

"Then for heaven's sake, man! Why did you ask me to come here?"

"Rodney discovered you had been living together. He confronted Lauren with the knowledge and I overheard."

"And Lauren didn't tell you we were wed?" he asked in exasperated tones.

Lauren's grandfather shook his head and he looked curiously at Julian. "No. She admitted to living with you but said nothing about your marriage." He was very confused. "Why all the secrecy? When did this marriage take place?"

"I made Lauren swear not to tell." Julian was just beginning to realize what a terrible blunder he had made with Lauren. "It's a long story. Let's go in the library and I'll tell you all about it."

As Julian proceeded to outline their meeting (glossing over their first night together) and subsequent marriage, Julian remembered his conversation with Lauren and how his anger had been fueled by the belief that she had betrayed his trust. Now he knew she had let everyone think ill of her rather than tell the whole story and redeem herself. A deep remorse came over him, and he knew it would not be easy to tell Lauren of his previous doubts without an-

gering her further. He had wronged her and
severely misjudged her. Would she ever forgive
him? he wondered.

The Earl brightened when the story was finished. "Your motives might be in doubt, but at
least you are honorably married to Lauren. Will
you take Molly with you? Lauren is very at-
tached to her."

"Aye," Julian said shortly. "I only want Lauren to be happy." And he knew in that moment
it was true and he would do everything in his
power to make Lauren content.

Molly scuttled around the room and collected
all the necessary objects while Lauren sat fum-
ing on the bed.

"I knew Lord Keaton would come for you,"
Molly said in a matter-of-fact voice.

"You knew nothing of the kind!" Lauren said
coldly.

"He loves you," she said simply.

"Ha! He knows nothing of love. He may lust
and chase with the best of men, but his heart
is cold."

"He was kind to you when you first arrived
in London," Molly said. "He was kind when all
others were cruel."

"Oh, he was kind so he could use me to his
own end! Fool that I was, I bedded the beast and
have had no peace since."

"He's accepting you as his wife. You once told
me that was all you desired," Molly reasoned.

"I thought it would be enough, but it isn't."
Lauren sniffed and wiped away a tear. "If he

wanted me to be his wife because he wanted me to be his wife, then it would be different."

"You make no sense!" Molly admonished. "If and so and because... You want him and he wants you; be grateful for that."

"I'll not be grateful to that swine! He thinks he's doing me such a marvelous favor! Well, favors be damned!"

"A lady doesn't talk like that!"

Lauren gave Molly a bitter smile. "I'm no lady, just an unwanted wife."

A heavy sigh escaped Molly as she folded Lauren's nightgown. "I've never met two such proud, foolish people in my whole life."

Lauren glanced at Molly and was about to make some scathing remark when her eyes alighted on the scant gown in her maid's hands.

"Why are you taking that thing?"

"Tonight's your wedding night in the true sense of the word. I thought you'd be wanting something a little provocative."

"Put it away!" she ordered. "I'll not dress myself up for his pleasure and he's not sharing my bed."

Molly ignored Lauren and placed the gown with the rest of her belongings.

"Did you hear me?" Lauren demanded.

"I'm thinking the whole house can hear you."

"Then do what I say."

"No! You can throw your tantrums and put on your fancy airs with the other servants, but I'll do as I please."

"Are you sure you're really a maid?" Lauren asked nastily. "You have a decided disrespect for your betters."

Molly placed her hands on her hips and grinned at Lauren. "If the way you and Lord Keaton are acting is supposed to be better than me, then I'm glad I'm a servant!"

"Ooooh! Why doesn't anyone understand?"

Molly's smile disappeared and she sat on the bed beside Lauren. She gave her an affectionate hug.

"I understand, my girl. Truly I do. And that's why someone around here has to use some sense. You love Lord Keaton and I think he loves you."

Lauren shook her head back and forth, a pained expression on her face.

"There, there, love. You know you love him."

"I don't want to love him! I refuse to love him!"

"Seems like I've heard all this before," Molly smiled.

"What am I going to do, Molly? What am I going to do?" she wailed.

"You're going to get dressed and I'm going to finish packing. Then we're going downstairs and leaving with his lordship."

"But—!"

"No buts!" she said firmly. "If I know Lord Keaton, he'll come up here and fetch you himself if you don't go down."

Lauren started to cry, rocking gently against Molly.

"Shhh, Lauren. I don't like to see your fine, fiery spirit beaten down like this."

"How can I live with him knowing he bears me no love?"

"Just take one day at a time and everything will soon be clear."

"Oh, Molly. What would I do without you?" Lauren smiled through her tears.

"I don't know," she grinned. "It's a good thing I'm here to make you see reason"

"I'm going to need a friend, Molly."

"Aye! And I'll always be that friend, don't you worry."

Lauren watched as Molly finished the packing and then they were ready to go downstairs. Lauren almost panicked and rushed back to her room when she saw Julian standing at the foot of the stairs.

Unconsciously, she stiffened as she walked down to join her husband. When he took her arm, she involuntarily flinched and saw his look harden.

"I'm sorry I could not tell you about my marriage, Grandfather," she said with a sad face.

"I understand everything now," he assured her with a smile. "Just be happy and you'll make me happy.

She kissed his cheek before she left with Julian. They did not speak as the carriage carried them off into the night to a future she deemed at best uncertain.

Seeing no danger, we disarm our mind,
And give our conduct to the waves and wind.
—Matthew Prior

Chapter Ten

Felice impatiently tapped her foot as she watched Julian eat his breakfast. He calmly ignored her glowering looks as he enjoyed the food set before him.

"This has gone on long enough, Julian," she finally said, refusing to keep quiet any longer.

"What has?" he asked mildly. He lifted his cup and sipped the hot tea.

"You're married but you both act like strangers. You hardly exchange two words when you're together. And I know that you don't share a bed."

"It's none of your concern, Felice," he said shortly.

"It is my concern when I see how thin you're becoming! Lauren isn't looking well, either."

Julian looked up at her words and frowned. "Lauren is unwell?"

"She hasn't complained or anything," Felice explained. "But then she doesn't confide in me." Her lips twisted wryly. "I think she considers me as part of the enemy force since I'm you're

240

sister. She's very polite to me, but she's wary of letting me get too close."

"What do you propose we do?" Julian leaned back in his chair, shaking out the lace on his cuff.

Felice brightened. "I just received a letter from Cousin Nicolet. She married Simon de Palissy last year and is now a duchess. She's invited us to visit, and has secured invitations for us to attend the wedding of Louis's grandson to the Archduchess Marie Antoinette."

"You know how I dislike the French court. All the petty intrigues and jealousies among the nobles bore me."

"But it will be such fun, Julian! And think of Lauren. She's half-French, you know. I'm sure she'd like to return for a visit."

"Have you already mentioned this to Lauren?" he asked, raising an inquiring brow.

"Of course not! I wanted to see if you'd agree first."

"It might not be a bad idea," he mused aloud.

"It will be good for you both. I know it can't be easy for her to parry all the looks and innuendoes that are being bandied about."

"What are you talking about, Felice?" Julian's tone was curt.

"Don't you know?" She was surprised. "Everyone's speculating on your quick marriage. I mean, it was so sudden and there wasn't an announcement. You must have known there would be gossip."

Julian shrugged. "Gossip has never bothered me."

"I know. I sometimes think you relish being

the focus of the gossip. It lends you a certain air." She grinned as she watched him scowl. "But you must think of your wife. She doesn't enjoy the sort of notoriety she now has."

He sighed heavily. "You're right." He paused a moment to think. "All right, Felice. We'll go to France and give the tongues a rest." He smiled wickedly. "But what will they have to talk about once we're gone?"

She gave him a pert look. "Oh, doubtless they'll find someone else to bother."

"I'll inform Lauren of our plans. Have you asked the husband if he wants to go?"

Felice looked exasperated. "I wish you wouldn't refer to Brendan as 'the husband.' He does have a name."

Julian laughed. "I like Brendan, as you very well know. I admire the man's remarkable endurance. Look how long he's put up with you."

She threw her napkin at him, which he laughingly dodged. "Monster!"

"Brendan will think you're the monster if you run up the kind of bills I think you will while we're in France."

She smiled mischievously. "The French do have such excellent taste in clothes. I know I won't be able to resist all those luscious confections."

"Just keep Lauren away!"

"You can well afford to spoil her!"

"I don't mind her buying a new wardrobe, but between the two of you I doubt there'll be enough dresses left for the Frenchwomen."

"All's fair in love and fashion," Felice said as she gaily danced from the room.

* * *

Once the trip to France was mentioned to Lauren, Molly spent days organizing Lauren's wardrobe. Visits were often long, protracted affairs and in this case, they planned to stay several months in France. Molly even bought herself a few new things to take to France, exclaiming that the "Frenchies" had an eye for the ladies and she wanted to catch every eye she could.

"And what makes you think I'm taking you along?" Lauren had teased.

"With you cold-shouldering his lordship and him ignoring your bed like it was poison, there's no one else to do up your dresses and lace your underclothes. Not take me? Hmph! I'd like to see you leave me behind."

Lauren knew she could not and would not argue with such delicate, well-phrased logic.

On May 17, 1770, Marie Antoinette wed the future King of France. The ceremony was the beginning of a week of parties and balls that would celebrate the union.

Even Julian was caught up in the air of festivity that engulfed Versailles and Paris. He laughed and danced with an abandon that made his sister give a secret smile of delight. She rightly attributed this change to Lauren, who had dropped her aloof air and enjoyed the gaiety of Paris.

Lauren no longer shied away at Julian's touch, although she still would not let down all her barriers. Julian had hurt her very badly and she was afraid to let him get close enough to hurt her again. Her tender heart was still bruised. He was being very kind and charming, and that helped in a small way to narrow the wide gulf that was still between husband and wife.

They were attending a ball being held in the new Salle de l'Opéra and everywhere Lauren looked there was a display of opulence. The men had gone to seek refreshments while Lauren waited with Felice and Nicolet de Palissy.

"Ah, look," Nicolet whispered, nodding her head toward the dance floor where a man was leading a woman to the center of the room. "The Princess of Lorraine is going to dance the minuet."

"I'm glad you were not so foolish as to be hurt by this action," Felice murmured as they watched the couple slowly go through the motions of the dance.

Nicolet laughed. "Oh, I think it's rather funny, really. But the other duchesses of France think they have been slapped in the face by the King."

Lauren shook her head. "I don't understand what the problem is." As she glanced around she could see the anger on many people's faces as they watched the couple dance.

"The aristocracy jealously guards its rights and privileges. Some think that by letting the Princess dance before the nobles of France another rank is being placed between the princes of the blood and the dukes and duchesses of France. It's nice to know that Simon is not so petty. He refused to sign the petition the nobles sent to the King requesting that he not allow the Princess to dance before them." She laughed.

"Simon said it was merely a way for the King to show the Empress of Austria, Maria Theresa, that all is going well between France and Austria." She lifted her hand in a dismissive gesture. "There is no great political disaster occurring."

Even as Nicolet spoke, Lauren noticed that many people were refusing to dance and some were leaving the room as a gesture of their displeasure.

"I haven't seen Madame du Barry tonight. Will she be bold enough to appear?" Felice asked.

"I doubt she will let any opportunity pass to flaunt her power over the King." Nicolet grimaced, then laughed. "I heard an amusing piece of gossip about the King's mistress, but I don't know if it's true."

"Tell us!" Felice said eagerly.

"When the King went to meet Marie Antoinette at the Forest of Compiegne, he then escorted her back to the château on the outskirts of the forest. There, he gave a dinner for a few people of the highest rank. Well, who do you think was there?"

"Not Madame du Barry!" Felice exclaimed in horror.

Nicolet nodded. "The one and only."

"Did Marie Antoinette know she was the King's mistress?" Lauren asked.

Nicolet shook her head and giggled. "No. She innocently wanted to know what the Comtesse du Barry did at court. A woman sitting near her reportedly blushed and said the Comtesse amused the King."

All three women laughed. "And then," Nicolet continued once she had caught her breath, "Marie Antoinette said that she would be the Comtesse's rival!"

"That poor child!" Felice cried. "Only fifteen years old and having to fend for herself in this place."

"There will be many seeking to use her for their own ends," Nicolet said sadly. "Of course, Madame du Barry is the one to toady to if you really want something from the King." She stopped talking and her eyes widened. "There is the Comtesse with the Duc d'Aiguillon."

Even as Lauren followed Nicolet's gaze, her heart started to race furiously. D'Aiguillon was a name she would never forget, for he had been the man in charge when the attempt to take Brittany had failed. That had been the British defeat which had sealed her father's fate.

"Ah, here come the men!" Felice said, unaware of Lauren's troubled countenance.

It was much later, when they went into the palace gardens to watch the fireworks, that Lauren found herself standing by Nicolet.

"I was wondering," she said hesitantly. "Is the Duc d'Aiguillon the same gentleman who was once the Governor-General of Brittany?"

"*Oui!*" She looked curiously at Lauren. "Do you know him?"

"No. I've just heard of him."

"He might once have been Governor, but the people of Brittany have no love for him."

"Why?" Lauren was curious, even though she hated to reopen an old wound.

"The Parliament of Rennes refused to collect a tax he ordered and he became angry. I'm not sure if he dismissed the parliament or if they resigned, but then d'Aiguillon tried to form his own parliament. After that he was recalled from Brittany.

"Perhaps I should explain that our parliament is not like the one you have in England. Ours is more like a judicial court, and is composed of rich lawyers.

"Well, d'Aiguillon is the Duc de Richelieu's nephew, and some say Richelieu, along with Madame du Barry, plans to make him the new minister."

"But what of Choiseul? Isn't he now the minister of the government?"

"True, but Choiseul takes every opportunity to slight the new mistress and his hostility toward her has been noted by many. I've heard from reliable sources that Choiseul had hoped his sister, the Duchesse of Gramont, would be the King's mistress when Madame de Pompadour died. You can imagine their fury when the King chose to take a common prostitute into his bed over a woman of the nobility."

"But Madame de Pompadour was not of the nobility," Lauren protested.

"Yes, but still she had not been the kept woman of no telling how many roués. The man she was living with when the King became enamored of her is nothing more than a procurer! Jean du Barry called himself Comte but it is really his brother, Guillaume, who holds that title. The King insisted that du Barry be married before she came to him, so Jean paid his brother to marry her and then he quietly disappeared."

"And this woman now has enough power that she can choose the new minister?" Lauren asked.

"Oui! She is the most powerful woman in France because she has the ear and the affections of the King. So you see how much it is to one's advantage to have Madame du Barry on his side?"

"Yes, of course," she said absently. It all seemed rather strange to her, due to her sheltered upbringing in the convent.

"Ah, there is Choiseul with his wife and sister. I also see Mademoiselle de Lespinasse with Monsieur d'Alembert. Oh, and the Duc de Romoulet as well as the Comte de Bernave."

Lauren's head swiveled sharply at Nicolet's words. "Where is the Duc de Romoulet?" she demanded.

The past was again rushing in on her, gripping her as names heard long ago were now re-emerging. All those years ago the Duc de Romoulet had signed the awful letter that had been responsible for her father's disgrace. If the man was here, perhaps he held the key to that mystery and could clear her father's name.

"That is him standing alone," Nicolet said.

Lauren followed Nicolet's gaze and saw a tall, thin man with thick black hair. His face was sharply defined with a long nose and high cheekbones. He was not exactly handsome, but he did draw the eye with his somber expression and aristocratic bearing.

"Could—I mean, well, could you introduce me to him?" Lauren asked hesitantly.

Nicolet sent a swift glance to Julian, but he

was laughing at something Simon was saying and did not notice their conversation.

"I don't think that would be a good idea," she whispered.

"Why not?"

"I don't think Julian would like you to be associated with such a man. He has a terrible reputation with women. Some say he rivals Richelieu in his appetites."

Lauren gave a nervous laugh. "I don't want to go to bed with him, Nicolet. I just want to meet him."

"If it's all right with Julian, then I will."

"No! I mean, I don't want Julian to know."

Nicolet looked decidedly uneasy. "Are you telling me everything? I wouldn't want to do anything to hurt Julian."

"Nothing I do will hurt him," Lauren said coldly.

"I wouldn't be too sure of that. He has a certain look in his eyes when his glance rests on you. I think he might be the possessive type once he finds true love."

Lauren wanted to tell Nicolet that Julian knew nothing about love, but she held her tongue. Nicolet was, after all, Julian's cousin.

"Please. Just introduce me. No one need know."

"I'll think about it," Nicolet said.

As if becoming aware of someone's attention focused on him, the Duc de Romoulet stopped and looked around before his eyes settled on Lauren.

She did not know what to do, but her eyes

would not leave his face. He bowed and gave her a dazzling smile before he walked away.

"You see what I mean?" Nicolet asked.

"There is an air of wickedness about him," Lauren mused aloud before she turned her gaze back to the scene around her.

In the gardens jugglers wandered through the throng, as well as acrobats and other entertainers. Lights hung from trees, and a group of musicians softly played as couples danced in the woods.

Their party was sitting under a crystal chandelier that had been hung in a tree when a woman passed their table, stopped, and then returned.

"Julian!" she announced in gay tones. "What are you doing here?"

"Hello, Monica," he returned her greeting with a slight smile.

"And how are you, Monica?" Felice asked, sending a nervous glance at Lauren.

"I'm enjoying myself very much. The French really know how to treat a woman," she laughed, throwing the subtle barb at Julian.

Monica's gaze went around the table and rested on Lauren. Her eyes narrowed angrily, but then a smile touched her lips. "And this must be your wife, Julian."

He nodded curtly and then rose to his feet. "Come dance with me," he said, not wanting Monica's malicious tongue to harm Lauren.

Lauren, unaware that he was protecting her, could only see that he was dancing with the woman who had once been his mistress, and the one woman who had outlasted all his other affairs until she had demanded too much of him.

Felice saw Lauren's lips tighten and grinned to herself. If Lauren was jealous then there might be hope for them yet.

Anger boiled up within Lauren as she watched Julian and Monica. Did he have to hold her so intimately? she wondered. Did he have to laugh at what she was saying? They seem to be enjoying themselves, she thought angrily. Then, without giving herself time to think about the wisdom of her actions, she stood and moved away from the others. She was well aware that she was going in the direction of the Duc de Romoulet, but that did not stop her.

She saw him leaning against a tree, watching the lighted gondolas drift down the canal. He must have heard her approach because she was almost alongside him when he laughed.

"What took you so long, *chérie?*"

She froze at his words. He turned and gave her a devilish look. "I was waiting for you."

"H-how did you know I would follow you?" she asked nervously, for she had not known what she would do until the moment it had happened.

"Let us say I just knew."

She wondered if he knew who she was and that he was responsible for ruining her father, but then his words eased her worry.

"I have learned to recognize certain signs in women. I know when they are restless or sad. I know when they are tired of their matrimonial roles. You didn't look happy, and an unhappy woman is always searching for love."

"Perhaps I found love only to discover that it

is not what I thought it would be," she said, haughtily, not liking the way he talked about her. He was acting as if she wanted an affair with him.

"Ah, a disillusioned woman is even more eager for love. You see, no matter how many times women might be hurt by a man, they still cling to the hope that there is that one perfect man out there just waiting for them to find him."

"Are you saying that we are tenacious, monsieur? Or that we are foolish?"

He took a step toward her until he was looking down into the violet depths of her eyes. He caught his breath at her beauty and felt desire rise in him.

"Never foolish," he murmured huskily. "I admire women who never lose faith in mankind."

"Even if it was a man who was unkind to her?"

"Certainement!"

Lauren was at once repelled and attracted to this man. She was repelled by the lustful gleam in his eyes and the bold way he seemed mentally to strip her of her gown, but she was also drawn to him by the need to know the man who had been partly responsible for her father's disgrace. Playing the coquette had never been her forte, but she suddenly knew that she had to do something to get his interest or she might never learn the truth about his role all those years ago.

"I think I could have faith in you," she said, making her voice soft and seductive. "Could you reaffirm my faith in men?"

"Avec plaisir!" He growled deeply before he reached for her.

Lauren was appalled. She had meant to tease him, to lead him along, not realizing how potent her charms were or how hungry he was to sample them. She tried to step back, but his arms caught her, pulling her close to his chest.

"Let me go!" she cried.

He pulled back, surprise on his face. "What is wrong, *ma petite?*"

She quickly calmed herself. He shouldn't think she was afraid, even though she was.

"Th-this is not the place. M-my husband might come upon us."

He grinned. "How true. I should learn to curb my impetuosity. When and where shall we meet?"

Quickly, Lauren searched through her mind and found an answer. "I go riding every morning in the forest near the Palissy estate. Perhaps we could meet there and talk."

"Talk?" He lifted an inquiring eyebrow. "Shall we want to talk?"

"Talk," she repeated firmly before she turned away.

She left him and walked away into the shadows, when Julian moved from behind a tree to stand in front of her.

"Is your little tête-á-tête finished?" he demanded in a rough voice.

"Oh, you startled me!" she gasped.

"I was sure you were too busy to notice me," he said.

"The last time I saw you, you were dancing with Monica. I thought it would take you longer to discuss old times," she scorned.

"Leave Monica out of this! We're discussing you and your behavior!"

"But Monica is so very much a part of us. You wouldn't have married me had she not decided she wanted to be your wife."

He sighed. "I didn't make her my wife, though, did I?"

"No, but you're probably thinking you can take up where you left off!"

"Monica doesn't interest me. Can you say the same for that man you were with?"

"I *am* interested in him, but not for the sordid reasons your tiny mind has worked out!"

He caught her arm, shaking her. "The Duc has a reputation with women and I don't want your name linked with his."

She laughed. "I wonder how many husbands said the same thing about you when they lectured their wives on their infidelity?"

"The women were always well aware of what they were getting into. They weren't innocents like you are."

"I'm not innocent! You saw to that!"

"Enough of this, Lauren! I want you to stay away from the Duc."

"I want you to stay away from Monica!"

"If I didn't know better, I'd think you were jealous!" he blurted out.

"I'm thinking the same thing about you!" she returned with equal heat.

"Ha! I just don't want my wife's reputation to be in doubt."

"Oh, it's not in doubt! You ruined it long ago."

Felice approached and was immediately aware of the tension between them. She had thought they were beginning to get along together.

"Julian! Lauren! Anyone could come upon you and hear you arguing like children!"

"Children don't get into the kind of trouble Lauren's pursuing!" Julian snarled.

"What do you know about children?" Lauren taunted. "You're too busy chasing their mothers!"

"Stop it!" Felice urged. "Can't this at least wait until we're back at Nicolet's?"

Julian stormed off, leaving the two women alone. Felice noticed that Lauren was shuddering.

"What was that all about?" she asked quietly. "I've never seen Julian so angry."

"Oh, he's always like that when he's with me. All we ever do is argue."

Felice gave her a mischievous look. "I wouldn't say that. I seem to remember a time when Julian couldn't stay away from you. You must have been happy together once."

Lauren blushed. "That was a lifetime ago."

"Not so long ago." Her eyes were filled with tenderness. "Don't you think you've punished Julian enough?" she asked in a soft voice.

Lauren looked incredulous. "I'm not punishing Julian!"

"I think you are. I think you're both punishing each other by not admitting you care for one another."

"I don't care for him! He only married me to save himself from Monica. He made me leave my grandfather when I wanted to stay with him.

At least I knew Grandfather only wanted my happiness."

"It seems to me that he caused himself more trouble by marrying you than he saved. He's irritable, short-tempered, and hasn't been eating well. Oh, I know that he's always been the very devil when he's angry, but he's different now. His bad temper used to be short-lived, but now it's part of his personality."

"I'm sorry, Felice. I-I want us to be friends, but I don't wish to discuss my marriage with you."

"Then discuss it with Julian! Get everything out in the open and maybe you'll both see reason."

"Here comes Nicolet," Lauren interrupted. "Let's go and join the others. We've been away too long."

Felice groaned inwardly, but there was little she could do but follow Lauren as she made her way toward Nicolet.

The night was turning to dawn when the three couples found themselves on their way home.

Lauren rested wearily against the velvet seats and gazed out at the slowly lightening landscape. Julian lounged beside her, his eyes closed, giving every appearance of being asleep. Lauren dreaded having to go back to the estate because she knew her argument with Julian was not finished.

They arrived at the Palissy château and once inside, Nicolet wanted them all to come into the sitting room and enjoy a drink before going to bed. They agreed and followed her into the room.

Nicolet was a tall woman with beautiful blond hair, while Simon de Palissy was as dark as she was fair; they made a striking couple. Everyone was aware that they were deeply in love and Lauren felt very sad seeing them, as well as Felice and Brendan, so content. If only things had been different between her and Julian. If only he had loved her to distraction as Simon seemed to do with Nicolet. Even Brendan and Felice were cooing at each other like lovebirds, while she and Julian sat on opposite ends of the sofa, ignoring each other.

"I had a wonderful time tonight," Nicolet's voice bubbled with enthusiasm. "Weren't the fireworks beautiful? All those exploding colors!"

"It was a dazzling display," Brendan murmured. "I must admit that hardened as I am to balls of every kind, this one will long live in my memory as the best."

"Versailles was like a fairyland tonight," Felice gushed. "All those fountains lit up and everyone parading around in their finery! Those gowns! Some of them must have cost a small fortune."

"I've heard that life at court is so expensive it ruins some of the nobles," Brendan added.

"That's true," Simon returned. "Many nobles leave their estates and flutter about the King hoping to get some petty privilege. I'm lucky that I live so close to Versailles. I can attend the King when I must and yet not neglect my responsibilities."

"Madame du Barry is very lovely," Felice sighed. "Did you see all those jewels she was wearing? Brendan is very generous with me, but her jewels were extraordinary."

Nicolet smiled at Felice's wide-eyed look. "She's about to bankrupt the treasury with her desire for jewels and dresses. Each article she receives seems to outdo the last."

"The King is infatuated with her," Simon shrugged. "Someone asked the King what he saw in her and he said that she made him forget he was growing old."

"She's lovely enough to make a man get up from his deathbed!" Brendan grinned.

"Just make sure you don't get tempted by her charms!" Felice sniffed.

"She has her eye on the King, my darling. She'd never give me a second look."

Lauren grew bored with the conversation and stood up, ready to leave. "I think I'll retire. It's been a long day."

"By all means," Nicolet assured her. "Will your maid be waiting for you?"

Lauren smiled. "Molly probably couldn't sleep waiting for me to return. She wants me to tell her all about the ball."

"There are celebrations in Paris tomorrow. Perhaps she could attend those. I know our servants are just as eager to enjoy the festivities."

"Thank you. I'm sure Molly would enjoy that."

The gentlemen stood and watched as she gracefully made her way from the room and up the stairs. When she reached her room, she saw Molly sitting in a chair, fast asleep. Lauren closed the door softly, but Molly stirred anyway.

Molly sleepily rubbed her eyes as she looked

at Lauren. "What was it like?" she asked eagerly.

Lauren closed her eyes on a dreamy sigh. "It was beautiful! You should have seen all the silks and satins reflected in the mirrors that lined the walls. I heard someone say that over four thousand people had been invited."

The door opened behind Lauren and she turned with a smile on her face. When she saw Julian enter, the smile slipped away to be replaced by a frown.

"What do you want?" she demanded in a cold voice. "It's late and I want to go to bed."

"You knew we did not finish our earlier conversation." His tone threatened her, making her temper come to the fore.

"I have nothing to say to you!"

"Then I shall do the talking," he assured her. He sent Molly a dismissive glance. "Leave us!" he ordered curtly.

"Stay, Molly!" Lauren insisted as Molly started to leave.

"Go!" Julian repeated and Molly placed her hands on her hips.

"What am I to do?" she queried in a sarcastic voice. "Am I to go or stay?"

Julian gave her a fierce look. "I said to leave!" he growled and Molly scuttled from the room.

"How dare you order my servants about!" Lauren said in an offended tone.

"She knows who pays her wages."

"Of course! How remiss of me to forget that money talks!"

"I want you to stay away from the Duc de Romoulet!"

She arched one eyebrow. "We only talked."

"His talk is aimed at getting on your better side. Did he ply you with words describing your beauty?" he sneered.

"At least some men find me beautiful and desirable!"

"If I find him in your bed, Lauren," his voice was soft and menacing, "then it will be the last bed he warms!"

Her eyes narrowed to two violet slits of rage. "How dare you speak thus to me as if I were some common strumpet seeking a man!"

"Perhaps I remember how easily I crawled between your legs!"

She flinched at his words as if he had struck her, and indeed she did feel a pain in the region of her heart. She had given herself so lovingly to him, but now his words besmirched that memory.

Julian immediately regretted his words, which had been fueled by anger and jealousy, but he did not know how to take them back.

"You, my lord, have shattered my last illusion! If you think me so lowly as to bed all and sundry, then I might as well comply!"

"Is that an offer for me to share your bed?"

"Certainly not!" she hissed.

"You once let me into your bed readily."

"That was before I knew what a fool I was!" she cried, turning her back on him.

He moved closer until he was almost touching her. He could smell the sweet scent of lilacs that rose from her hair and he wanted to touch her with a need that was painful. His hands touched her shoulders and she jerked, but he did not release her.

"Don't!" she said, trying to twist away.

"You used to like me to do this," he murmured huskily before his lips touched her neck.

"I did not!" she angrily refuted, throwing back her head so he could see the angry sparks in her eyes.

"Things don't have to be like this between us," he insisted as he turned her to face him. There was a tender expression on his face. "We don't have to deny ourselves the joys of the marriage bed."

"There would be no joy!"

"Let me show you," he entreated, pulling her closer.

"It seems that marriage was indeed the death of our love, for I no longer desire you," she lied, hoping he would go before she made a fool of herself.

He flinched and his eyes grew cold. "So I was right! Once a woman is secure in marriage then she has no need to play the lover!"

"Marriage would be wonderful with the right man, but you, with your strong dislike of the institution, you killed my love as surely as if you had run a sword through it! You can't disown me and then claim me when the mood is upon you!"

He pushed her away. "The mood, as you say, is no longer upon me, madame. Your shrill tongue would kill even the most devoted desire!"

"Good! Go then, and leave me alone!"

He bowed mockingly. "Just remember," he

warned. "Even though I do not want you, I'll not be cuckolded!"

"And will you deny yourself other lovers?" she recklessly retorted.

He smiled sardonically. "You deny me your bed. What else am I to do? Men were not meant to be deprived of such a basic need."

"And whom will you bed? Your old mistress?"

"Monica pleased me well enough at one time. She will probably suffice, and if not, then Paris is full of women eager to please."

"If you do, Julian—" she threatened.

His lips lifted in a small smile. "Of course, I could reconsider if I had a better offer."

She clamped her lips together and, turning away, she heard him chuckle as if he had scored a point.

"Go ahead! Seek out these women who are so eager for your attentions, but be careful they don't give you something more than satisfaction!"

"What a little cat you are when you're aroused," he laughed.

"Just go!" she screamed, rushing across the room and into the bedroom. She quickly locked the door and leaned against it as tears coursed down her cheeks.

The handle was tried, but when he found no easy admittance, he knocked impatiently. There was no response from within and he grew angry.

"Lauren!" he called through the portal. "Open this door!"

There was still no sound, so he hit the door with his fist. "Open this door or I'll break your bloody neck!" he roared in frustration.

A laugh came from behind and he whirled angrily to find Molly standing there with a grin on her face.

"What's so damned amusing?" he wanted to know.

"You are," she returned with a bluntness that halted him. "You're telling her to open the door so you can break her neck. I'm surprised she's still locked in there!"

"Oh, hell and damnation!" he cursed. "I'm beleaguered by snapping females!" he stormed before he left the room.

Molly leaned closer to the door. "He's gone!" she called.

She heard the click of the lock and then the door opened, revealing Lauren with red-rimmed eyes.

"Why do we treat each other like this, Molly?" she asked in a sorrowful voice. "Why must we tear each other apart?"

"You're both hurting and you lash out at the thing that hurts you the most."

"I don't even recognize myself of late," she whispered, wiping away a tear. "I never knew there could be so much bitterness within me."

"Why not go to Lord Keaton's room and apologize?" Molly asked eagerly.

"No," Lauren was quick to return. "He should apologize. He makes me the way I am with his taunts!"

"There can never be peace until someone makes the first move."

"I—I just can't!" She sharply caught her breath. "If he would but show me a little love then I would gladly throw myself at his feet and beg forgiveness," she softly declared. "But I'll not open myself up for his scorn by going to him when he doesn't really want me. Any warm body would satisfy him!"

"That's not true!" Molly denied. "I've heard the servants' gossip and they say he has no mistress."

"He probably will by tomorrow," she said as fresh tears fell. "I fear I have sent him into another's arms when that is the last place I want him to be!"

Lauren cried herself to sleep that night, and Molly climbed into her own bed, wondering what would become of the two proud people caught up in a desire so intense it would surely destroy them if they did not give in to it.

The next morning Lauren went down to the stables for her ride. A lovely white mare had been offered to her by Nicolet, and Lauren was free to ride her whenever she wanted. She saw the horse standing proudly by the gate, already saddled.

"Bonjour, madame!" the groom called, walking toward her. "Your horse is already prepared."

Henri was a kind man with a rotund belly and rosy cheeks.

"Merci, Henri," she returned with a smile. She noticed that several servants were searching the stalls. "Are they looking for something?" she asked, nodding in their direction.

Henri glanced over his shoulder. *"Ah, oui!* It seems that a strange man was seen lurking about. We told the Duc de Palissy and he ordered the grounds to be searched." He lifted his shoulders regretfully. "We have found no one."

"Do you think it was a poacher?"

"Who knows? Perhaps it would be wise if you didn't ride alone until this man is found."

She laughed. "I'll be fine."

"Are you sure, madame? It would be easy to get one of the men to accompany you."

"I like the privacy of my morning ride," she told him honestly. "I wouldn't enjoy the ride half so much if I knew I was being followed."

"Whatever you say, madame," he said, respectfully tilting his hat.

Lauren rode out of the yard and started down the road. When she saw Nicolet approaching in an open carriage, she pulled on the reins to stop the horse. They snapped in her hand and she went flying backward to land in a heap on the ground.

Nicolet stopped the carriage and rushed over to Lauren. She bent over her with an anxious exclamation.

"Oh, my dear! Are you all right? What happened?"

"I—I don't know." Lauren was very shaken. She tried to get up and winced as a shaft of pain lanced up her leg. "I think I've hurt my ankle!"

"I hope that's all it is," Nicolet said in concern before she ordered her servant to place Lauren in the carriage. "Send someone after her horse!" Nicolet ordered before they started for the house.

The carriage pulled up before the door and Lauren was carefully lifted by a servant and carried into the house. She was taken to her room where Molly exclaimed over her and bustled about pulling back the bedcovers so Lauren could be put to bed.

"I'll send for a physician!" Nicolet said worriedly. "It's too bad that Julian has gone hunting with Simon and Brendan. Will you be all right if I leave you for a few moments?"

"Molly will take care of me," Lauren insisted. "There's no need to send for a physician."

"But it might be broken. I must insist," she declared before she left the room.

"What happened?" Molly asked, pulling the boot off her uninjured foot.

"I don't know. One minute everything was fine, and the next I'm falling off the horse."

When Molly tried to take off her other boot, Lauren moaned in pain and a fine mist of perspiration broke out on her brow.

"It's swollen!" Molly grimaced. "Shall I leave the boot on your foot?"

"N-no," she whispered brokenly. "It will have to come off sooner or later."

Molly was very careful, but still Lauren could not help but cry out as the boot came off her foot. There was a large purple bruise on the pale skin of her ankle, and it hurt when she tried to move it.

"I'll get some hot water and we'll soak it," Molly soothed.

"I hope it isn't broken!" Lauren wailed.

"We'll find out soon enough. You just rest and I'll see about getting that water."

After Molly bathed her foot, she tucked the covers around Lauren and clucked about her like a mother hen. "I'll send a message to Lord Keaton," she began, but Lauren stopped her.

"No! There's no need to bother him over something so trivial."

"He'll want to know," Molly insisted, standing back to view Lauren with a disapproving expression on her face.

"I'm—I'm not hurt that badly. Just let me rest for a while and I'll be fine."

Molly made a face, but closed the curtains around the bed, creating a warm, dark resting place for Lauren. "I'll be back soon," she said softly, for already Lauren's eyelids were drooping with fatigue.

It was late in the evening when the men returned. They were in the library drinking brandy when Felice found them.

"I'm glad you're back," she said anxiously.

"What's the matter?" Brendan asked, attuned to his wife's distress.

"Lauren had an accident—" she began, but did not finish as Julian's glass slipped from his fingers to crash to the floor.

His face was white and his eyes were pained as he stepped forward.

"Lauren's been hurt?"

"Yes," she said, but added quickly, "It was nothing serious. She fell from her horse and twisted her ankle. The doctor was here and he said it wasn't broken, but she'll have to stay off it for a few days to prevent permanent damage."

"Thank God," he murmured fervently, and everyone in the room looked away in embarrassment at having witnessed Julian in the grip of such strong emotion. "Can I see her?"

Felice shook her head. "She's asleep now. The

doctor gave her something for the pain. Thank goodness he didn't bleed her, because she was looking very pale."

"That's strange that she should be thrown," Julian spoke in an undertone. "She's an excellent rider."

"Er—that's something else," Felice added.

"What?" Julian was instantly alert.

"It seems that her bridle had been cut. A man was seen earlier lurking about the stables, but when the grounds were searched, they could find no one. Nicolet saw Lauren riding away from the house and Lauren stopped to talk to her just before she fell. The head groom said it was a good thing she was not riding very fast and stopped when she did, otherwise Lauren might have broken her neck."

Julian slumped into a chair and Brendan hastily poured him a glass of brandy to replace the one he had dropped. Julian downed it without thinking.

"I must thank Nicolet for attending to Lauren. How lucky that she was on the road at that time."

Felice motioned to the two men to leave the room and when the door closed behind them, she came to kneel in front of her brother.

"This should be a lesson for you." Her words were spoken softly and he glance up.

"What?" he asked. He was still dazed by the events of the day.

"This should show you how foolish you have been acting. Life is too short to let pride stand in the way of happiness. What if she had died—"

"Enough!" he growled, his eyes narrowing in pain.

"But what if she had?" she persisted. "All this fighting and wounding would have been on your conscience. You love her, don't you?" she asked, gently stroking his hand.

"How do you know that?" he frowned, even now finding it hard to express himself with words.

"I saw the way you looked when you heard Lauren was hurt. You couldn't hide the way you feel. It was there for everyone to see."

"Everyone but Lauren," he said enigmatically.

"She didn't see it, but you can tell her."

He shook his head, looking into the empty glass as if it might hold another drink to sustain him.

"You can!" Felice breathed, tightening her grip on his hand.

"Lauren doesn't want to hear my lovesick words. She's finished with me. She says I killed any love she might have had for me."

"Words! Angry, impulsive words!"

He smiled sadly. "How can you be so sure? Can you read her heart?"

"I'm a woman and that gives me some insight. When you wound her she returns the pain without thinking. It is an instinct to guard the heart from destruction."

"I don't know, Felice."

She laughed. "Is this the proud Lord Keaton who single-handedly made a fortune? Is this the charming lover who wooed the loveliest women of England and kept them hanging on his every word? I thought no woman could resist you."

"Lauren is different," he said emphatically.

"I know. Only the truth will win her."

"The truth!" he muttered. "I don't know what the truth is anymore."

"Yes you do!" she urged.

Julian sighed heavily. "Yes, maybe I do....I love her."

"Was that so hard to say?" she grinned.

"No, but just because I can tell you it doesn't mean I can tell Lauren."

"But she is the one who needs most to know!"

"What a meddling, interfering sister you are," he laughed. "And how I love you for that."

"And I love you, dear brother. I only want you to be happy."

He suddenly grew solemn. "What if I bare my heart to her and she rejects me? I don't think I could stand it if she scorned my love."

"There are many gambles in life. If we want to live life to the fullest then we must sometimes take a risk."

He slowly nodded. "Perhaps you are right. But if she should reject me then I'll have to release her." A sadness entered his eyes. "That is a gamble I am loath to take."

"Why don't you go upstairs and see her. She's asleep, but it may ease your mind to know that she's all right."

"I think I will," he smiled, patting her hand. "Go to bed now, Felice." She moved away but his voice stopped her at the door. "And thank you for listening to my troubled ramblings."

"That's what sisters are for."

"Oh?" He cocked his head to one side. "Is that what they're for? I've often wondered what their usefulness was."

"Beast!" she laughed.

"Good night," he called.

"Good night, and pleasant dreams."

When he was alone, he leaned his head against the chair and closed his eyes. He felt drained of all energy, as if his confession to Felice had been too much for him. As he sat, a peacefulness came over him and he knew that a burden had been lifted. He had admitted loving Lauren, and the admission had been a true release for him.

Julian had fought against his heart, denied his feelings, but now he knew for sure that his love for Lauren was strong enough to face all odds. Love had fought a battle with his stubborn mind and his old resolutions—and won. He was glad to yield if only Lauren would return a tenth of the love he had for her. He was truly humbled now, for he would now take crumbs of affection if he could not have her whole heart.

There are two births, the one when light
    First strikes the new awak'ned sense;
The other when two souls unite;
    And we must count our life from thense:
When you lov'd me, and I lov'd you,
Then both of us were born anew.
                    —William Cartwright

Chapter Eleven

"I'm so tired of lying in this bed," Lauren moaned. It had been a week since her accident and she was thoroughly sick of the inactivity.

"The doctor said you had to stay in bed and rest until the bruises healed."

"I'm healed already!" she stormed, venting her frustration on Molly.

"Obviously your temper hasn't healed." Julian's voice came from the doorway.

Lauren's heart skipped a beat when she saw him standing so tall and handsome before her. Lately, Julian's attitude toward her had mellowed; his eyes caressed her and his voice became gentle whenever he spoke to her. But still she was wary of him, watching him like a nervous rabbit ready to bound off at the slightest hint of a trap.

"Good morning, Lord Keaton," Molly beamed.

"Have you come to have breakfast with your wife?"

Every day since the accident, Julian had joined Lauren for breakfast in her room. She did not realize it, but it was part of his plan to win her love.

"No. I've come to tell Lauren the doctor said she could get up." His eyes twinkled at the look of delight that flashed across her face. "I thought you might enjoy a walk in the gardens."

"That sounds wonderful."

"Then get dressed and I'll wait for you outside."

When Lauren came downstairs, she was amazed to see Julian through the window cutting flowers. As she went down the path to join him her heart beat faster.

He held out a bouquet to her. "These are for you, though they pale next to your loveliness."

"They're beautiful," she said, burying her nose in the fragrant blossoms to hide her blush. She found Julian irresistible in this light mood, and the morning air could not have seemed more pleasant as she strolled by his side.

"Let's sit beneath this tree," he said, taking her arm and pulling her over to a shady grove of fruit trees.

She spread her skirts around her as Julian sat down next to her. A bee buzzed by her and she shooed it away. She turned to Julian with a laugh, but it died on her lips when she saw the intent expression on his face.

He leaned closer, his senses stirred by her scent. Just as he was within a breath of his goal, Felice and Brendan came around the corner.

Julian jerked back with a groan and realized he had been outmaneuvered; he had failed to keep his eye on his flank. Frustration hardened his face.

"Lauren!" Felice rushed forward. "It's so good to see you're feeling better."

"I've felt fine for the last two days, but the silly doctor insisted I stay in bed. I would have ignored him, but Molly stood over me and made me obey."

"That Molly is quite formidable. And speaking of formidable, why are you glaring at me, Julian?"

Julian wiped the expression from his face. "What do you mean, Felice?" he asked, feigning innocence.

She was about to argue with him, but decided instead to sit beside Lauren and tell her of their trip into the village.

"I was just going to the stables, Julian. Would you like to come with me?" Brendan offered.

"Why not," Julian muttered.

The next day Lauren went shopping in the village with Felice and Nicolet, and the day after they went to visit a neighbor. It was not until the third day that Julian again found an opportunity to put his battle strategy to work.

Lauren was on the front lawn with her easel and paints. She was studying the house when he strolled lazily toward her.

"Do you need a subject?" he asked, stopping before her to strike a pose.

She laughed. "All you need is a chimney and I could paint you."

"You don't do portraits, I take it?"

She shook her head and laughed. "Some people might be unkind enough to say I do not do landscapes, either."

"Where is the rogue that would so defame my wife's fine art?" Julian demanded theatrically.

"Oh, please, sir," she pretended to beg. "Don't slay all my critics, for then there would be naught but you and me in this world."

"That would be ideal," he murmured. "I sometimes think we would get along together very well if we were just left alone."

Lauren became uneasy at the subtle change in Julian. She was discovering a new side of him, which she liked very much, but it was still too soon for her to open her heart to him completely. She could not bear the thought of suffering his rejection again.

"You would grow bored without other people to amuse you."

"I need no others," he said quietly.

"I once thought that, but you quickly proved me wrong."

"That is past history, Lauren. I have changed."

"You couldn't change that much. I don't think it's as easy as shedding an old cloak for a new one."

"Perhaps not, but my heart has indeed learned much these past weeks."

His words were meant to seduce, but their relationship was still new and fragile, and Lauren feared he might be teasing her. They were slowly rebuilding on a foundation that was yet too shaky to support trust. If he would but say he loved her, then she would eagerly rush into his arms. She waited expectantly, but the words did not come.

Julian, in turn, was wondering if now was the time to bare his heart to her, but he feared she might laugh at his words, thinking them a joke. He had played the light lover so well to her in the last few days that now he feared he had lost his nerve to try a bolder attack.

In an effort to appear relaxed, Julian leaned back against the tree, twirling a blade of grass between his fingers. His mind, however, continued to struggle with the need to let his heart speak.

Beside him, Lauren grew restless, interpreting his casualness as a return to the old cavalier Julian. She had thought him to be on the verge of a declaration of love, but she was mistaken. He seemed to have forgotten she was there.

A sob welled up in her throat. Not wanting Julian to see her cry, Lauren picked up her skirts and ran back to the house as Julian stared at her in complete bewilderment.

As Lauren came downstairs the next morning, she found the house full of preparations for the ball Simon and Nicolet had been planning for months; the event was now only a day away. Lauren felt a nervous expectancy within herself as she watched the servants bustle about polishing and cleaning everything in sight.

Slowly, she was coming to terms with her conflicting emotions: she wanted Julian to be the bold lover he'd been during their first encounters, as well as the friend who could tease her and make her laugh. But did he want this too?

Lauren hoped she had misjudged his feelings the other morning.

For the ball, she had bought a new pale gold gown the color of Julian's eyes. She had a gold feather to wear in her hair and gold slippers for her feet. The effect, she hoped, would entice him.

By the night of the ball, the floors of the ballroom had been polished until the reflection of the dancers could be seen in them. The chandeliers blazed with lights and the doors leading to the gardens had been left open to let the sweet scent of the flowers drift into the house. A table of delicacies had been laid out along one wall so the guests could nibble food when they took a break from the dancing to converse and flirt.

When Julian led Lauren into the first minuet, she felt her pulse flutter. She found she had only to look at him and the blood rushed wildly through her veins. She had to admit that he was the handsomest man there with his dark, somber coat and breeches and his impeccable linen. The other men looked like strange peacocks, she thought, since many of them wore colors that were too bright. Julian stood out among them, and she was proud that he was her husband.

"Are you enjoying yourself?" he asked when they came together in the dance.

"Yes," she smiled into his eyes, and then they parted as the steps of the dance demanded. It was as if they were fencing in some strange kind of duel as they came together and parted, only to find themselves face to face again. The dance was taking on a significance to her that she had never before noticed. He advanced and then retreated as she turned away. It was not unlike their relationship; she wanted him but always seemed to be turning him away because of her pride.

When the dance finished, he led her to a comfortable sofa where Felice and Brendan were sitting.

"It's a lovely ball," Felice murmured, glancing slyly at Lauren and Julian. It was good to see them at ease with one another and not bickering.

"And the women are even lovelier," Brendan said gallantly. He took Felice's hand and kissed it.

She blushed like a schoolgirl and Lauren looked away, feeling uncomfortable. She wanted Julian to act like that with her, she realized. With all her heart, she wanted his tender glance to touch her and his affection to enfold her like a warm blanket.

Had she ruined any chance they might have had at happiness, she wondered, by telling Julian that he had killed all love in her? It had been a lie, told in anger. She loved him with all her might. She had loved him even when he had denied her as his wife, even when he was overbearing and arrogant.

But their marriage would not survive if she continued to act as stubbornly as he did. Molly had said that someone had to make the first move. Lauren blushed as her thoughts tumbled quickly one over the other. Dare she make that first move? Or would she only be opening herself up to rejection?

Lauren did not want to spend the rest of her

life in a wary truce with Julian. She wanted to spend it in his arms. The thought of seducing her own husband almost made her laugh. Could she do it? she asked herself. The more she thought about the idea, the more merit it had.

"Lauren! Lauren!" Felice's anxious voice brought her back to the present, and she saw Julian and Brendan looking at her in concern.

"You were so far away from us," Brendan said. "Is something wrong?"

She gave a small smile. "No. I'm fine." But she could not meet their eyes.

"I don't think you are." Felice looked sternly at Julian. "She appears quite flushed. Hurry and get her something to drink."

Julian gave an exaggerated bow and left them.

Brendan stood up. "I'll be right back. I want to ask Simon something."

When they were gone, Felice turned to Lauren. "Would you like to tell me what's worrying you?" Her expression was kind and sympathetic.

"It was nothing." Lauren blushed again, knowing she could not tell Felice of the wanton, wicked idea she had of seducing Julian into her bed. She just could not talk about it to anyone. It was something that demanded action, not words.

Felice knitted her brow. "I know that I am Julian's sister, but that doesn't mean we can't be friends. I've always wanted a sister and I think I can be loyal to him as well as to you."

"I didn't mean to imply that I don't trust you!" Lauren looked upset.

"I know. I just wanted to let you know that

anytime you need someone to talk to, I'll be
there."

Lauren impulsively hugged Felice. "Thank
you," she murmured softly.

Felice's glance went to Julian, who stood
waiting to get a glass of wine. "He's my brother,
and I love him," she muttered. "But sometimes
I think he needs a good sharp nudge in the ribs!"

"And do you think the same thing of me?"
Lauren asked mischievously.

"I certainly do!" she laughed, and Lauren
joined her.

Julian returned with the wine and Lauren
slowly sipped it, watching while the dancers
went through their paces on the floor. She did
not see the woman approach until Monica was
standing by Julian.

"Julian!" she said seductively, putting her
hand on his arm. "I wondered where you were?"

"I'm with my wife, Monica." His lips twisted
contemptuously, but she did not choose to notice.

"I would have thought you would find domesticity confining after all this time," she said,
giving Lauren a resentful stare.

"We haven't been married a year yet, Monica," Julian laughed.

"But you were never known for your—uh,
constancy."

Lauren's eyes glittered angrily and Julian,
seeing the warning sign, quickly pushed Monica
toward the refreshment table.

"Let's get a glass of wine," he ordered, leading
her away.

"Oh! That woman!" Lauren's voice was frosty.

"Why doesn't she chase someone else's husband!"

"Don't say that!" Felice said, trying to lighten the situation. "She might go after Brendan."

"But he loves you," Lauren sounded wistful. "He wouldn't look twice at another woman."

"Don't underestimate Julian's powers of resistance. He's never liked pushy, clinging women."

"Then perhaps Monica is the exception," Lauren said tartly. "I heard that she lasted the longest of his mistresses. He must have seen something in her."

"Yes, but when one has had gold, tinsel does not seem so bright," Felice said softly.

"What do you mean?"

"Never mind. That's a beautiful dress you're wearing."

The evening passed and it was nearing midnight when Lauren slipped from the room, seeking the coolness of the balcony. She did not realize that someone had joined her until a man leaned over the railing beside her. Looking closely at him, she recognized him as the Duc de Romoulet.

"Good evening," she said, her voice cool.

"*Bon soir*, Lauren."

"How do you know my name?"

"It was easy to find out the names of Simon's houseguests. I asked who the loveliest woman in all of Paris was, and you were named."

"Don't try your flattery on me, monsieur. I'm immune."

He laughed. "I thought all women wanted men to sing their praises."

"False flattery fools no one."

"I waited for you at the forest, but you didn't come."

"There was an accident and I couldn't come." She swallowed. "It was a mistake to say I would meet you."

"No it wasn't. Why not meet me tomorrow."

"No!"

He sighed in exasperation. "A man likes a little chase, but don't be too coy."

"I'm not being coy, monsieur, and if your head was not so swollen with conceit you would see that I have no interest in you."

Instead of being shocked or angry at her tirade, the Duc seemed to be amused. He propped his head on his hand and lazily watched the agitated rise and fall of her breasts before his gaze drifted leisurely down to her narrow waist and then up again.

"I admire fire and spirit, especially when it is encased in a lovely form. Your form is exquisite."

"Will you leave me alone!" she demanded.

"But it was you who sought me out, madame. You were the one to whet my interest."

She sighed angrily. "I wasn't interested in you as a lover!" she scorned. "I wanted some information, but now I find it no longer matters. I intend to forget the past and look to the future."

"Information?" A puzzled frown appeared on his face. "What kind of information?"

"It was about something that happened a long time ago."

"If I can help you, then I will."

She looked at him closely. Could he be sincere? "My father was accused of treason years ago. The main piece of evidence was a letter from you thanking him for the information that led to the defeat of the British force at St. Cast."

"And what was your father's name?" he asked calmly. For some strange reason Lauren felt he already knew her father's name."

"Stephen Warwick."

"Stephen Warwick?" He paused and rubbed his chin. "The name doesn't sound familiar."

"Did you get information from someone in England about the proposed invasion and then pass that knowledge on to the Duc d'Aiguillon?"

"That was a long time ago, Lauren, and my memory is not what it once was."

"I see that you have no intention of enlightening me, so you might as well be on your way!" Her tone was bitter.

"Listen!" he growled. "No woman talks to me like that!"

"I just did!"

He glared at her and then caught her arm, jerking her into his embrace.

"Let me go! How dare you!"

"I shall find great pleasure in mastering you, *ma belle!*"

"Let her go!" A stony voice came from the doorway.

They both turned and Lauren swallowed nervously at the furious look on Julian's face. Surely he did not think she wanted this embrace.

"I said to let her go," he repeated, and the Duc moved away, releasing her.

"It seems your wife is not the constant type, either!" Monica grinned.

It was only when the woman spoke that Lauren noticed her looking so smug and triumphant as she stood beside Julian.

"Be quiet, Monica!" Julian's eyes seethed with angry golden lights.

Lauren wanted to proclaim her innocence, but could find no words. The cold, bitter man facing her now bore no resemblance to the kind companion of recent days.

"Your lovely wife and I were just talking." The Duc flinched at the fury in the other man's eyes.

"My idea of talking and yours are vastly different, monsieur!" Julian said tautly. "Go inside, Lauren," he ordered, and she quickly obeyed, rushing past him into the lighted room. He gave Monica a hard glare. "As much as I know you're enjoying this little scene, Monica, it does not concern you."

"Hmph!" she said, and with a flounce of her skirts she left.

"Stay away from my wife," he said now that he and the Duc were alone.

"I rather enjoy her company." Outwardly the Duc was cool, but inwardly he was quaking. This man looked like he could murder him.

"Then it will be pistols at dawn!" Julian almost shouted.

The Duc laughed nervously. "My dear fellow. I never wake before noon. Besides, I have no intention of tramping around in the damp grass just to appease your outraged sense of betrayal. Nothing happened between us."

"Very well, but if I ever catch you with her again, you'll not be able to slink away like the

snake that you are." Julian turned on his heel
and marched away, leaving the Duc to wipe his
damp brow.

"Where's Lauren?" he asked Felice when he
could not find his wife anywhere.

"She's gone to bed. She said she had a head-
ache. The poor thing looked quite shaken."

He nodded curtly and left the ballroom, making his way up the stairs to the second landing.
He threw open the door to Lauren's room and
stopped abruptly at the sight of her sitting in a
tub full of bubbles.

She blushed at his bold look and lowered her
eyes. "I w-wanted to wash the touch of that man
from my skin," she said quietly.

He stood stiffly, fighting down the urgings of
his body. She looked so lovely there with the
bubbles around her, her long dark hair escaping
from its confining knot.

"I—" he cleared his throat. "I just wanted you
to know that I overheard part of the conversation. I know that you didn't seek his attentions."

"Th-thank you, Julian."

"Why should you thank me?" His voice was
strained.

"For not thinking me guilty. Thank you for
trusting me."

"I do trust you," he said wryly. "It's every man
in breeches with eyes in his head that I don't
trust."

She giggled. "Am I really that lovely?"

"You are lovely beyond my wildest dreams."
His voice was deep and husky.

Lauren was suddenly shy and nervous. She
had planned to seduce Julian, to be a true wife

to him, but now that the moment was at hand, she did not know if she could go through with it, as she was a mass of nerves. She felt burningly alive, and if he should touch her she feared she might go up in flames like a torch put to dry tinder.

"D-do you wish to stay?" Her voice was meek and she could not meet his eyes.

"Are you playing a game with me?" he asked coldly. "The chase is fine, but then comes the capture. I don't think my thwarted desires can stand another night without the taste of you."

Her eyes flew to his and she saw the hungry yearning in his gaze. "If you want me, then I am yours for this night."

"Never doubt that I want you." He gave an exasperated smile. "For some reason you have worked your subtle sorcery on me until all I can think about is your saucy smile and your silken skin. Others fade into insignificance when I remember the way you once clung to me with wild cries of delight."

"Your words woo me most persuasively, my lord," she said breathlessly.

"Are words enough, Lauren?" he entreated.

"No, words are never enough, my lord."

In two long strides he was across the floor, lifting her into his arms. She placed her damp arms around his neck and touched his lips with hers. "But remember that I will never be any man's passive plaything."

He did not speak, but bent his dark head and captured one pert nipple between his lips. Slowly, deftly, he moved up her breast and she threw back her head to give him access to her lovely neck.

She grabbed his dark hair and pulled him closer, smelling the sweet scent of wine.

"You are truly a devil, Julian," she moaned as he carried her to the bed. He placed her in the center of the covers and leaned back to look down at the wild, wanton woman stretched so temptingly before him.

"I never thought you were a passive plaything, my love," he said before he pulled the ruby red drapes around the bed, enclosing them in a world of their own.

"Make love to me," she whispered in reply, opening her arms to him. Quickly he came to her, savagely taking her lips in his as he sought to consume the very essence of her. He reached for the buttons on his waistcoat, but she rose and gently pushed his hands away.

"Let me," she said huskily. Lauren was a little clumsy with the buttons but soon she had them loose and then she was pulling apart his linen shirt, staring hungrily at the wide expanse of his chest. It had been so long since she had seen him like this that the sight of him sent a wave of warmth down her spine. She leaned forward and placed her lips on his chest, playing with his nipples as he had played with hers.

He growled deeply then stripped off his breeches. With eyes like molten gold he continued to feast on the sight of her sitting naked in the middle of the rumpled bed. Julian's desire was growing with a fiery intensity when he finally reached for her. Lauren rolled away from him, putting a look of surprise on his face, but it quickly disappeared as she pushed him back onto the covers and leaned over him.

"I said I would be no passive woman," she taunted lightly. She began to work a magic on his body that was every bit as potent as any witches' brew. Up and down his body her mouth teased and caressed him until he was aching as never before. It was such an exquisite agony, but soon it became too much for him and with a husky endearment, he rolled over, imprisoning her beneath him.

When he entered her, she felt a flame begin to flicker in her belly that grew into an expansive blaze, consuming her with heat. Higher and higher she rode, taking him with her to a crest of ecstasy until in a blinding flash of blissful release, they reached the ultimate peak of pleasure.

She felt the slippery moisture of their bodies molding them together and she smiled as she ran her hands down his muscled back.

"I think you have burned me to ashes," she whispered into his ear. Julian shuddered in her arms as her breath teased him.

He lifted his tousled head, smiling warmly at her. "And like the phoenix that rose from the ashes, so shall my desire smolder and burst anew!"

With a gasp of rapture she felt him move within her as they found a mutual pleasure in the ageless triumph of desire.

As Lauren rested in the crook of Julian's arm, she listened to his deep, even breathing. Had she made the right decision? she wondered. Was this shared desire enough?

Her eyes traveled lovingly over Julian's sleeping form and she gave a secret smile. Oh, yes! she thought. She had done the right thing. She might not have his love, but she would cherish every moment they were together, hoarding up all the joy, until the day when all the pieces might be enough to make her forget that she had hoped for lasting love.

She sighed as she thought of her father. Lauren had promised herself that she would clear his name, but she was no nearer to the truth now than she had ever been. But she knew that her father would not have wanted her to spend her life searching out the villain who had caused his downfall. He would have wanted her to find her own happiness and let him and the charges against him rest in peace.

Realizing this, she snuggled closer to Julian, finding comfort in his slowly rising and falling chest. She only wanted to live for the here and now, and to forget the bitterness of the past. A contented smile appeared on her face as she drifted off into sleep.

She did not know what woke her in the early hours of the morning, but when she opened her eyes she was aware immediately that Julian was no longer with her. Frantically, Lauren glanced around the room, to find him standing before the window. He was gazing out at the faint beginnings of a new day.

"Julian?" she called drowsily from the bed.

When he looked at her she was leaning on

one elbow, watching him with sleepy violet eyes. Her raven tresses were spilling around her shoulders like a silk cloak, appearing even darker against the paleness of her skin.

"Is something wrong?" she asked.

"No."

"Then come back to bed. I miss your warmth."

"Are you cold?"

"A little," she murmured.

"Then I'll gladly be your blanket," he said as he slipped between the covers. He gazed into her wide violet eyes, still misty with sleep. "You have fairy eyes."

"Fairy eyes?" she asked, yawning.

"Yes. They're so beautiful and compelling. I could gaze into them all day. Your eyes speak for you; sometimes they smile and sometimes they glow with mischief, but usually they tell me all I need to know."

"And what do they tell you now?" she asked with a naughty grin.

"They tell me that you are hungry."

"Hungry?" She was surprised at his words.

"Aye," he leered. "And I'm also hungry for the sweet meat set so temptingly before me."

"Would you have others call you a glutton, sir?" she protested, holding him off with one hand.

"Everyone knows what a sweet tooth I have, and you are the sweetest dish I've ever seen! I'll gladly suffer the gout if this kind of feasting causes it."

"Come here, you hungry man," she insisted, holding out her arms. "I can't have you going to bed without nourishment."

"That's true," he laughed. "It's a punishment I couldn't bear."

Julian found in her arms that perfect haven of peace which every man searches for but few find.

Later, Julian found himself gazing down on the sleeping figure of his wife, much as she had done earlier with him. Her sweet, innocent sleeping face contrasted with the wild, passionate creature he had held in his arms only an hour ago. He wanted to bury himself in her sweet softness and never leave.

From the first moment he saw her he had been hers, though he had been too proud and vain to admit it. She had woven a silken ribbon of delight around him and now he did not want to break that bond—that very bond he had once raged against. No, he did not want to break it for anything; in fact, he wanted to tie a knot to keep him securely tied to her forever.

But Julian was afraid to speak words of love to Lauren, lest she reject him and fly away again. She had not mentioned love. She had not demanded anything of him as she gave of herself so willingly. Dare he risk it all by asking more from her than she could give? He couldn't forget that once she had said that he had destroyed her love. Was it still dead, or might he still be able to rekindle the feelings she once had?

He pondered this question as daylight beckoned. He was still no closer to an answer when Molly pulled back the bed drapes and grinned at him with evident pleasure.

"It's about time," she whispered before she scuttled away, chuckling to herself.

* * *

Happily Lauren made her way down to the
stables. She felt like dancing a jig or humming
out loud, but she contented herself with a wide
smile.

"Good morning, Henri," she chirped gaily.

"Bonjour, madame," he returned. "You are
looking very happy and very lovely today."

"Thank you." She glanced around. "Is my
husband here? He said we were to ride together
this morning."

"He was here earlier, but Monsieur Taylor
and the Duc de Palissy came down and wanted
him to see the livestock in the far pasture. He
said to tell you that he would join you as soon
as he could."

She looked disappointed. "I think I'll go on by
myself. Please tell him that I'll be riding down
near the woods."

"Oui, madame," Henri replied as he helped
her mount her horse.

Lauren set a brisk pace for the mare and soon
they were flying across the meadow. The house
was a small dot behind her when a gust of wind
caught her hat and whipped it from her head.
She laughed as the breeze tore through her carefully arranged curls, and she shook her head to
let the tresses tumble down her back. Enjoying
her newfound happiness with Julian, Lauren
felt more carefree than she had in years. Today
everything looked brighter and better to her.

As she entered the thick forest she slowed her
horse. She dismounted and carefully walked the
mare in between the trees, guiding her with a
sure and steady hand. When she reached the

small pond she'd been heading for, she stopped and tethered the horse to a bush, pulling off her boots at the water's edge and slipping her feet into the cool water. Like a small child Lauren kicked her feet up and down, splashing water every which way. This had become her favorite place at the Palissy estate ever since she'd found it the first day there.

Suddenly Lauren heard the whinny of a horse and sat up, looking into the undergrowth.

"Julian?" she called. When there was no answer she slowly got up, peering into the darkness made by the closely set trees.

"Julian?" Is that you?"

A horse and rider came into the clearing, followed by two other men on horses. They looked rough and unkempt with a day's growth of beard on their faces, their clothing soiled and wrinkled.

"Wh-who are you?" she demanded in a quaking voice. They did not look friendly. "Th-this is private property and you'd better leave at once."

"*Hélas!* And who is going to make us leave, *petite?* You don't look big enough to carry us off."

The other men laughed, and one made a coarse remark in French to the other.

"Are you Lauren Warwick?" one of the men demanded.

"How do you know my name?"

"We just know it," another man said, giving his partner a warning look.

"G-go away and I won't tell anyone that you're

poaching." Her breathing was rapid, showing her fear.

The first man's gaze passed over her with a lecherous slowness, and when his eyes again met hers, she flinched at the lust she saw in them.

"We did not have it in mind to poach, but seeing you, I think you might be worth taking."

"No!" she cried, running for her horse. But one of the other men managed to pull his horse between Lauren and the mare, blocking her path of escape. "You'll be much better than a scrawny rabbit," the man laughed.

The only route open to her was behind her, so she whirled and rushed into the woods, running as if the hounds of hell were nipping at her heels. Frantically, she pushed aside the low-hanging branches, but several caught and scraped her smooth cheeks. Panting breathlessly, Lauren knew she must keep running because she heard the curses of her pursuers as they fought against the undergrowth. They must be close, she thought.

On and on she ran, jumping over rocks, darting in and out of the trees as she tried to escape the men. Her feet stung without her boots, which she'd had to leave at the pond, but she did not stop to look at the damage. She had to elude those men, no matter what it took.

Out of breath and ready to collapse, Lauren spied an old barn in a clearing ahead. She rushed toward it and pushed open the old rusty door, slipping into the cool, musky dimness inside.

Several bundles of hay were scattered around, and a mouse ran squeaking by her feet. The roof had rotted away in places, letting the sun come through in smoky streams. There was a loft, but it looked so ramshackle that Lauren feared it would not hold her weight. She jumped when she heard the men enter the clearing, and without giving her safety another thought, she scampered up the ladder and quickly made her way to the corner, crouching behind a stack of hay.

Soon after, she heard the hinge of the door creak and then the shuffle of feet on the dirt floor.

"She wouldn't come in here," she heard one man say. "She'd know this would be the first place we'd look."

"Quiet!" Another man ordered in gutteral French. "Search over there in that stall."

Lauren started to tremble, but still she remained hidden while the sounds of their search came to her loud and clear.

"She's not here, Jacques!" a voice said in a disgusted tone. "She's probably long gone from this place by now!"

"Look up in that loft, Claude!" It was the order she had been dreading. She held her breath in fear.

"Non. Not me! I'll not break my neck."

"I'll break it for you, fool, if you don't get your carcass up there!" Jacques said.

The ladder creaked with the man's weight and Lauren flattened herself to the floor. She peered through a hole between two bales of hay and saw the man as he gingerly tried one of the floorboards. It broke and crashed down, barely missing one of the men below.

"Watch what you're doing up there!"

The man named Claude looked around the loft, but all he noticed were rotten boards looking ready to give way at any moment. His glance stopped on the bales of hay, but he did not think the girl would be foolish enough to come up here, much less to cross this precarious floor to get to that hiding place.

"She's not up here," he called down.

"Are you sure?"

"Very sure! If you don't believe me perhaps you would like to search the place for yourself!" he muttered sarcastically.

"Very well," the voice was grudging. "Come on down and we'll look elsewhere."

"With pleasure," and he hurried down the ladder as if he feared it might collapse at any moment.

Lauren held her breath until she heard their receding voices. Unable to believe she had not been discovered, she remained behind the hay, afraid to come out in case the men might still be lurking outside.

Time passed slowly, and finally Lauren moved, groaning at the stiffness of her arms and legs. Proceeding slowly, she stepped from one board to the other, testing their strength as she went. She let out her breath in relief when she reached the ladder, and then hurried down it and started for the door.

The sound of a horse outside halted her, and she jumped behind the door, flattening herself to the wall. Her eyes darted nervously along the wall where she saw a pitchfork standing in the corner. Inching her hand along the wall, her fingers finally closed reassuringly around the wooden handle. Lauren clutched it to her breast and moved slowly back behind the safety of the door.

A shadow fell through the doorway, lengthening as a man came forward. She closed her eyes, murmured a prayer, and then charged out from behind the door, aiming the weapon at the man's back.

"What the devil!" the man exclaimed, catching the prongs and twisting them from her hand.

Lauren stared in stunned amazement at Julian. He looked equally disturbed, a confused expression on his face.

"Were you trying to kill me?" he demanded.

She shook her head and placed a trembling hand to her temple.

"I-I thought you were those men."

"What men?"

"There were three of them. They chased me through the forest." She looked down at her bare feet. "I left my boots by the pond."

"I saw them as well as your horse." His voice was deep and shaken. "I thought you had gone for a walk. I didn't realize you were in danger." He pulled her into his arms.

"Oh, Julian!" she cried. "It was terrible!"

He gathered her closer, resting his chin on her head. "You say these men were chasing you?"

Her head nodded. "I-I don't know what they would have done to me if they had caught me."

His grip tightened at her words. He knew what would have happened and it made him angry that he had not been there to protect her.

"They were probably poachers," Julian reassured her. "Simon said he gets them all the time."

"They said they weren't poachers!" She started to cry, burying her face in his chest.

He led her over to a bundle of hay and sat her down on the loose straw. "It's all right now, darling. They're gone."

"I was so — so frightened. I kept thinking that I might never see you again!"

"*Sssh!* Don't talk like that!" What would he do if something happened to Lauren? She had become so very precious, so very necessary to him.

It was in that moment that he knew he had to tell her of his feelings. Life was too short and time too fleeting for him to hope that the right moment might come someday. Now was for the taking and he had to bare his soul or regret it for the rest of his life.

"I—" He was hesitant. "I don't know what I would do should I lose you. You are my most precious possession."

She moved back, wiping away a tear. "You can't own other people unless they give you the right."

"I love you, Lauren," he said quietly.

Lauren turned away, picking up a handful of hay and letting it sift through her fingers.

"Did you hear what I said?" he asked in an agonized voice. Was she already turning away from him? Were his words too hastily spoken?

"How can I believe you?" she finally said in a small voice. "You once told me you didn't believe in love."

"I was but a walking shell of a man when I

uttered those banal words. Now I realize you were heaven-sent when you blundered into me on the wharf. Little did I know then that I was saving myself as well as a frightened girl. I was cold and cynical about love. You showed me what a barren wasteland I had been living in and how different life could be."

Lauren could not look at him. She wanted to believe him, but could she, dare she, risk that pain again? Should she trust him not to bruise her fragile heart?

It was strange, but once she decided to take second best, she had accepted that as her lot. But here was Julian offering her heaven on earth and she was too afraid to reach out and grab it with both hands.

Julian watched as she nervously twisted a blade of hay in her fingers. He could sense the doubt in her and wanted to take her in his arms and make wild, passionate love to her. He wanted to show her with his body what his mind struggled over, fearing that his words sounded hollow and false to her ears.

All those times they had lain together, he had taken her in love, but he had not realized it, thinking it was only desire. But he could not take her again until she knew that his words were sincere and his heart was at her mercy.

"Look at me, Lauren," he asked, but still she remained turned away from him. "You have every right not to believe me, and I have given you little reason to trust me, but I speak only the truth when I say I love you."

She turned then and looked at him. He had always been so proud, seemed so sure of himself and others. Now he looked rather desperate, hoping with all his heart that she would not reject his love.

Lauren saw all this and so much more when her violet gaze met his golden one, now he was allowing her entrance into that most private place in his very soul. She knew he spoke the truth and she could give him no less in return.

"I gave my love to you once, thinking it would be returned. Yet you only felt chained by my passion. So last night, when I gave myself to you, I told myself that I would settle for whatever you were willing to give. Today I find that the love I have for you is reciprocated; the only thing that would make me happier would be for you to take me in your arms and claim me body and soul!"

With a cry of happiness Julian caught her in his arms, swinging her round and round until they both became dizzy. He then laid her on a bed of straw that was more lovely than any downy bed, and lifted her feet and kissed them.

"Your poor feet," he murmured.

"They do not hurt nearly as much as your cavalier treatment had hurt me."

"I had no way of knowing how a husband should act. It is a new experience for me," he grinned. "Besides, I thought my treatment of you last night repaid my earlier debt."

"Oh! Does everything come down to your prowess in bed?"

"But you would miss it if I were unable to satisfy you."

She gently stroked his cheek. "You satisfy my deepest desires. Even if you were not able to make love to me tomorrow, I would still love you and find satisfaction in being loved in return."

"I must have done something right in my life to deserve your love." His eyes were warm.

"And the luckiest day of my life was when you happened to find me on the docks of London."

"We were destined to be together."

"I love you so," she said, no longer afraid to speak the words.

"And I love you," he groaned huskily.

"Then show me how much," she begged, arching up to him.

He claimed her lips in a long, warm kiss, sliding his hands under her jacket to feel the silken smoothness of her skin. She was breathless with desire, wanting him even closer, when a sound came from outside, jerking them apart.

"Lauren! Julian!" Felice called.

"Ignore her and maybe she'll go away," Julian whispered.

"Maybe they're not here," Brendan answered her.

"Don't be ridiculous. Here's Julian's stallion, and I know that was Lauren's mare down by the pond." Her voice was insistent.

Julian lightly began to nibble Lauren's earlobe, sending shudders of delight down her spine.

"Felice. I think we should turn back," Brendan said.

"They must be here somewhere! I can't go back until I find them," she announced in a petulant voice.

"I don't think she's going to leave," Lauren gasped as Julian continued to tease her senses.

Regretfully, Julian broke away from her. "She chooses the worst times to interfere! Stay here. I'll make her leave."

He walked outside and Lauren giggled when she heard Felice's exclamation.

"Julian! We've been looking everywhere for you!"

"You've found me now, Felice, so perhaps you'd be good enough to go away," he said calmly.

Lauren heard Felice gasp. "But where's Lauren?"

"She's with me."

"Oh!" was all she could find to say.

"Is there anything else?" he asked, cocking his head to one side.

"Well, yes. Monica is at the house. She says she came to visit Nicolet, but I really think she's here to see you. A sentence doesn't pass her lips without her remarking on your absence."

"If I stay away long enough, perhaps she'll leave."

Felice shook her head. "I don't think so. I get the distinct impression that she won't leave until she's seen you. I believe she's hoping to revive your old passion," she laughed.

"She can forget that!" he announced with feeling, and Lauren, hearing his words, smiled to herself.

There would only be room for one woman in Julian's life and in his bed, and she intended to be that woman.

"I've got my hands full with a dark-tressed, violet-eyed witch," Julian said.

"And does this witch finally know how you feel about her?" Felice asked with a smile.

"She certainly does!" Lauren said, coming from the barn to stand beside Julian.

Felice chuckled at the sight of Lauren with straw stuck in her hair and her lips full and swollen from kissing.

"I take it his affections are returned?"

"Returned in full measure!" Lauren's voice was husky as she gave Julian a loving look.

"It's about time!" Felice nodded.

Julian chuckled. "That's what Molly said, although I don't think she was talking about quite the same thing."

"Will you be coming back to the house anytime soon, Julian?" Brendan asked. "Or shall we tell Monica we don't expect you back until tomorrow?"

"Tell her I'm unavoidably delayed."

"And he'll be delayed forever as far as she's concerned!" Lauren added with a mischievous grin.

Julian hugged her close to his side and smiled down into her upturned face.

"Do you really want me to tell her that?" Felice demanded.

"Tell her whatever you like." Julian looked at her, narrowing his eyes against the sun. "Just go away for now and leave us alone!"

"Yes, sir!" Felice said impishly as she whirled her horse away. She glanced at Brendan. "You knew they were in there all the time, didn't you? And that's why you wanted us to leave."

Brendan shrugged. "I thought they might be, but by then you had already disturbed them."

There was a decided gleam in his eyes. "What do you say to us finding our own little trysting place in the woods?"

"It sounds wonderful."

Julian and Lauren laughed as they watched them ride away.

"Shall we take up where we left off?"

"By all means!"

They entered the dimly lit barn, but they did not see the dust and the cracks in the roof. They paid no attention to the spiderwebs in every nook and cranny of the building. The ramshackle barn was a palace to them. And there, within its dusty confines, they created a world of their own where no one could intrude.

As far as the lovers were concerned, the old barn roof was a covering of silver clouds, the hard, straw-covered floor a bed of tulips, the dust about them gold dust and the wooden walls a silken drape to hide them from prying eyes.

Everything is beautiful when one is in love.

Death calls ye to the crowd of common men.
—James Shirley

Chapter Twelve

The weeks went swiftly by and soon it was July. Lauren and Julian found that their love was growing day by day, making them happier than they had ever been.

One morning Lauren came downstairs to hear voices in the sitting room. Curiously, she made her way into the room, stopping when she saw Monica Ridgley sitting on a sofa, conversing with Julian, Nicolet and Simon.

Lauren experienced a twinge of anxiety at the sight of the woman, but it quickly passed as she remembered that Julian was all hers now. She smiled at them all, entered the room and sat down on the arm of Julian's chair.

"Monica has just brought us some interesting news," Nicolet said. "Do you remember my mention of the Duc d'Aiguillon the night of the ball celebrating the marriage of the King's grandson?"

"Yes, of course."

"I told you then about how he had placed such high taxes on the people of Brittany that the parliament wrote to the King complaining. The King did nothing so the parliament resigned in disgust and d'Aiguillon was recalled to Paris after he tried unsuccessfully to form his own parliament.

"The court of Brittany accused d'Aiguillon of wrongdoing and wanted to take him to trial. The Duc agreed, but only if the Parliament of Paris were to try him.. He seemed to think he would be declared innocent by them, and he knew the Parliament of Rennes harbored a strong dislike for him. Well, it soon became evident that d'Aiguillon was not coming off well at trial and would probably be found guilty. Madame du Barry came to his rescue and asked the King to step in and save d'Aiguillon, and he agreed."

"How did he manage to do that without angering the parliament?" Lauren asked. "After all, you said that d'Aiguillon had agreed to the trial."

"The King said that the hearings had to be stopped because of state secrets or some other nonsense. He pronounced that d'Aiguillon was innocent."

"I hear it is still rather touch-and-go in Paris," Monica added. "The parliament wants to ignore the King's orders, claiming that he unlawfully interfered with the flow of justice. But I doubt they will go that far—that would be open revolt."

"Yes," Nicolet nodded. "But the parliament has asked that d'Aiguillon relinquish his position as peer since his reputation was seriously harmed by what came out at the trial."

"Oh, he'll come out of this without a scratch," Simon said in disgust. "If Madame du Barry is behind him, then the King will follow her wishes."

"But that doesn't seem fair!" Lauren was indignant. "Why do you have courts if their laws are not upheld?"

"France is different from England," Simon smiled. "Here the King's power is absolute. In theory he has to answer to no man, only to God."

Monica rose to her feet. "I must be going now. I have an appointment.

"Thank you for telling us about d'Aiguillon." Simon walked her to the door. "We haven't been to Versailles lately and we've missed all the excitement."

"It was my pleasure." She glanced to where Julian stood with his arm around his wife. He looked younger and more carefree. As if in answer to some unspoken question in her eyes, he left Lauren's side and crossed the room to stand before her. Simon discreetly moved away.

"Was the thought of marrying me really so horrible?" She could not resist asking the question.

"Of course not. It was the chains of marriage I fought against, but now Lauren has shown me how necessary loving bonds are in life."

She gave a bitter smile. "I would have made you happy."

He shook his head. "We would have destroyed each other. Would you really have wanted that?"

"I just wanted you," she said, forgetting to mention his title and money had also interested her.

"I hope you find love, Monica," Julian said sincerely. "I didn't used to believe it existed, but it does." Across the room he sent Lauren a loving glance that finally killed all Monica's hopes. She knew he would never look at her in that way.

"Don't pity me, Julian," she scorned. "I can do without that."

"I don't pity you. I simply wish you the best," he returned gently, instantly quelling her rising temper.

"Good-bye," she nodded, resigned to the fact that he was lost to her forever, and just beginning to understand that he had never been hers in the first place.

After she left they went into the sitting room and Nicolet served tea. They made light conversation, discussing the latest fashions and how the crops might be that year.

When Felice entered the room on Brendan's arm, everyone immediately knew that something had happened. Her cheeks were flushed and her blue eyes twinkled with a lively light. Even Brendan looked excited, a grin of happiness on his face.

"Are you going to tell us what's happened?" Julian laughed, "or shall we take turns guessing?"

Felice shyly lowered her eyes. "There's to be an addition to our family early next year."

There was a moment of silence until everyone guessed her meaning, then bedlam broke loose. Lauren rushed across the room to hug Felice and they giggled like schoolgirls. Julian and Simon vigorously shook Brendan's hand and offered their congratulations.

Nicolet joined Lauren and Felice, warmly

clasping Felice's hand. "I'm so happy for you. I know how you have longed for a child."

Felice was too emotional to speak, nodding her head as tears filled her eyes.

"I think it had something to do with the French air," Brendan grinned.

"Or trysts in the woods?" Julian said with a twinkle in his eyes.

"Could be," Brendan returned, and everyone laughed.

Lauren and Felice lazily walked through the gardens. It was a beautiful day full of sunshine and flowers. Everywhere they looked they found a profusion of blossoms, each one appearing to outdo the other.

They were wearing cool muslin dresses. Lauren's was blue, embroidered with silver threads. She wore a straw hat with a wide blue ribbon around the crown that tied in a large bow under her chin.

Felice was wearing a yellow gown with tiny green flowers painted on it. She also wore a straw hat to protect her from the sun, but hers had a yellow plume in it.

"I have never felt so complete in my whole life," Felice murmured dreamily as they reached the open meadow.

Lauren played with the bow tied under her chin and tried to adjust the angle of her hat. "I'm very happy for you, Felice," she smiled. "I know how much this child means to you."

"I've always wanted a child of Brendan's, something tangible from our love. Besides," she tilted her head, "I've always adored children. I used to gaze longingly at my friends' children."

"Do you want a boy or a girl?"

"Oh, I thought Brendan would want a boy so he would have an heir, but he told me the other night that he didn't care what sex our child turned out to be, as long as I came safely through the birth."

"You will. I know you will," Lauren said fervently. So often women died in childbirth, but she could not bear to think of Felice dying to give life to her own child.

"I'll be fine. I don't know, I just have this kind of intuition that tells me I'll have a son and I'll live to see him grow into manhood."

Lauren slowly placed her hands over her womb. Even now such life might be growing and flourishing within her. She had refrained from telling anyone yet, not wanting to take away Felice's uniqueness. She wanted to wait a little longer until she was absolutely sure.

"I would like to have Julian's child," she said hesitantly.

Felice smiled shyly. "If I know Julian like I think I do, then you'll no doubt have hundreds of little babies running around before you know what hit you."

"Heaven forbid!" Lauren looked scandalized. "Two or three will be plenty."

Felice chuckled. "I can just see you now with fifteen little boys all looking like Julian."

"Felice!" she exclaimed in mock horror. "I thought you were my friend! How could you wish such a thing on me?"

"I'm sorry." She dropped her eyes to hide her

mirth. "I guess I just wasn't thinking. You can blame it on my condition."

"Oh, look!" Lauren said in an excited voice. "What lovely wild flowers!" She pointed across the meadow where a group of trees divided the property from the road. "Let's take some back to the house."

Felice lifted the hem of her gown and they strolled toward the trees. The ground was covered with blue, purple and yellow flowers growing without rhyme or reason along the rocky path.

"These are the color of your eyes!" Felice held up a delicate violet flower. "You should place some in your hair."

Lauren picked some and haphazardly stuck them behind her ear. "How do I look?" She gracefully pirouetted.

"You look like a wood nymph," Felice giggled.

Lauren untied the bow under her chin and pulled the straw hat off her head. She threw it to the ground and picked some more flowers, slipping them into her dark hair. "They make me feel quite saucy!" she laughed.

"Look, Lauren," Felice began, reaching for a yellow flower that was different from the others. Suddenly two men stepped from behind the trees.

Felice stepped back with a cry, drawing Lauren's attention. She saw the two men and recognized them as the ones who had chased her into the woods.

"What do you want?" she demanded haughtily. She would not let them frighten her this time.

"We want to take you for a little ride," one grinned.

"I'm not going anywhere with you!"

"Oh, but we were told to take you and that's what we're going to do," the other man snarled, grabbing her wrist and jerking her against him.

"Let me go!" She angrily twisted in his arms, but his grip only tightened. She kicked him, catching him on the shin, and he uttered a curse and wrenched her arm painfully.

"Watch that, or you might get your lovely little neck broken!"

"Let her go!" Felice started forward, but the other man stepped in front of her.

"You're a pretty little thing," he drooled.

"Leave off, Claude! We're only to bring this one!" the other man snapped.

"This is the Duc de Palissy's estate! You could be shot for trespassing!" Felice warned in a frightened voice.

"They'll have to catch us first," Claude laughed.

The other man started to drag Lauren into the woods, and Felice stepped forward. Claude pushed her back and she tripped, losing her balance. She fell on her side and gasped in pain.

"Don't, Felice!" Lauren cried. "Don't try to stop them or they might hurt you!"

The man clamped a dirty hand over Lauren's mouth before he rushed into the woods.

Felice stumbled to her feet and ran after them. She reached the edge of the road and peered from behind a tree. She watched as the two men shoved Lauren into a black coach and shut the door. A hand came out of the carriage window and threw the two men a sack of gold. The men mounted their horses and rode off in the direction opposite to the coach.

Felice slid down the tree, painfully scraping her hands on the bark. The last thought she had before she slipped into unconsciousness was that the man in the carriage had looked like the Duc de Romoulet.

When Felice opened her eyes, she was lying in her bed. Brendan and Julian were standing over her with concern on their faces. Nicolet and Simon were standing anxiously by the door.

"How are you feeling, my darling?" Brendan bent closer, and she could see tears in his eyes.

"I'm a little dizzy," She quickly sat up. "Lauren! They took Lauren!" she cried, suddenly remembering everything.

"Who took her?" Julian's voice was strained.

"I don't know." She weakly rubbed her forehead. "We were picking wild flowers and these two men stepped out in front of us. They grabbed her and pushed me down. I followed them and saw them put Lauren into a black coach that was waiting in the road. I'm almost certain I saw the Duc de Romoulet inside."

"Rest now, Felice," Brendan urged, gently pushing her back onto the pillow.

"All of a sudden her eyes widened in dismay. "Our baby! Our baby, Brendan! Is it all right?"

He sat on the edge of the bed and took her in his arms. "It's fine, my love. But you must rest and keep up your strength. Remember you're talking care of two now."

She gave him a faint smile and closed her

eyes. "I'm so thankful," she murmured sleepily. "Now all we need is to get Lauren back."

When her breathing was even, the two men moved away from the bed to converse between themselves.

"Could she be right about the Duc de Romoulet?" Brendan asked.

Julian looked grim. "I fear it could be so. She refused him at the Palissy ball, and I don't think he's the kind of man who likes to be thwarted by women."

Simon stepped forward. "The Duc has a château on the outskirts of Paris. He doesn't have the funds to keep it up as well as his other property, so he's let it fall into disrepair. There aren't any servants and the place is rather secluded. He could reach it before nightfall, and it would be just the place to take her if he means to seduce her without anyone interfering."

Julian's eyes were a hard, glassy gold, and his fingers itched to be around Romoulet's neck. "Yes, I think that might be the place he's taken her. I swear I'll kill him if he's harmed her in any way."

"Let us go with you," Brendan urged.

"No!" Julian was emphatic. "This is my concern. You stay here and take care of your wife. She needs you."

"Then I'll go," Simon said.

Again Julian refused the offer. "Thank you, Simon, but I must settle this with Romoulet by myself."

"Are you sure, *mon ami?*" Simon persisted. "He might be a coward, but he's a mean coward. I wouldn't put it past him to have set a trap."

"Regardless, I must still go alone."

He walked back to Felice and bent to kiss her on the forehead. His eyes were gentle when he looked at Brendan. "Take care of her. She's very precious to me."

"No more so than she is to me," Brendan returned with a small smile. "And you bring Lauren back," he added gravely.

"I intend to."

The three of them saw the anger on Julian's face and they had little doubt that he would. They also knew that Romoulet would be very sorry that he had tampered with the Earl of Keaton's wife.

Lauren was dumped unceremoniously into the carriage, and before she could get her balance it was moving. She pushed back the hair that had fallen into her eyes, and saw a man in the shadows.

"I'm so glad you decided to join me," a voice murmured.

She gasped as she recognized the Duc de Romoulet leaning casually against the seat.

"What do you think you're doing?" she demanded angrily.

"I thought it was obvious. I'm abducting you."

"But—but why?"

He idly studied his fingernails. "There are many reasons, and you'll know what they are soon enough."

"I demand that you take me back at once!" she ordered. He merely laughed at her.

"Just sit back and enjoy the ride. I've no intention of taking you back."

Lauren was really frightened now. At first she thought it was some kind of silly prank, but the determination in his face convinced her otherwise.

She moved toward him, but he lifted a pistol, aiming it at her chest. "I wouldn't try that if I were you."

"And what if I prefer death to what you have planned for me?" she asked contemptuously.

"I don't think you'll find it so bad," he drawled. "I have quite a bit of experience with women. I've never yet had one go away unhappy."

"What a large ego you have!" she sneered.

He shrugged. "But what I have planned for you will have to wait." He was silent for a moment and then he grinned. "Ah, I forgot to tell you that you have a visitor waiting at my house."

"A visitor?" She was confused.

"Oui!" He appeared deep in thought. "But I think I shall save him as a surprise."

"I've had enough surprises for one day!" she said with a trace of sarcasm.

"Nevertheless, you shall have to wait. Now sit back like a good girl and relax. We'll soon be there."

Lauren did as she was told, not because she was suddenly timid and meek, but rather because she felt she had to conserve all her energies for the coming ordeal. She pondered the Duc's mention of a visitor, but decided it was unimportant. Probably he just wanted to keep her guessing until the moment was ripe for him to show her what he really had planned for her.

* * *

It was almost dark when they reached the château. Lauren could just barely make it out in the darkening gloom with all its windows devoid of light. It was a large house, almost massive, with two wings off the central building, reminding her of large bat's wings.

It was rather forbidding as it stood starkly outlined against the backdrop of a slowly sinking sun. A shiver went over her as she realized how isolated she would be here. She could be killed by the Duc and it would be years before anyone found her bones.

The Duc took her arm and led her up the steps to the door. A heavy lion's head was carved into the woodwork and Lauren could almost believe it snarled at her before the Duc pushed the door open and propelled her inside.

The furniture was covered with cloths to protect it from the dust that was everywhere. Their footsteps echoed hollowly in the hall as they crossed the marble floor and stopped before two double doors. The Duc opened one and bowed to her, waving his hand for her to precede him.

Lauren warily entered the room, noticing the flickering candelabra set in the middle of a long rosewood dining table. Chairs lined either side, looking like guests at a dinner party. The Duc closed the door behind him and Lauren jumped at the sound.

She started trembling, not wanting to turn around and face the Duc. She hoped that in delaying the inevitable, she might find a way out of her predicament.

"Welcome to our humble abode!" a sarcastic voice came from a dark corner of the room. Lauren peered into the darkness and gasped in disbelief when Rodney stepped into the light.

"I told you you had a visitor, did I not, *chérie?*" the Duc laughed.

"What are you doing here?" Lauren asked in amazement.

"After you left England my father had another attack of conscience. So boring these plebeian ideas he sometimes has." He shook his head sadly. "It appears that he plans to divide his fortune between us. The house and title are entailed and must go to the next male heir, but there's no such stipulation on the money." He calmly walked to the head of the table and sat down. "Now, I can't let the old fool do that, can I?" he asked in a reasonable voice.

"What are you going to do?" Her voice was a tiny whisper.

"The only thing I can do. I'm going to kill you," he said matter-of-factly.

"You can have the money! I don't want any of it!" she cried, wringing her hands in front of her. She thought he had gone mad.

He waved her words away with one hand. "It doesn't matter what you say. I've already decided that the money shall be mine, without your generous offer."

Lauren gasped. "It was you who sent those men to abduct me that day I went riding in the forest!" she said, finally beginning to understand.

"Of course! You conveniently told the Duc where you like to ride." He leaned back in his chair and tapped his lips with one finger. "You're very hard to get rid of, niece. First we cut your bridle, but you lived through that. Then we tried to take you, but you got away from those fools. You're like a cat with nine lives!"

"You'll never get away with this," she snapped.

"Of course I will! No one linked me to Stephen's disgrace and no one will think I had anything to do with your death. I have someone in England who will swear that I never left that shore."

"So you admit that you were the traitor and my father was an innocent victim?"

"Why not? You'll not live to tell anyone, so I might as well confess." He grinned. "They say confession is good for the soul."

"A soul as black as yours must have a lot to confess!" she nettled, moving forward to hold on to the back of the chair at the end of the table. "I'm surprised you didn't kill my father instead of just settling for ruining him."

"But I would have had a widow and small child to contend with, and then have to wonder if Father would take pity on them. You see, it was I who told Father that he should urge Stephen to flee England instead of waiting for a trial."

"How convenient that my father listened to him."

"Yes, wasn't it?"

The Duc leaned against the door in a bored manner. "Don't forget you promised her to me before you kill her," he said in a conversational tone. "I didn't bring her here just to hear you prattle on about your past."

"Don't worry!" Rodney taunted. "You'll get her." His eyes rested consideringly on Lauren.

"I always wondered if Stephen ever suspected me."

Lauren shook her head, tears coming to her eyes. "No," she whispered in a husky voice. "Mother mentioned it, but he would hear no ill of you."

"What a dear brother!" he scorned. "I knew he was weak."

"He wasn't weak!" Lauren hissed, pushing away the chair and slamming her fists on the table. "He was good and honorable! You're the one who's weak, having to use others to get what you want! You're too weak to rightfully earn what is due you!"

Rodney came to his feet and his face was creased with rage. "Rightfully?!" he sneered. "What chance does a second son have? I had no rights; they were all given to Stephen just because of an accident of birth!"

"He wanted to share everything with you! But you didn't want to share! You had to have it all!"

"That's right! I wanted it all, and I had it all until you came around sticking your nose in things that didn't concern you and opening all the old doubts in my father's mind!"

"You ruined my father! You ruined him because of your greed!" Lauren cried angrily.

"Yes! And it was so easy," he taunted. "I was sending the Duc information about the British forces in exchange for gold. When the Foreign Office began to get suspicious, Father told me all about it. It seemed the perfect opportunity to give the French information and give the war office its traitor. I had Romoulet send me some letters incriminating Stephen. It was relatively simple to see to it that those letters came to the attention of Father."

Lauren glared angrily at Romoulet. "You belong together!" she scorned. "You're both vile, evil men!"

"Enough reminiscence," the Duc said drily. "I think it's my turn to ply her with sweet nothings!"

Lauren pressed back against the table and her legs trembled. "I won't go with you!" She flinched at the look in his eyes.

"You think not?" He glanced at Rodney. "Are you quite finished with your tale?"

"She's all yours," he laughed. "Make it good, Romoulet," he smiled nastily. "It will be the last time she lies in a man's arms before she goes to her grave."

The Duc moved forward and Lauren kicked the chair at him, but he deftly dodged it and caught her around the waist, swinging her over his shoulder. She beat his back with furious fists and kicked him with her legs, but he placed one arm across the back of her knees to stop her.

"Cease, you vixen!" he ordered.

Rodney laughed. "Are you sure you can handle her, *mon ami?*"

"I can handle her."

Up the dark staircase they went, with Lauren twisting and turning in his grasp. He stumbled once under her weight but he regained his balance, smacking her soundly on the rear. He finally reached the landing and opened the first door he came to, hurrying inside with his bundle.

A cloud of dust came up, as he threw her down

on the bed. The Duc reached for a candle beside the bed and lit it.

"I want to see the ecstasy on your face when I take you," he laughed.

She rolled away when he reached for her, scampering across the wide bed, but he was after her. Her feet found the floor and she made a run for the door, but he caught the back of her gown, ripping it off one shoulder.

As her hand caught the handle of the door, he grabbed her arm, jerking her back, and she let out a cry of pain.

He pulled her over to the bed, despite her resistance all the way. Lauren sank her teeth into his wrist and the Duc cried out in agony.

"Bitch!" he growled, and then he slung her across the bed and threw himself down on top of her. "You'll pay for that!" He slapped her across the face and she whimpered in pain.

"Let's see what's under these skirts!" he snarled, lifting them.

She clawed wildly at his face, leaving a bloody mark down his cheek. He jerked back angrily and slapped her again. Then his hands were on her body, touching her smooth, satiny skin.

Anything would be better than this degradation, even death, she thought. Lauren screamed, and then screamed again before the Duc put his hot, sweaty palm over her mouth and silenced her hysteria.

Feverishly, Julian pushed his horse forward, urging it across fields and pastures as he hurried toward Paris. He did not use the road since it was too winding. He needed to make up for the lost time.

The sun was setting, but still Julian rode on, only stopping once to water the horse. He was covered with sweat and grime, but he did not care. His personal appearance was the last thing that mattered to him now.

It was dark when he entered the gates that led to the Duc's château, and he raced the horse up the drive to the door. A black carriage, bearing no coat of arms, was in front of the house.

Julian gave it a hard, grim look before he mounted the steps and threw open the door. He stormed inside and, glancing around, saw a light coming from a room off the entrance hall. Moments later he was in the room.

Rodney was sitting on a long table with his feet planted on the seat of a chair. In his hand was a long, thin rapier that he had taken from the wall when he heard Julian arrive. He did not look frightened or upset, but had an arrogant tilt to his head and a slight look of amusement.

"The great Lord Keaton has come to the rescue," he mocked.

"Where is she?" Julian demanded.

"Where is she?" he queried, looking bewildered. "Why, who are you looking for, my lord?"

"What is the point of all this, Rodney?" Julian growled, stepping forward.

Rodney flourished the sword and Julian halted. "Stay where you are!" he warned. "Or you might indeed get the point!"

"What are you doing here—what part did you play in Lauren's abduction?"

Rodney lightly touched the point of the blade, as if testing its deadliness. "She should have stayed in France when her mother died. She made a bad mistake in thinking she could come back to England and rejoin the family."

"And why should that bother you?" Julian asked, clearly not understanding Rodney's animosity toward Lauren.

"She knew I had something to do with her father's disgrace and constantly pried where she had no right. Father now wants to divide the inheritance between us, and I have no intention of letting that happen."

"And did you plan her father's disgrace?" he asked coldly.

"Yes. I don't mind telling you as I did her, since neither of you will live to tell another."

Julian took a step closer and Rodney pointed the sword at him. "Don't come any closer unless you want to meet your maker sooner than I had planned."

"Where's my wife?" he shouted.

A scream came from above, quickly followed by another one.

"I believe I hear your wife now," he chuckled. "It sounds like she's enjoying herself," he said, glancing at the ceiling.

Before Rodney knew what happened, an insane bellow of rage came from Julian. The sword was knocked from Rodney's hand, and a furious fist landed a numbing blow to his chin, knocking him off his seat. He landed on the floor, where he lay stunned and aching.

Julian was out of the room, taking the steps two at a time. He threw open the first door on the landing, and inside, the candlelight illuminated two figures on the bed. The man on top looked around as the door crashed back on its hinges.

"Lauren!" Julian's voice was tense. "Lauren! I'll kill you, you bastard!" he exclaimed as he furiously advanced.

The Duc pulled his pistol from his pocket and aimed it at Julian. "I don't think I shall be the one to die, monsieur."

Lauren reached up and knocked the pistol from his hand. The Duc watched in fear as the pistol hit the floor and skidded out of reach.

Julian lunged at him, taking him to the ground. Lauren watched, at first unable to discern who was who in the shadows until she lifted the candle, bringing a soft glow of light over the figures.

Julian bent over Romoulet, hitting him again and again, until he slumped unconscious to the floor. He turned to Lauren, who was sitting in the middle of the bed, and saw her torn gown and the bruise on her cheek. His eyes simmered with anger.

"I wanted to kill him, but he passed out on me."

"Oh, Julian!" she cried, and he rushed over to sit by her, taking her into his arms and smoothing back her tumbled locks.

"He—he was touching me, and it was awful! I wanted you and you came!"

"But not soon enough, my love, or else I would have saved you from this misery."

"It wasn't your fault," she said. "Neither of us knew Rodney was in France."

"And neither of you shall leave it!"

When they heard Rodney's voice they turned and saw him standing in the doorway. He had the sword in his hand and there was an ugly look on his face. Lauren could see a bruise already swelling on his chin. His dark eyes narrowed as he watched them.

"Stand up slowly," he ordered, waving the sword menacingly, "and don't try what you did before because I'm ready for you this time."

Julian slowly stood up. Rodney glanced at Romoulet and then back at Julian. "Is he dead?" he asked.

"Unfortunately no, but he'll pay for his crimes just as you will."

Rodney laughed harshly. "There will be no witnesses to speak against me."

"I speak of a higher authority than that on earth."

"Be quiet, and move away from Lauren!"

Julian took a step away.

"I think I'll kill my dear niece first," he said. "She's been so much trouble it will be a pleasure to know I've finished with her."

Lauren scrambled off the other side of the bed, taking Rodney's attention away from her husband. Julian grabbed the bedcovers and rushed forward as Rodney began to brandish his sword. The two men fell to the floor with grunts of pain. Lauren came over to Julian to take the sword that he had miraculously managed to twist from Rodney's grasp.

They stepped back and watched as Rodney battled his way out of the covering. He was breathless when he stood and saw that Julian had taken his sword from Lauren and was now holding the weapon on him.

"Go on and kill me then!" he glared.

Julian shook his head. "Oh, no, that would be too easy for you!"

"What do you plan to do?"

"I'm taking you back to England so you can be tried for treason. No doubt you'll hang someday, but until then you'll enjoy living in a cold cell."

Rodney looked wildly at them and started to curse.

"Never! I'll not go back to some dark cell! I've had enough of cells to last me a lifetime!" He was mumbling incoherently. "Nobody's going to put me in a hole again! Nobody!" he screamed.

He ran over to the window and before Julian could stop him, he had jumped out and fallen to the courtyard below.

Lauren covered her eyes and Julian walked over to the window to stare down at the broken, twisted body lying on the stones.

"Hold me, Julian," she cried, reaching out for him. He enfolded her in his arms. "Thank you for coming for me!"

"I'd gladly risk my life for yours," he murmured into her hair. "Without you my life has no meaning."

My love is of a birth as rare
As 'tis for object strange and high:
It was begotten by despair
Upon impossibility.
                    —Andrew Marvell

Chapter Thirteen

Alone in their big bed, the Earl of Keaton and his wife held each other and breathed sighs of pleasure. They were finally back in England after clearing up all the problems that Rodney's death had caused. The Duc de Romoulet was facing charges of abduction and was being suitably scorned by his former friends.

Lauren's grandfather had been saddened not so much by his son's death as by the fact that he had never had a chance to make amends with Stephen before he died. The Earl had kissed Lauren on her return and then taken to his bed, saying he had no wish to live. But that was before Lauren told him her secret. Upon learning that he was soon to be a great-grandfather, he began to take a new interest in life.

Now Lauren snuggled closer to her husband, running her hand through the hairs on his chest.

"You have truly trapped me, my lord," she whispered. "This latest bit of your mischief makes me so large I could not flee even if I so desired."

"Never say trapped, my love. If two people love each other then it is a joy to be together. My parents were trapped in a loveless marriage, and they never knew true happiness."

"I was only jesting," she said. "I didn't mean for you to be so serious. I forgot about your mother and father."

He had told her everything about his parents. He did not want to have any secrets from the love of his life.

"I know, Lauren. I suppose I shall always remember them with a certain sadness. Their marriage will always be a point of pain to me."

She lovingly stroked his hair. "Our child will have no such pain. He will grow up in a house full of love." They were silent for a moment and then she giggled. "Do you think you'll be as silly over our child as Brendan is over little Michael?"

Felice had safely delivered a beautiful little boy a fortnight earlier, and Brendan could not stop remarking on the miracle of his birth.

"I'm sure I'll be much worse," Julian grinned. "After all, we Keatons are very possessive of our families."

"Oh, look!" Lauren exclaimed, sitting up in bed, unaware that the covers had fallen around her waist, baring her beautiful breasts to his gaze. "Isn't it lovely?" she asked, awe in her voice.

"They're very lovely," he groaned huskily, and she glanced at him, gasping in surprise when she saw where his gaze was directed.

"I was talking about the rainbow," she laughed. "Look out the window! It's beautiful!"

There on the horizon was a lovely, glowing rainbow, set against the pale blue sky. And even as they watched, it seemed to move nearer, to magically hover over their home.

"I'm so happy, Julian." There was a warm heaviness in her chest, as if her heart were expanding with joy.

Julian's hand slid slowly over her swelling stomach and his eyes glowed with fierce pride. "I'll keep you with me forever, my darling," he whispered, bending to kiss the place that harbored their child. "But it will not be a trap that harms."

"And how shall you hold me, my lord?" Her voice was breathless and she thought there surely must be stars in her eyes.

"I'll hold you always within the circle of my love."